We Turn To Face The Sun

STEPHANIANNA LOZITO

ISBN: 979-8-9856849-3-3

Formatted by Michael Davie - grimhousepub.com

For Melissa
and all the things I couldn't understand.

Chapter One

APRIL, THE YEAR IT HAPPENED

I run my fingers along the rough fibers of the rope, and I remember everything.

As the coarse braid grazes the surface of my skin, I am once again asleep and dreaming on the morning everything fell to pieces.

It still feels so real.

I can still smell the salt air and hear the crash of waves before me. The water is cold, like icicles slamming against my legs, numbing them. The wet sand crunches under my knees, grit collecting under my fingernails as I grab it by the handful. My left sleeve looks shredded, as if someone pulled a piece of it away.

I am still here.

Tara is gone.

She is in the churning water somewhere, lost, the current pulling her toward the unknown.

I don't know why we are at the beach. I don't know where my sister Tara is.

My phone rings.

Half-awake, I reach for it. But I am of two worlds right now. Eyelids heavy, mind fuzzy, I am both sleepy and no longer asleep. The phone rings in my ears, but the beach still appears in my mind. It is hard to understand what I am dreaming and what is real.

Just a few minutes ago, in my mind, it was a cloudless night, and the full moon shone a bright ray of light across the choppy surface of the water. I was in the ocean with Tara, where I was trying to swim against the rip currents toward the shore. She kept reaching for me, but I kept pushing her off to save myself. When I made it to the beach, I looked back, and Tara had disappeared, the only sounds remaining the crashing of waves and my pulse beating like a bomb about to explode.

I can't see.

I can't breathe.

She was my sister, and she was there for a moment. She was grasping at my arms and legs to use me as an anchor that would pull her safely to shore. Then she was gone. Now I am alone on the beach, kneeling in the sand, confused and tired.

I don't remember why we were in the water.

I don't remember if she called my name as I made it toward the shore or if she went down silently.

My T-shirt is damp from sweat, and my hands shake from the memory of my struggle in the sea. I can still feel the force of the cold water pushing me further and further away from shore. I can still smell the sea air and feel the seaweed clutch at my ankles like handcuffs, threatening to pull me under the water's surface. I can still see that my sister is not there. I can feel that the darkness has swallowed her up.

The phone is still ringing.

I take a breath before answering it.

My mother's voice is agitated on the other end of the phone.

"Dad and I can't find Tara."

I am disoriented. My mother's call confuses me. I am still in that in-between time, partway from dreaming to being awake, between imagination and reality.

"Jen, did you hear me? Tara is missing."

And I am suddenly afraid that my mother sees into my dreams and is devastated that I left my sister in the water to die so I could survive. In my mind, I see my mother joining me in my dream, looking for Tara from the sand, waiting for her head to surface above the waterline. I imagine I'm watching my mother stumble by the waterline, grasping at shells and reeds as if she can tow Tara back ashore with them. I can hear her calling for Tara, cursing the currents that pull her daughter further and further away.

It can't be true. It was just a dream.

My mother asks, "Jennifer, are you there?"

I reply, "What do you mean she's missing, Mom? Where is she supposed to be?"

She says, "Tara didn't come home last night and isn't in the guest room now. I can't get in touch with her. We've called and texted her all morning."

I don't understand why this warrants a phone call. I am not convinced that anything is unusual, despite the dream lingering in my mind. But my mother is quietly insistent in her concern for my sister's whereabouts.

"She was supposed to go to the city with me today. We were going to meet Leslie and her mother for dinner and a show. We bought the tickets months ago."

My sister didn't often commit to spending time with our family, but I assume her best friend Leslie's inclusion in the plans made them both more appealing and likely to happen. Yet, despite Tara's promise to go to New York with my mother later today, I am still not worried.

I sit up and rub my eyes. I try to be patient as I fumble for my glasses. The world around me is a collection of vague shapes without them, disorienting me even more. I put my glasses on as if they would help sharpen my mental focus, with my mind still fuzzy.

I look at my clock, and it's only eight a.m.

"Mom, it's early. You know she never wakes up this early. There's plenty of time for Tara to come home from wherever she is. She probably drank too much and is crashing on someone's couch."

"Maybe. But what if something happened to her?"

My irritation is growing in equal measure to my mother's concern, but I try to comfort her as best I can.

I say, "I'm sure she'll be home any minute."

My mother presses the point and says, "Jen, you're not taking this very seriously. Why can't we get in touch with her?"

"Mom," I insist. "This has happened so many times before—"

My mother cuts me off and says, "Jen, I want to know where your sister is. She's my daughter, and I'm worried. Something isn't right."

It is happening again.

Tara's whereabouts are unknown.

My parents are worried.

My day will become consumed by my sister.

It is my family's pattern, one artfully perfected after years of practice.

I genuinely believe Tara is somewhere—perhaps sleeping off too many Chardonnays—immune to the storm of concern slowly brewing in my parents' minds.

For the sake of peace and moving on this morning, I hope my sister will be reasonable with her emotions and leave a small trail of meager breadcrumbs to keep us satisfied and hopeful as we try to catch up with her, wherever she is and whatever she is doing.

She could appear at their house any minute now.

I can see Tara now, as I've seen her so many times before, creeping in the front door in the early morning with tousled hair and slept-in makeup. She would pass me sitting on the couch and say something like "What are you looking at?" if I asked her questions about where she'd been.

While her behavior has often been slightly irresponsible and often frustrating, it's also been consistent. So, I'm not sure why today is different. I can't imagine that it's different.

We've been down this road so many times before.

Tara has been drifting in and out of our daily lives for years, orchestrating absences to prove her point when family discussions went wrong. She has long exercised her perceived right of rebellion. She has so often made us wonder when—and if—we'll see her next. Yet Tara's absences were not only physical. They could also be emotional; she would simply go through her daily routines of life without the need to talk to us or return our calls or texts.

I assume she has seen my parents' attempts to contact her and turned away from them as she often does when she feels bitter or slighted about something. Tara has inflicted this treatment on all of us, cycling between rage and detachment, only peppering in a presence measured and temporary. It always seems to be our fault, even if we're not aware of the source of her anger. Even if we are, unwittingly, the source of it ourselves.

I honestly don't care anymore.

My father has taken the phone from my mother. "Look, Jen, I think your mom might be overreacting. I'm sure Tara is fine. But maybe reach out to her?"

"I agree, Dad. And I will text her as soon as we hang up."

My father has always been less likely to jump to conclusions than my mother. While she has always envisioned some disaster awaiting us, he has always been more likely to chalk it up to one of us simply being irresponsible. So much like Tara and I are, my parents are so different in their personalities. But when dealing with Tara, they are very similar in that they put love first. No matter what Tara does, they find a way to keep loving her. Even when she is unlovable, they have told me so many times that they are her parents, and while they can't explain why she behaves the way she does, there is some goodness in my sister and that she is their daughter and that is the end of it.

My father hands the phone back to my mother.

"Jen, it's Mom again. I'm not overreacting. I know how Tara is, but this doesn't feel right today."

Tara has always played by her own rules, defying my parents' authority and living just beyond the boundaries they have set to keep her safe. Go where you say you're going, make good decisions, hang out with the right people, come home when you say you're coming home. Simple tenets she has so often thrown aside over the years.

Basic rules she has thrown aside once again today.

I need more information.

I ask, "Mom, did you see her last night? Did anything happen?"

She replies, "We saw her yesterday afternoon. I asked her if she would be home for dinner, but she said she wouldn't be around last night. She didn't say anything about not being here this morning."

"Well then, I don't know what's going on. But I think you might be overreacting." I say.

"Jennifer?"

"Yes?"

"Can you please come over?" My mother pleads with me.

I challenge her, "Do you need me to come over? Can't I just try to get in touch with her—"

She cuts me off before I can continue. She says, "I'm very

worried."

I tell myself that this will be the last time. But, if this happens again, I will need to put my foot down and insist that we no longer operate this way. It just isn't fair.

I tell her, "I'll be there in an hour."

I press the button to hang up, wishing I could slam the receiver down onto its cradle. It would be such a powerful and satisfying punctuation to a frustrating phone call, a gesture that cell phones have erased, where no matter how hard I press the disconnect button, it doesn't have the same effect.

My mother's request to come over infuriates me, and I feel guilty for it. But, like so many times before, I know that we will put everything aside to extend our olive branches for some unknown slight, a gesture intended to draw Tara back into our orbit, if even just for another short while.

And, honestly, I have no interest in having my sister around. I don't want to try to get her back from wherever she is right now. I don't want to do the work it requires and then suffer for it.

That work entails spending our time trying to solve Tara's mysterious disappearing act, only to be told we're ridiculous and that she's an adult and doesn't need to tell us where she is all the time. And maybe Tara's right—perhaps we play the role of seeker too much. But today, my mother feels the need to seek.

But I still see no evidence to indicate that Tara is in trouble. She is in her thirties, for fuck's sake. She's not a defiant teenager staying out past her curfew.

The guilt creeps into my mind again. I am directing my frustration at my mother when I feel it instead for Tara.

All my mother has ever wanted is family harmony. So, for her, family peace is the most important thing. My mother tempers worry with comfort. She is the only child of a single mother. My grandmother set firm boundaries around my mother to protect her, a feeling of protection my mother has always blanketed upon

Tara and me. Despite us being adults, she still does this because she's incredibly kind and sensitive and places the value of family above all else. Which is part of the reason my mother refuses to turn my sister away, even when she's had enough of her behavior. Even when Tara's behavior tortures her.

I had always shared my mother's vision, which is why, despite every time Tara has pushed me away, I had never stopped trying to make her love me, even when it seemed impossible. To this day, I persist in seeking her approval even when raging against her unacceptable behavior. It's irrational and painful, proving endlessly fruitless and exhausting.

I have never known what to do about Tara.

My parents have never known what to do about Tara.

And we still don't.

My sister has created an environment where no one wins; she is either in trouble or not. In either scenario, it's emotional chaos. She'll become angry that we made a big deal over nothing. Or it won't be nothing. I don't know which scenario is worse.

All the other families I know don't deal with shit like this, at least from what I've seen firsthand. With no real-life examples that I can use to explain our family dynamic, I have always turned to the stories I've seen in movies or on TV to explain just how broken our situation is.

I think about this one episode of *The Sopranos* that has always struck a nerve in me. Adriana is a young woman engaged to the mob boss's nephew. She becomes trapped in an impossible choice to become an FBI informant or go to jail for selling cocaine. She will lose her life either way. Adriana is a beautifully pathetic character, positioned between two terrible options with no apparent way out. Die physically or die emotionally—a tragic victim of circumstance, of forces greater than her comprehension. She tries resisting the currents that throw her around like a rowboat in a monsoon, breaking her into pieces with every wave that crashes down.

Someone like my parents. Like me.

People who must choose between two painful but inevitable outcomes. But either path incurs a type of death. We can choose to separate from Tara forever or keep her in our lives and pay the emotional price that feels increasingly dear. It's a type of emotional death because we lose either way.

My parents and I have chosen to die emotionally in our relationship with Tara. Consistent happiness simply does not exist when you love my sister. And while my parents' emotional death isn't necessarily more significant than mine, it is different. They have two daughters who are rarely happy at the same time or for the same reasons. While my happiness rests on harmony and order within our home, it often seems like Tara relies upon chaos. So, my parents have to choose. And so often, they choose her.

When I contact Tara, I will let her have it. I can't be her tracker, putting everything aside to hunt her down once again. I want to let her go.

But my parents need me to help them more than I need peace or emotional resolution.

So, once again, I relent.

I walk into the kitchen to make coffee as I consider my options. If I call Tara, there is very little chance she'll answer. If she does, she'll be irritated that I called. She will manipulate my concern into yet another disagreement, miscommunication, and misreading of my intentions. I decide to text her first, hoping that even a one-word response would reassure my mother that there was nothing to be worried about.

Hey, where are you? Mom and Dad are worried.

I keep it short and to the point. It's all I have the energy to write. I need this to be over to get on with my day.

I also call Tara's phone because it might be more challenging to avoid a call than a text. But Tara has perfected the art of avoidance. The phone rings again and again, and she does not pick up. I am not surprised; Tara can go days without responding to calls or texts. Then she'll resurface and text me but be economical with her words. One minute, she's there; most minutes, she's not.

I think about the dream I woke from earlier. In it, Tara had disappeared into the water. I try to remember if she disappeared because she chose to or because I pushed her away. My memory of the details fades as each minute passes, but the power of her disappearance remains the same.

Tara was there in the dream and reality, and now she's not.

Before heading over to my parents' house, I prepare for my day, which will include my usual Saturday morning errands and seeing some friends for dinner. First, I start my shopping list, noting that I need coffee, yogurt, Windex. I search for a coupon for Bed Bath and Beyond, remembering that I need to replace the guest room comforter. I call the new Thai restaurant around the corner to make a reservation for tonight.

I quickly scroll my work email, remembering that I have a department meeting on Monday for which I need to prepare. I also need to write the final exam questions for the Constitutional Law seminar I'm teaching this semester. I add these additional tasks to my list, confident I can finish them this afternoon, even if it pushes off my other errands. Of course, I can always hit the Bed Bath and Beyond near the Rutgers campus on Monday if I don't get to it today.

I check my phone for texts, and there are none. I reach out to a few of Tara's friends, young women we have known since grade school. I rarely contact any of them aside from Leslie. Most of them show me the same level of disinterest and animosity that

Tara does, likely because she has written me as the enemy in her story. I am the wicked sister who has continually done Tara wrong through my words and actions. I am the villain in her narrative, paired with her through some existential error—an outsider to her life.

I have their numbers on my phone because I sent the invites for Tara's college graduation party a few years back. I remember it so clearly. It was one of the beautiful, peaceful resting spots in our family's emotional marathon. The conversation that day was as light as the breeze that swayed the cap and gown decorations that hung above us. One of those times that made me optimistic that Tara had turned a corner, that things could be different between us.

As the party continued that summer day, I watched Tara mingling with friends, glowing with her achievement, moving quickly through the crowd, and accepting her accolades. I felt like she was on the verge of something different that day. I had hoped she had finally found herself after so many years of searching. Of course, it's impossible to know if she felt that way, but I have been a perpetual student of my sister's expressions and mannerisms, and amid the champagne and cake and balloons, I was sure I could see a spark of hope in her.

I had hoped it was real.

I had hoped it wasn't a carrot I would devour, not knowing the stick would soon follow.

But the stick soon came. As it always did.

I've kept her friend's numbers on my phone for years, knowing I would need them for something someday. But then, it was just a feeling. And today is the day.

I send out a few texts.

Hey, have you talked to Tara today? My parents need to get in touch with her.

```
Can you please text me if you hear from Tara?
            I want to talk to her.
```

My phone finally dings, and I hope it is Tara, so we can simply be done with this today.

It's my best friend, Joanna. We text for a few minutes as I wait for other responses.

```
                   Are we on for dinner tonight?
```

```
I just made the reservation for 7 — Tara
drama going on. I'll text you later.
```

```
                                        What now?
```

```
Her usual disappearing act. Same annoying
shit. I'm done.
```

```
    Sorry Jen. She'll turn up, like she always
        does. We'll drink all the wine later.
```

```
Thanks. See you there.
```

I should also text Matt, Tara's ex-boyfriend. It's a long shot, but I reach out to Matt anyway.

```
    Have you talked to Tara at all today?
```

When I asked Tara why she and Matt broke up back in January, she told me to mind my own fucking business. Of course, it is not unusual for her to withhold information like that, especially if it is painful and she perceives it as making her look foolish or guilty. But I imagine Tara did something that was finally a bridge too far for Matt.

It wouldn't be the first time she overstepped with him.

I overheard Tara telling our cousin Pamela once that she smacked Matt in the face during one of their fights. Another time, she threw a bottle into his new flat-screen TV. No matter how I imagine it, this latest fight was indeed something like that; a disagreement brought to a fever pitch by Tara, who likely had no end game for resolving it peacefully.

It would make total sense that she is either with him now or distancing herself from some new development in their occasionally tumultuous relationship. As I wait for Matt's response, I can see Tara now, standing wild-eyed on his front lawn, slashing his tires, keying the driver's side door of his car. I spin the scenarios beyond Matt alone. I can see her driving to a motel in Pennsylvania to hide out for a few days and make everyone worry about her. I can see her leaving a bar last night and getting pulled over, now too proud to make the call to ask to get bailed out. I can see her doing many things to explain why she hasn't appeared yet.

I'm not sure if or when Matt will respond. I don't know how frequently Matt and Tara were in contact, if at all. My sister lived with him until recently when a fight sent her back to live at our parents' house while they worked it out.

I find it ironic that Tara now lives with our parents again, even temporarily. I don't know why she just didn't buy her own house or rent an apartment. Tara certainly has the money. It just seems so odd that she ran back to my parents after all those years of running from them. I don't understand it.

Just like I don't understand why they would take her in. I know it's because they love her and won't give up on her. And that is the decision they've made, as they've told me many times. I guess we all have to live with our choices whether others understand them or not.

I hear my phone beep and see it's a text from Matt.

```
I haven't heard from her in a while. I'll let
        you know if I do. Sorry Jen.
```

Not what I wanted to hear, but not surprising either. My phone beeps again, and it's a text from my father.

```
Would you please come now? Police called and
             want to talk to us.
```

My hands begin to shake as I put down the dishes I had started unloading from the dishwasher. I feel uneasy, a dread beginning to build as I wonder what has happened to my sister.

The mention of police causes concern for me, but only because I can imagine the gravity of what Tara must have done to require the police to be involved. My first instinct is that Tara has once again fucked a situation up beyond repair. When Tara's emotions erupt, they can be destructive. I imagine that she has once again unleashed her rage on someone or something and crossed some physical or legal boundaries that the police could not ignore.

But my mind goes further than that.

Visions of car accidents and aneurysms and abductions take over my mind. I get dressed in a hurry as I endlessly spin out potential tragedies that might have transpired. Any of these would devastate my parents beyond repair; Tara's stroke of bad luck would plague our whole family with a sadness triggered by never having had the time to make things right between us.

I shake it off. The police would have come to the house if the news was that bad.

I am again in my dream, and I see Tara sink below the water's surface. I wonder what it means. My breathing quickens, making me feel lightheaded.

Tara has always made us work so hard for peace. She has never made it easy to be her parent or her sister. She has never been considerate about how her actions affect our feelings. She has always been selfish and temperamental.

And today is no different.

Chapter Two

I pull into my parents' driveway and see my father pacing out front, picking at weeds, straightening planters on the porch. He looks up as I come to a stop. In his face, I can see the expression I've seen so many times before. Lonely terror.

The face of someone who loves someone who lies continually out of his reach.

The expression of someone who knows that the love and concern he shows far outweighs those he gets in return.

The realization that his younger daughter exists in his life but is not connected to him.

The fear that even though he knows she cannot reciprocate his love, he might one day lose her for good and that today is possibly that day.

And he has tried so hard with my sister. He has always been more of a free spirit than my mother, the older of two children who explored the world under less strict supervision. I remember hearing the stories of parties and pranks and punishments and feeling like my father must have been a fun guy in his youth. He still is.

But he is more measured now than he was then. Still, he sometimes sees himself in his daughters—perhaps too much of himself —in his daughters. I assume this is why he doesn't immediately jump to conclusions when one of us appears to have fucked up. But, like my mother, my father doesn't turn my sister away. Even when his face contorts with worry. Even when his pain is evident in his eyes. Perhaps there is something familiar in her rebellion to which he relates. And my sister can be so much fun when she isn't behaving dreadfully.

I exit the car and approach him.

I ask him, "What did the police say?"

His eyes ignite. I can see the scenarios spinning around in his head. I place my hand on his arm.

"Only that they need to speak to us about Tara," he says. "Nothing else."

My father looks at me like he's waiting for the executioner. Like he knows that something terrible has happened. But I tell him my theory this will be nothing more than a hand-slapping Tara is getting for doing something crazy.

"It will be okay, Dad. I'm going to go check on Mom and make sure she's ready to go."

I stop in the guest room doorway where Tara has been staying. Everything looks in order. But I'm not sure, and I'm not sure if that's comforting or not.

Honestly, I don't know Tara well enough to read her signs. I can't tell if she is not here by her own choice. Would she make the bed if she were going to disappear for a while? Would she pack the suitcase for an extended stay, or would she wing it once she got to her destination? If she was going to do something drastic—like slash Matt's tires or vandalize the house of a friend who has wronged her—I don't think she would've taken the time to leave such order in her wake. Instead, I assume she'd let her fury swirl up a storm of laundry and bedsheets and trash in her furious path. But I am reading signs written in a language I don't understand.

Or maybe not everything means something.

I walk back toward the kitchen and see my mother standing there, running her hand across the kitchen counter. I watch as she feels something on the countertop and beings mindlessly wiping it while she waits, a habit borne from years of meticulous cleaning. I can feel her desperation as if she can wipe this morning away and give our family a clean slate. As if her productivity can disrupt this trajectory toward an unknown destination. As if she can summon my sister's whereabouts by sheer will.

But I want Tara's purported and temporary disappearance to have an uncomfortable outcome. I want consequences for whatever she has done and how she has made my family worry. Again.

I want there to be a punishment of some kind. I want Tara to feel some pain, whether it's an injury, a scare, or something else. I want her to face a sentence that we could never effectively inflict upon her to effect change in her.

Short-term suffering will save us all in the long term.

A rock-bottom moment will help Tara decide that she wants to change.

But Tara has never been good at change.

I say, "Mom, let's get in the car, okay?"

My mother looks up in my direction as if she's hallucinating. She focuses her gaze just beyond me, and I can tell that she hears my voice but does not see me.

"Everything will be okay, Mom."

My mother stops wiping the counter and looks into my eyes. She says, "No, it won't, Jen. The police called. No matter what happened, everything is not going to be okay."

There is an edge to her voice that is unfamiliar to me. I've never heard my mother be this direct with me.

I nod in her direction and turn to walk outside to give her—and myself—some space.

My parents meet me in the driveway, and I convince my father that I should drive instead of him. My father can become so absorbed in his worry, turning inward with such a laser focus that everything else turns to background noise. While I can tell he is desperate to retain control of some aspect of today, he reluctantly hands me the keys. I am sure my father feels like everything is out of control—now, and often, with Tara—and he will look for any opportunity to wrestle it into submission.

I empathize with him.

The police station is not far, situated a few towns over, the route familiar to me from my youth. It sits at the end of a series of back roads and two-lane highways that I traveled many times over in high school, on my way to football games and the local diner, to parties in the woods, and to the bank to deposit paychecks from my summer job. A visual history of my early life seems so different now; back then, it was my entire universe, yet it seems so far from me. While driving here again brings me a kind of nostalgia, doing so for this purpose makes me yearn for the days when things weren't as complicated. When I had choices of lesser consequence, and when I was fortunate enough not to have to await updates about my sister from strangers.

We arrive in the lobby of the police station and see a young officer at the desk. My father speaks first.

He says, "Hi, we received a call to come down. The last name is Rossi."

I catch a slight flicker in the officer's eye. I wonder if it is a hint to what she knows awaits us. She consults some paperwork on her desk and says, "Yes, that was Detective Marshall who called. I'll let him know you're here."

I look at my parents and smile weakly.

"It will be okay," I say to them as I squeeze their arms, hoping to calm them for whatever news awaits us.

They do not smile back.

I walk around the lobby as we wait, looking at photos of newsworthy local cases, precinct announcements, and awards of recognition. Anything to keep my mind distracted. As my father turns inward during times of stress and uncertainly, I turn outward, looking for something to take its place in my mind.

The door to the lobby opens, and a detective appears. He says, "Mr. and Mrs. Rossi?"

My parents walk toward him, nodding frantically.

My father responds, "Yes, that's us. And this is our daughter, Jennifer."

He nods in return and gestures us toward his office, just beyond the main door. We follow him past the buzz of activity in the space outside his office: the furious tapping of computer keyboards, the ringing of desk phones, the walking to and from the enormous copier taking up the center of this bullpen area, filled with detectives looking to get to the bottom of the cases they're working. For them, this is just another day filled with other people's missteps, poor decisions, and bad luck.

Including ours.

Detective Marshall closes his office door behind us and motions for us to sit. I can sense something in his mannerisms that unsettles me.

"Detective, what happened to my sister?"

"I am afraid I have some bad news. We found Tara at a Ramada Inn on Route 70 this morning—"

My mother jumps from her seat and interrupts him. She blurts out, "Is she okay? Can we see her?"

He looks at her, his face deflated, his expression limp. "No. I'm sorry," he says. "Tara is dead."

His words knock the breath out of me, disorienting me as if

I'm observing this room from somewhere else. I can't tell if time is slowing down or speeding up. I hear wailing but don't associate it with anything until I hear a slam. My father has punched a filing cabinet. He cradles his hand, wincing, his face red. My mother has melted into her chair, crying violently, hands over her face.

I rise to stand behind my mother and place my hands on her shoulders.

I ask the detective, "How did Tara die?"

"It appears to have been a suicide. But we will know more after the autopsy."

My mother screams, pulling the hair on the side of her head. She rocks back and forth in her chair, almost falling over until my father races over to steady her. Tears stream down his face.

"I am very sorry," Detective Marshall says because perhaps there is not much more to say.

Suicide. Tara took her own life.

I think about my wanting her to suffer to change, and the thought seems grotesque to me now.

It's hard for me to comprehend that Tara has killed herself because she was notoriously stubborn, digging her heels in toward whichever path she was currently pursuing. But for her to have ended her life just doesn't fit how I perceived Tara saw the world. It always seemed to me that her rage kept her alive, that her absolute belief in her righteousness within her life and our family was enough to keep her internal flame lit for a century as if she could feed off that energy forever.

I ask the detective, "How did she kill herself?"

I ask him this question because the curiosity is killing me. For it to be real, for me to understand it, I need to hear it. I need to see it in my mind. Is the body on the coroner's table intact, or is it visibly injured? Are there bruises or cuts, or holes in her skin? Or is the damage instead inside her, inflicted by a bottle of pills?

I hear my father speak.

"She did it, Jennifer. Does it fucking matter how it happened?"

My father rarely curses. His rage is palpable. I can feel the force of his despair, for he lacks the words to express it. He is also never short-tempered or belligerent with me—it makes his sadness even more powerful. His hand cradles the left side of his face, fingers splayed across his mustache, his eyes bewildered. For him, no matter the reason, the outcome is the same. This morning, he had two children, and now he has one.

But it matters to me. I need to know. In my parents' hearts, they must, too, despite how painful it will be to hear.

The detective begins to tell us what he knows.

I follow his story, one that is both ordinary and utterly unbelievable. It is equal parts typical and beyond comprehension. A hotel housekeeper—who is now fucked up for life, I suppose, a tragic byproduct of circumstance—found Tara in her hotel room, no longer alive at checkout time. The day before, Tara parked her car in the hotel lot and checked in with what I assume were the typical niceties as she handed the desk clerk her credit card and headed up to her room on the seventh floor, knowing what she came there to do. She then hung herself on the back of the hotel door. At least, that is what appears to have happened.

My mother explodes with grief once again, collapsing further into her chair, the sound of her visceral experience of this pain traveling across the first floor of the station, triggering pathetic glances I can see through the glass of this office. I can see in their eyes that they have witnessed tragic plot twists like this before.

My father has begun to shake his head back and forth as if the sheer physical effort can expel it from his mind. An unfortunate soul in a poorly fitting suit, this detective has told our family what Tara has done. He has collapsed the floor out from under our home with a broken mother, a brooding father, and a confused sister all inside.

By the time we realized Tara was missing, she was already dead. The last time we saw her, perhaps she knew she would be dead soon, and that is the most shocking part of it for me. I have gone through my life dreading the moment I would no longer be alive, and Tara decided which moment that was for her. As someone who has never considered suicide in either theory or reality, I can't understand how she could design this outcome, an outcome that so many of us tirelessly fight against until our last breath. I didn't know she felt this way.

What else do I not know about my sister?

My inability to understand her has now come full circle; I could not access Tara while she was alive, and now, I can't access her in death either. She has always been a puzzle I couldn't solve. I had long ago given up trying because it has been too painful for me. But now, I need to solve it. It's too sudden, too shocking to let it be.

Yet, it doesn't feel like anything could ever be solved. Tara has left us with only questions, an existential mess that I will need to help my parents clean up to the best of our abilities. Another emotional hurdle I will need to help them overcome. Another absence that I will need to fill on her behalf.

I have that dreamlike feeling again.

I imagine my sister lying on a stainless-steel table, awaiting the coroner's blade. Her eyes are closed, her face frozen in a half-smile. I'm standing over her body, studying her. I am rarely this physically close to my sister, and the imagined feeling surprises me. It feels dangerous and unfamiliar. I notice birthmarks and scars I've never seen before. I extend my hand to touch her face. I feel myself wanting to pry her eyelids open, to look her in the eyes when the detective speaks again.

"I am very sorry for your loss."

I pull at a bracelet on my wrist; it's a nervous habit. It feels cool on my skin, much like I imagine the coroner's table feels on my sister's back.

I bought the bracelet in Rome almost ten years ago. I saw from across the street in a jeweler's window. It is made of a bright yellow gold chain and reminded me of a necklace my father always wears, so I felt like it was a sign and bought it. I've always believed in signs and felt like I saw them all over Italy during that trip.

As I sit here in the detective's office, sitting in the news of my sister's death, I think about those signs.

So many of those signs were about life. Food and wine and music and art hit every single one of my senses, making me feel more alive than I ever had.

But there were an equal number of signs that referenced death. The Italians are incredibly passionate about their history and feel almost fueled by the demise of their ancestors. Their memories run long and deep.

I remember visiting a crypt in Rome. It was the same day I bought the bracelet.

As I walked down the stairs into the basement of a church in the Via Veneto, I could feel the temperature drop. The coolness of that space under the earth sharpened my senses to the memorialization of death that suddenly appeared all around me.

The bones were everywhere. Skulls, collarbones, and femurs lined the walls and hung from the ceiling. I could taste the dust on my tongue, historic atoms left behind by the skeletons that filled the room. I felt the history of this place in my bones, sensed the tingle of death on my skin.

The only thing that set me apart from the bones displayed in that crypt was that I was still alive. But I would be them someday.

There, in that crypt hidden under Roman streets that were still very much alive, I stood face to face with death in a way I never had before. I had attended many funerals as a child and was intimately familiar with the rituals of mourning the dead. But I had never seen anything like that. I had never felt anything like what I felt as I stood there.

I felt the weight of being temporary and meaningless. I was alive at that moment but would undoubtedly be dead one day like everyone else. I would ultimately rest somewhere, reduced to bones and dust, like all the skeletons around me.

I look down again at the bracelet on my wrist and realize I am still in the detective's office.

I feel like I'm suffocating.

I can't tell if it's the memory of the crypt or sitting in the room with the news of my sister's death.

I need some air. I've always felt like I've needed more air when it comes to Tara. Usually, it was when she was around. But, today, it's because she's not.

I walk out of the office with no specific destination in mind. My sister is dead, words I never expected to speak. I have never been on this end of a tragedy, nor have I ever looked in the face of someone who has delivered this type of news. While my life with Tara was generally unpleasant, it proceeded in a way that I understood, for it had become routinized to me, even in its frequent pain and instability. But it had never reached the point of tragedy, which breaks loose the expected order of things. This is not what we planned.

I don't know what to do. I've always lived with the feeling that Tara is not a part of my life, and now she's not. Forever. I know what this will do to my parents. I understand that all other things will be put aside for the sake of Tara as we begin the emotional clean-up after the storm. But, once again, it will be me who must coordinate the aftermath of her leaving, of her permanent absence. I am overwhelmed.

"She's dead, she's dead, she's dead, she's dead."

I announce my sister's death to myself in a low whisper as I step into the lobby, unaware that I am speaking robotically, peppering words into the room, bullets of truth that shatter the world as it previously existed. But I am talking to no one except myself. There is no emotion in my voice, no indication of anything but a need to declare this new world order of which Tara is no longer part. When my father got the call to come down to the police station earlier this morning, we were unaware that Tara would not be awaiting bail for crashing her car, burning down her boyfriend's house, or stealing a pack of gum on a whim. We came here to learn that she is no more. Tara was here one minute and gone the next.

I lean my head against the cool marble wall in the front hallway of the station. Last week, my parents and I met Tara for dinner in Newark. She made small talk with me over shrimp scampi and joked about my obsession with bread and olive oil. She talked about buying her own house. She checked her eyeliner in a compact mirror routinely pulled from her purse. She was the occasionally and accidentally kind version of my sister, the one I experienced once or twice a year when she could tolerate an evening alone with us.

She *was*.

The thought that she might have known she intended to die while we sat together that night at dinner takes my breath away. As she joked with us that night, perhaps she was already dead in her mind. I replay the evening repeatedly, looking for a sign, a signal that I couldn't interpret at the time, but I come up empty. I sink into a chair in the lobby and hold my head in my hands.

Our story has ended with the most unsatisfying finish. A sudden exit of one of the characters will develop an endless list of "what ifs" and "whys" in the audience's mind, a gaping hole that the other actors cannot fill except by speculation or nostalgia.

A sadness rushes over me, but it is mostly for my parents, for they have done the best they could despite the situation, and they are now left with this outcome as the reward. But it is also a sense of sadness for our family, which will now bear the scar tissue of this sudden loss, a wound that I know will fester and ache for my parents for the rest of their lives. And I will once again need to be the salve that brings some momentary relief, the healer that finds a way to fix it, the distraction that gives my parents some reason to smile when they think it is no longer possible.

Even though I don't necessarily feel sad that Tara is gone. From my perspective, we are the victims in this situation. And I know resentment and relief are not the right emotions to express at this moment. Or maybe ever.

But I feel all these things anyway, and I will keep that to myself.

I need to go back to my parents.

I head back from the lobby toward the detective's office. As I approach the door, I notice a crack in the glass of the small window above the door handle. I hadn't noticed that before. The smooth feel of the stainless steel in my hand and the weight required to push open the wooden door are both strange to me. This door previously stood between my family and the answers we awaited. It was a means to an end. When I walked through this same doorway last, only ten minutes ago, I believed my sister was still alive.

How the world changes within minutes, preventing us from walking through the same door twice.

It never looks the same, feels the same, or holds the same destination on its other side the second time around. Now, this door stands between me and my reality as an only child. It stands between me and my parents, who will never understand my perspective on the change in our family status, nor will I theirs.

There is nothing more to say at this police station, no more information to be provided to us, no paperwork or conversations or questions. Tara's deed has been done. And so is our time in this small office that has been exploded open by the painful delivery of news larger than all of us. We will walk out of this police station as a family of three, and there is nothing we can do to change that.

When I return to the office, it is cloaked in silence, awkward and heavy to the touch.

I say to my parents, "Mom, Dad. We should head home."

I help my mother from her chair and feel her lean against me as we walk to the door. My father follows behind us and says to the detective, "Thank you for letting us know."

Detective Marshall nods to acknowledge my parents and offers a final, "I am very sorry for your loss."

Before the office door closes behind us, the detective calls for my attention, "Jennifer?"

I tell my parents I'll meet them at the car and turn back to the detective.

"Yes?"

He hands me a clear plastic bag.

"These are the personal items that we found in Tara's hotel room."

I look down at the bag and take it from him. It feels heavier than it should.

"Thank you, Detective."

I walk out to the car holding a bag of my sister's final possessions; they are the last things she touched before she died. In this bag, I carry the weight of her death, and on my shoulders, I carry the burden of her choices, both old and recent.

My mind races to think about what will happen now. A list of tasks forms in my mind.

After the initial revelation of tragedy comes its necessary administrative counterpart. After the rug has been ripped out from under us, we must rearrange the furniture and vacuum the newly revealed debris that long sat under it. First on the list is transporting my parents back to their house, where they will become prisoners of their grief, surrounded by photos and memories of Tara, former daughter, and future ghost, haunting their dreams and waking hours.

The trip home does not take long, for Tara has chosen a town not too far away in which to end her life. More than fifteen minutes in the car would not have been possible for my parents, and I sense their emotional stamina grows shorter with every red light. Every moment I force them to stare out of the window at a world that no longer holds their youngest daughter is one too many. I can hear their quiet sobs. I can feel their broken spirits. Parents who are usually talkative and funny are silent and sullen.

I wonder if I've lost them forever. I wonder if I have lost myself as well.

I am both here and not here, just like Tara. I feel like this is happening to someone else, even as the pain of dealing with my sister is so achingly familiar. It's like I am watching the patterns of grief from afar, as the narrator of a story who can see and know everything happening but does not feel genuinely connected to it in any meaningful way.

I steel myself to endure delivering this news to friends and family. To explain it to them. To try to express sadness for my sister that I don't yet feel. To make our private hell public knowledge.

I can see some of my parents' closest friends—the Millers and the Tuccis—having a drink on the Millers' porch next door. They begin smiling and waving in our direction. My parents stare out their windows, oblivious to their friends' greetings, focused solely on their grief. I gesture to the neighbors as I usually would, for they are unaware of the news we have just received.

I don't want to cause any unnecessary attention or concern until I can usher my parents into the house. I don't want to have to report my sister's death to them in the driveway, surrounded by azaleas and concrete birdbaths, answering question after question about what happened as my parents listen to their daughter's death story again and again.

Later, I will talk to the neighbors to protect my parents from questions and assumptions. But I can't protect them forever. The news will spread throughout their neighborhood, a tidbit of information that will race along the lines of the game of telephone, spreading from house to house until we are surrounded by people who know what has happened in whatever version of the story arrived at their stop in the chain. I know that my parents will now be the parents of the daughter who killed herself. I can just see some of the neighbors out for their morning walk one day, whispering to each other as they pass, "Did you hear about what happened to their younger one?"

I wouldn't blame any of them. The wondering is inevitable.

They all mean well. They all care about my parents. I just don't feel like being the family spokesperson right now.

My mother heads straight into her bedroom and closes the door. I will check on her later. I assume she will try to sleep, a temporary escape from the nightmare she now faces: her child, dead by her own hand.

My father wanders out to the backyard and will likely continue his daily set of chores—watering, weeding, checking—because it will keep him from falling apart. And from the outside, no one will be the wiser that things are crumbling within this house's four walls. No one will be able to see through the orchestrated up-lighting and carefully potted plants that our newly downsized family is attempting to tackle a tragedy of such great magnitude that I question our ability to survive it intact.

I begin to make phone calls—to friends, aunts, uncles, cousins, Leslie, Matt—to let them know what has happened. Each conversation begins with telling them Tara has passed away and ends with letting them know the circumstances. Sometimes I phrase it as "It was self-inflicted," and to others, I say, "She took her own life."

No matter how I say it, it's emotional shock and awe, and I

feel bad delivering this kind of news. And I hate having to answer the question I'm asked call after call: "Why would she do this?" I hate having to hear, "She never seemed like someone who would do that." I am as unclear on that answer as they are, and I can't offer anything that will comfort them. The best I can do is reassure them that my parents are trying to cope, and no, they're not doing okay right now, and yes, I'll let them know when we have the arrangements made.

A strange thought occurs to me: when does someone die? Someone can die physically, but that person is not yet dead until you learn that they are dead. Even after that person takes their last breath, they are, to you, still alive in your mind. It is not until a person's death is announced that it becomes real. And those time-lines can be messy; they can overlap. Tara was dead before we thought she was. And now telling others she is dead brings that dreaded moment to life repeatedly.

After several hours of phone calls, I am exhausted and dying for a cigarette. I sneak out to the garage, and honestly, I feel like it's the best cigarette I've ever smoked. Smoking has always calmed me down, a habit that allows me to focus on its mechanics alone and distracts me from everything else. My father walks by as he surveys the yard, lost in his distractions. Usually, I would hide from him when I smoked—taking up the habit is the one way I've disap-pointed him, and he's always been furious with me for it. But today, he is so consumed by Tara that he has no energy to spare for me. As a result, I am invisible to him.

I head back into the house, unsure what to do with myself. People will start arriving soon, and I am glad to have a moment alone. It is the only time I will be alone for a while. I open a bottle of wine, sit on the couch, and look out the window. I see the neighbors' grandchildren riding their bikes in the cul-de-sac out front.

The kids seem so carefree, so content with riding around in a circle. I wonder if Tara was already unhappy at that age or if her discontent came later. I can't remember. But then, I was too absorbed in my own childhood to notice. And now, I'll never know.

I look at my watch and realize it's approaching dinnertime. I call to order a few pizzas, so there is food in the house when people begin to arrive. Then I go to check on my parents.

As I walk through the kitchen, I see a soft light coming in through the window. It's the turndown of the day, the late afternoon with its golden color signaling that darkness is approaching. This time of day always made me sad, as if something were ending before I was ready for it. But, as I turn to face the sun, it is disappearing before my eyes, eluding me.

I approach the door to my parents' room.

I hear my mother say, "Robert, I can't do this."

She moans, and I can hear the physicality of her grief.

She cries, "Robert, what are we going to do? I can't live without her."

I imagine that losing a child is a unique type of sadness, one that reverses the expected order of things. I worry about my mother's ability to cope.

My father opens the door and is startled to see me standing there.

He says, "Your mother isn't feeling well, so I'm going to give her something to help her rest."

I ask him, "Do you need anything, Dad?"

"No." He pauses as if he just remembered something. "Are you okay?"

"Yes, I'm okay. I love you."

"I love you too," he says.

He hugs me more forcefully than usual. It feels like he is trying to ensure that I don't disappear like Tara did. As if his grasp can keep me here forever. As if he can hold onto someone and make them permanently fixed in his life.

I see my mother over his shoulder. She's lying in bed and staring at the ceiling. Her features are reddened and contorted, wrenched into a display of distress. Her eyes are fixed to the space above the bed. Is she trying to find Tara somewhere? Does she imagine her daughter to be an angel, a heavenly being hovering above her for eternity?

I try to place myself within my mother's grief. If she closes her eyes, she'll fall asleep, and if she sleeps, she'll have to wake up. When she wakes up, she'll have only several seconds of peace before she remembers. The breath before the rush of remembering, a pause that brings relief for her brutalized psyche, a few precious moments in time where her daughter is still alive. Those hazy moments when you first wake from a dream and can't tell what is real.

It's the way I felt this morning when my sister disappeared into the water before I knew she had disappeared from the world.

My father returns with the pills and a glass of water.

He says, "Jennifer, I'll be out in a little bit, okay?"

"Sure, Dad. I'm taking care of everything. Don't worry."

As I stand in the doorway watching them, I fear that I will become invisible to them because of this, the child who remains and does not need their care. The one who is alive and therefore does not need their attention.

The one who wanted to live.

My parents' bond will now include the loss of their daughter, something to which I can't relate. I don't fault them, for they are immersed in their grief and the power of the sadness that now blankets them. I am now the only child who remains alive in our family, but one who has been able to survive on her own—the daughter who never turned away from her parents in life or death.

I close the door to allow them some privacy because there is nothing else that I can do for them right now.

Before I turn and walk away, I realize that this is yet another door closing on my previous life. What lies on the other side is my parents, now different people, forever and finally changed by my sister. I am on this side, alone again, sitting in loneliness that is especially painful even though I have felt Tara's absence for years.

So, I am mad, even furious, at my sister. My mother's tears fuel my fury. As I hear her sobbing on the other side of the door, I remember my mother crying when Tara walked out of Thanksgiving. I remember her crying with worry when Tara disappeared for a few days after throwing a party and trashing my parents' house. I remember her crying on Christmas mornings and at birthday parties. I remember thinking I could feel my mother's heartbreak so often.

And it was always Tara's fault.

The only time I remember breaking my mother's heart was when Tara was born. I don't remember my parents leaving for the hospital after dropping me off at my grandmother's house. I honestly don't even remember my mother being pregnant, having my limited worldview. Instead, I remember that I did not want to share my parents with anybody.

I was perfectly content as an only child, sitting on the rocking horse in my playroom, listening to *The Monkees* for hours on end. The soundtrack of my early years was "Daydream Believer" and the squeals of the springs of the rocking horse as I rode back and forth. I can remember looking at the rows of books on the shelves, the green shag rug, my Raggedy Ann and Andy dolls, and thinking that this was all mine, and I could stay here by myself, forever.

On the day Tara was born, I remember it being cold with a lot of snow outside. In the closest parking spot, my grandmother left the car—an olive-green Chrysler Plymouth that smelled like leather and Chanel No. 5. We braced ourselves against the wind that blew snow into massive frosty dunes across the front of the hospital. Even as we rode the elevator up, I don't remember realizing what we were there for, so I asked my grandmother, "Is Mommy sick?"

"No, sweetheart. Mommy is not sick." She removed my hat and smoothed my hair. "She had a baby, and now you have a little sister!"

My grandmother smiled at me, hoping I would share her enthusiasm. Instead, I vaguely remember being confused, heartbroken. I would now have to share my family and my things with someone else. I pulled my hand away from my grandmother's and crossed my arms in protest.

The elevator doors opened to my mother's floor, and I immediately saw her sitting there, her auburn shag perfectly combed for my visit, her eyes hopeful. Perched on the edge of the sofa in the maternity visiting room, my mother was a vision in a long brown tribal-printed nightgown—so beautifully seventies—and held out her arms to greet me.

I can still see her sitting there. It's one of the mental snapshots of my mother that persists to this day.

"There's my girl," she said.

I walked up to her slowly, cautiously.

I don't remember all the details about this day, but I remember feeling like I had lost, rather than gained, something. That I had lost my specialness. I feared I would no longer be able to play any record I wanted. I would no longer choose the flavor of ice cream at the grocery store. I would no longer have all my mother's time when I begged her to read me just one more book so that I could fall asleep. She would have to take care of a baby now, and I thought my mother would leave me on my own, an afterthought in her daily routine.

I frowned at her and turned away.

"Don't be like that, Jenny." My mother playfully fluffed my hair.

I pulled my crossed arms tighter against my chest and said, "No."

My grandmother tried to intervene. "Jennifer, you're hurting your mother's feelings."

"I don't care," I replied. Then I ran down the hallway away from them, unsure where I was going but knowing I didn't want to stay there. I wanted them to chase me, to make me feel special again.

My grandmother eventually found me, and after a quick scolding, she told me it was time to leave. My mother needed to feed the baby and rest. I don't remember asking what my sister's name was. I don't know if it even occurred to me to ask.

When we returned to my mother's side, I refused to let her button my coat. I shrugged off her kiss and wouldn't look at her. As the elevator doors closed in front of my face, I remember seeing tears in my mother's eyes. She was crying, and I'm sure she didn't want me to see that. She had covered her face, the wide sleeves of her robe draped across her chest.

When Tara finally arrived home, however, my sister became real to me. She was no longer the anonymous and theoretical baby sister I had envisioned; she was a little doll that smelled like Baby Magic and made cooing noises. I offered to help change her diaper, and my parents would tell me, "You are such a big girl, so helpful."

I offered to help my parents with everything. When Tara dropped her pacifier, I would rinse it off before handing it back to her, and my parents would tell me, "What a great big sister you are." I took on the role happily because it gave me a chance to shine in all their eyes. I no longer cared about not being an only child. I was a big sister now.

And now I am again taking care of Tara. Only she is no longer alive. Instead of picking up her pacifier from the floor, I am ordering catering for her funeral. Instead of changing her diaper, I call aunts and uncles to tell them Tara is dead.

What a mess. What a fucking disaster.

I turn on some of the lights in the living room and make sure there is toilet paper in the powder room. I put a few more bottles of wine on the kitchen counter. There is nothing else for me to do. Except to wait and think.

I attempt to remember life before my phone rang this morning, marveling at how one phone call can disrupt the order of things, thrusting us into a new world that feels like a foreign, unfamiliar landscape, upending our previous orientation to it. Even if we have previously traveled on smooth seas, it does not make us good sailors. It simply means that fate has smiled upon us thus far with generosity instead of malice. How we will ultimately fare is tested when those placid waters lose their hold to storms that churn the surfaces around us.

I am now fearful that my parents and I will succumb to the storm in whatever form it might take. I worry that the well-practiced defenses and deflections I have deployed to protect the foundation of our family over the years will prove useless in the face of what has happened to Tara. That we will thrash around helplessly in the wake of what she has done.

And so, my emotions are complicated. I feel sad that my sister has taken her own life because even though we were not close, I am not a monster. She was my sister. But her death raises more in me. I can't tell anyone because I am still trying to understand it myself. But it feels like a type of liberation.

With Tara's death, I can breathe. I can feel comfortable in my skin, knowing that I will no longer need to defend myself or my parents against her. And yet, the relief is unsatisfying. The endless battle between us is over, but only because one of the combatants has chosen to leave the battlefield, not because the source of the war has been resolved. I am now left alone and invalidated, even as I am liberated.

What I don't feel right now is broken or battered by her death. I don't feel hopeless in my ability to continue without my sister. I don't feel anything except the nagging fear that perhaps I am a kind of monster after all. And that is something I will keep to myself. I can't imagine that anyone else would understand anyway. It makes me feel guilty and even more alone. And angrier at Tara, too, since she is the source of all of this.

Joanna is on her way over, and so are family, the neighbors, and some of Tara's friends. I hear the doorbell ring and prepare myself to receive our visitors' sympathy. I prepare to explain the things I can't. I prepare to comfort others as they try to comfort me. As I walk toward the front door, I steel myself to bear the burden of the family on my shoulders. But I am angry at Tara for leaving me behind with this, the tears, the arrangements, the explanations.

But they will not be my tears.

I will be the lone island of detachment in a sea of sadness, forced to have ship after ship of mourning passengers dock on my shores and drain my resources.

Tara has once again ruined everything.

The lack of sadness I feel is her fault.

The anger I feel is her fault.

The guilt I feel is her fault.

She is the fucking worst, even now.

And I hate her for it.

Chapter Three

"Jesus, Jennifer. I am so sorry," Joanna says as she hugs me tightly.

"Thanks for coming, Jo," I reply.

"I can't believe this," she says, shaking her head.

"Me either," I say as I drain my wine glass. A trickle of red wine runs down my chin, and I use the back of my sleeve to wipe it.

Joanna grabs my empty glass and turns to say hello to my aunts and uncles and cousins, the neighbors. Everyone is milling around my parents' living room, eating pizza, and wondering why Tara is dead. Joanna is my best friend and knows our family history well, but Tara's death is still a shock to her.

Like it is to all of us.

Joanna returns to my side with a refilled glass of wine. She says, "I can't believe Tara did this. I can't imagine what you're going through."

I respond, "I know. I never thought it would come to this."

I didn't.

I place my pizza down on my plate. I'm not very hungry.

My father walks in, and Joanna hugs him.

"Mr. Rossi, I am so sorry about Tara," she says.

"Thank you, Jo." My father smiles at her, but I can tell his mind is somewhere else. My mother still hasn't appeared from the bedroom.

"My parents will stop over tomorrow. My mother made a pot of soup, and I put it in the fridge for you."

He nods his head and responds, "That's very sweet. Please thank her for me."

He leaves us moves to say hello to the rest of the room.

As my cousin Pamela pulls Joanna into a conversation, I think about Joanna's family. I just had dinner with them a few weeks ago, which seems like a lifetime ago.

And it was a lifetime ago—Tara's lifetime.

As Joanna's mother, Marie, set the table that night, I noticed how much the pattern on one of her platters looked like my grandmother's china: an oval plate with lilacs wrapped around gold keys along the edges. I remembered all the meals my grandmother served on plates just like that one and how I wished she were still alive.

I remember my grandmother Sadie so well, even though I was young, maybe eleven or twelve, when she died. I felt like the world was falling apart. I felt like some of the glue that held our family together had cracked and split open. I was nine when she passed, but my love for her was so deep I thought I would drown in it.

I felt that grief in the core of my being. I cried at the very thought of my grandmother no longer being alive. I believed she was in a place called Heaven and thought it was an even more magical place now that she was in it. That she would love and care for everyone in heaven like she did for me while she was on earth.

Joanna's mom handed me the platter, now filled with vegetables, and said, "Jennifer, taste this new marinade I put on the asparagus. I want to see if I should make it for Thanksgiving."

"Mom, Thanksgiving is seven months away," Joanna said while smirking at me.

Marie laughed and said, "Oh, stop it—you can never prepare too early, Jo."

Marie was sitting on the edge of her chair, her eyes eager for my feedback.

Joanna's mother has always loved trying out new recipes on me. Joanna has been my best friend for years, and each time I have dinner with her parents, her mother experiments with something she hopes will please me. I know this because Joanna has told me she always raves about my mother's cooking. Since Marie can be slightly competitive, she always asks for my blessing on her culinary experiments.

I stabbed a spear of asparagus with my fork and took a bite. It was delicious: a mixture of garlic and lemon with a hint of something that tasted like dill.

I nodded with approval and said, "Delicious. You should make it again."

"Oh, good!" She smiled at me. "I'm sorry you weren't able to spend Thanksgiving with us last year. Maybe you can join us this year."

Joanna's sister Tracey smiled at me and said, "Yeah, we missed you, Jennifer."

"What you missed was Tracey accidentally putting cumin in the pumpkin pie instead of cinnamon," Joanna said as she laughed, looking at Tracey and pretending to vomit on the table.

Tracey pleaded her case and said, "Cinnamon and cumin look exactly the same."

We all laughed while Tracey slapped Joanna's arm and said, "Jerk."

I wish Tara and I could have been sisters like that. It seemed easy. Effortless. It was the after-school special of sisterhoods, the one I always wished I had. The one I read about in books and watched on sitcoms. It was what I thought love was. Simple and uncomplicated.

I've been envious of Joanna and Tracey's relationship for as long as I can remember. When Joanna and I were ten, Tracey would let us come into her room while having sleepovers. She would play the latest *REO Speedwagon* album for us as we tried on her new lip glosses. It always seemed so easy, so natural. I rarely saw Tracey and Joanna fight, but when they did, I always saw them make up.

And it was always strange to me, the outsider who was waiting for the explosion that never came. It made me question whether Tara and I were the typical sisters or the outliers. Or maybe I just saw what I was looking for in everyone else.

Marie was insistent and said, "Promise me you'll come this year, Jennifer."

Joanna yelled, "Mom, drop it! You're going to make her run away." They all laughed.

I laughed too and said, "That sounds nice."

Joanna looked at me knowingly. She was my first stop after Thanksgiving dinner last year. I drove right to her house from my aunt's and stormed right into her living room, yelling about what a bitch Tara was. Joanna watched me cry and scream that night. I swore that I would never spend Thanksgiving with Tara ever again.

I've spent the occasional Thanksgiving with Joanna's family, and I was sorry to miss it. But last year, I had to be with my family. Thanksgiving came right after a particularly rough patch with Tara in the early fall, and I didn't want to abandon my parents.

I had sensed that things weren't going well with Matt at the time, and Tara was emotionally volatile, overly touchy, and irritable at everything. She fought with each of us at the slightest provocation. She even got angry with my parents because they redecorated the bathroom Tara and I shared as kids. She said she didn't know why they had to change it, said it was fine, in her opinion. She reacted as if the guest bathroom in a house she no longer lived in had a material impact on her life. It was bizarre to me.

It always amazed me how oddly sentimental Tara became about certain things, how unwilling she was to see anything from her childhood transform into something different. She was perpetually unhappy most of her childhood and yet wanted the look and feel of her life in our childhood home to remain the same forever, as a specimen pressed between glass. Or maybe Tara was just uncomfortable seeing other people being so comfortable with change.

I have always had such high hopes for Thanksgiving in particular. The purpose of it—coming together to be grateful for what you have—always made me hope things could be different. As if the holiday could wave a magic wand to transform us entirely into new beings. That perhaps our story would rewrite itself, casting Tara and me into the picture-perfect scene complete with soft lighting, scored like an eighties movie with a song orchestrated to show how much we loved each other and that everything would be okay.

Without the hope of that transformation, I've had to focus more on the aesthetics of the holiday rather than the experience. I remember driving to my aunt's house in Central New Jersey that day, noting the signs of Thanksgiving all around me. Pumpkins lying in thoughtfully designed arrangements across front steps. It made me think about the foods of my childhood—spanakopita, stuffed mushrooms, pumpkin bread—coming to life under my mother's watchful eye. Passing driveway after driveway filled as far as the eye could see, minivans and SUVs with license plates from New York, Delaware, and Pennsylvania. Listening to the first day of Christmas music on the radio.

My family scattered themselves across my aunt Diane's living room—Pamela, my aunt and uncle, my parents, Tara—pouring drinks, making Black Friday plans, picking at cheese and crackers. We had mingled with ease early in the day, high on seventies music and the smell of pumpkin spice candles.

To keep the peace, I had stayed out of Tara's way most of the day and was relieved that she had stayed out of mine. I have always known how easily we could escalate to conflict, how one misspoken comment, one misunderstood glance, could quickly launch us back into battle.

The implicit social agreement in our family, between Tara and me and our aunt, uncle, cousins, parents, friends, was that we all knew to tread lightly around Tara, to keep it light, fun, and funny always.

Honestly, I've always felt like I signed that agreement with a gun pointed at my head, for part of Tara's good time often included ostracizing me. For years, and because she did it primarily through humor, others saw it as funny. But I never saw it that way.

As Thanksgiving dinner ended, I knew a fight was coming. I could never envision which form the conflict would take. Still, I could sense it was on the horizon like rain before it fell: I could feel the pressure change, sense the energy in the air, smell the humidity clinging to the corners and curves of every surface.

As my aunt and uncle cleared the table, I could sense that our family web's tensile strength was about to collapse, setting the free fall in motion, a fall most terrifying because you can't assess your position relative to the bottom. As my aunt began to serve dessert, I walked into the kitchen to refill my glass of wine. I could hear the murmur of agitated voices—Tara's and my mother's—as they stood near the sink, their voices sitting just below the soundtrack of *The Bee Gees* coming from the other room.

Tara and my mother disagreed about something, which I assumed was the paycheck story my father just told over dessert. It was a funny and innocent story, but Tara always overreacted. After all the stories she told about me, I couldn't believe her skin could be so thin to the same treatment. But it always was, even when I had hoped for it to be different.

I went back into the dining room, greeted by somber glances thrown over the picked-over plates of pie and half-filled cups of coffee. My cousin Pamela had stepped outside, and my father was staring at the fireplace.

Tara has always been an equal opportunity offender with her tirades, but my dad was in the crosshairs on this most thankful of holidays. He was drinking more than his usual glass or two of wine that day, one of the telltale signs that something was amiss. Alcohol has always been the silent member of our family; it primes our social pumps and anesthetizes our wounds. It sometimes makes us better and other times worse people, sometimes more fun and others more sullen. Sometimes I think we rely on alcohol to help us solve the riddle that continually stumps us: what causes our family to fall apart regularly?

But there is no valid logic to it. If you were to trace these episodes and try to draw correlations between people, places, settings, and words, they would appear simply as a cluttered collection of pins and strings and photos, like the frantic ravings of a madman trying to plot the course of his crimes.

Sometimes the trigger has been something as small as forgetting a critical detail that Tara deemed essential. Other times, it has been more direct, like my father making Tara accountable for some misstep. But that day, it all started with a harmless story poorly received.

Tara walked back into the room, walked right past my father, and ignored him.

I stood in the doorway observing them.

My father tried to smooth the situation over, joking with Tara, referring to her by her childhood nickname, T-Rex. She was not responding to it. She veered from simply uncooperative to mean.

My father stared at his glass on the table, running his fingers along the rim. The look on his face—focused, determined, frustrated—told me his mind was racing, searching for an escape that he knew did not exist. I could feel his pain and frustration viscerally, and I needed to make it stop. I needed my family to operate without drama. I needed to free us from our captivity. I envisioned my parents as emotional hostages ripping off their blindfolds and rushing into my arms as I rescued them.

But rescuing them required me to rush into the building, shooting at the enemy while defending my position. It required me to throw fuel on that smoldering fire. Still, I needed to protect my father.

I stepped between them.

I said, "Tara, stop it. It's Thanksgiving."

She replied, "Shut up, Jennifer. You always take his side. You always think it's my fault."

She set her drink on the buffet table. The warmth in the room immediately created a ring of condensation around its base. As if her glass itself was perspiring with nervous anticipation of the trouble brewing.

This time I would not back down.

More loudly, I said, "Tara, it is always your fault."

I could feel my bracelet tapping against my wrist and realized my arm was shaking. With every tap, I yelled at Tara in my mind.

Tap-tap-tap-tap. *Fucking bitch.*

Tap-tap-tap-tap. *You ruin everything.*

Tap-tap-tap-tap. *I wish you would just go away.*

The fury inside my head was radiating out to my wrists, jolting my fingertips, electrifying my body.

I couldn't help myself; I had started down the path and couldn't turn back now. I remember thinking that Tara always ruins everything. That she always causes a fight. That I hated her and everything she says and does.

I yelled, "Why can't you just give Dad a break? Why do you always have to start a fight?"

My mother tried to intervene and said, "Jennifer, Tara, Robert, please. Please don't do this."

My father erupted, finally having hit his limit. He finished his drink and wiped his mouth on the back of his sleeve.

He roared across the room, "You know what, Tara, you're right, I'm wrong, you're perfect, and I'm an asshole."

I was glad to see him respond like that. It helped me feel less alone in the fight. But it wasn't anything more than a frustrated capitulation. He had no more tools in his bag to try and repair the situation. He had no other move than to sacrifice himself at Tara's altar, hoping that it would end the conflict.

Tara spat back at him, "Yeah, Dad, you are an asshole."

His eyes darted away from her; his face strained from absorbing the blow. He refilled his glass, nearly tipping the Scotch over the top of the rim. I worried that Tara had again upended any dreams he had for a relationship with his daughter. That his every expectation for his family was once again disintegrating in front of his own eyes.

"That's it, Tara," I intervened.

I walked right up to her, pointing my finger in front of her face. I wanted to grab her by the neck and squeeze until she relented.

I said, "I can't take it. You do this every time. You ruin everything."

She slapped my finger away, which sent me back a few steps. My aunt and uncle rose from their chairs. My mother and cousin yelled for us to knock it off. My hands began to shake, and I couldn't control the words coming out of my mouth. Days and months and years of resentments were manifesting themselves.

I didn't back down, moving closer to Tara again.

I said, "Why do you have to hurt everyone all the time? I am so tired of this shit."

Tara's eyes were on fire.

She replied, "Fuck you, Jennifer. I hate you."

With those words, Tara raced to the foyer to retrieve her coat and purse.

My mother tried to stop her. "Sweetheart, please stay. We love you. It's a misunderstanding."

Despite Tara's frequent missteps, my mother has always tried to comfort her during these episodes. She was trying to glue broken glass back together, even though each shard sliced her fingers as she collected them.

And with every injury my mother has sustained, my resentment has grown.

My mother avoids conflict at all costs. It's not in her nature to rock the boat or confront people. She is a gentle soul who is only looking for a similar gentleness in return. She loves deeply and doesn't always need that love returned in kind. But she does want peace.

Tara grabbed her things and said, "No, Mom, I don't want to be here anymore."

And with that, she opened the front door to leave.

We all gathered in the foyer, spilling out onto the front steps.

My cousin Pamela stepped forward and tried to intervene. She said, "Tara, come on."

Tara responded, "No, Pamela. It's not fair."

Pamela grabbed her arm and became more forceful with Tara, "You can't do this. It's Thanksgiving. Just make peace with them, please."

Pamela immediately softened, tugged on Tara's sleeve, and smiled, her eyes pleading for Tara to reverse course.

Tara said, "No. I'm always the bad guy. Perfect Jennifer can stay. They love her more anyway."

She looked back before leaving. I moved to stand next to my father and grasp his arm in defense. When Tara saw that, it reignited the fire in her mind. She opened the door and walked out. She shouted at us over her shoulder as she marched toward her car.

"Happy fucking Thanksgiving. All of you can go fuck yourselves," she yelled across the lawn.

Though Tara ended it just as I knew she would, her words still stunned me. If I were watching this scene as an outsider, I would think it was some bad movie, a poorly acted melodrama with too much unnecessary dialogue, too many hair-trigger personalities.

We stood there and watched Tara make a scene on the front lawn. Her long legs stomped her feet into the grass; long brown hair spilled from the loose bun she hastily fashioned, her sharp features undulated between rage and satisfaction.

Tara had her purse slung clumsily through her right elbow, and a leftover bottle of Chardonnay swung in her left hand. The keys in her pocket jingled with each frantic step as she descended the steep driveway. Her exit from the family holiday was severe but swift, something everyone was undoubtedly thankful for.

I was glad to see her leave. Her exit allowed me to breathe more air. I had always felt like the room got more expansive, more comfortable when she left it.

Tara turned and peppered us with one last edict. She yelled, "Jennifer, I hope you're fucking happy. I know this is what you wanted." Then she started her silver Honda Accord and slammed the door shut behind her.

Maybe it is what I wanted.

It is what I expected.

Tara has usually stormed out of family meals somewhere between taco dip and turkey. Somewhere between light banter and pointed criticisms. That time she had made it to pie.

And as much as Tara believed we would place the blame on

her, I knew I was the one who would be at fault. While others treat Tara with kid gloves all the time, I have refused just to sit back and take it from her. I had stopped being diplomatic and passive years ago. Because of this, my family often sees me as an instigator, an agitator of already explosive situations. Since Tara never stuck around to be blamed, I was the next best thing. I was the sounding board for all the frustrations that my family felt.

I knew it was coming.

My mother said, "Jennifer, why did you have to start with her?"

She spat the accusation at me, her eyes oscillating between sadness and rage. She was searching for something to fight; I was the flint in the tinderbox. For this, I don't blame my mother; my parents have also been victims of Tara's emotional crimes. With no ability to reprimand Tara to any effect, my parents have often assigned me as the target to bear the responsibility for inciting Tara's wrath. Because they know I will never leave them. Because they know I understand. Even if it hurts us all.

I crossed my arms in front of my body, not ready to take the blame.

I said to my mother, "I couldn't let her speak to Dad like that."

She replied, "I know. I don't know what to do."

I didn't know what to do either.

My mother began to cry, and I hugged her.

"Why is she like this, Jennifer?"

I don't know. I never have.

"Everything will be okay, Mom."

I wasn't convinced of it. But my mother needed to hear it.

My aunt appeared by my side and ushered my mother into the living room.

I heard her say, "Ann, everything will be okay. I'm sure she'll feel bad about how she left."

I didn't share her optimism, for I've never seen evidence of Tara feeling regret—about anything.

But my parents have never given up, and as hard as it is to witness, I admire them for their persistence. No one has ever known what to do about Tara, though, so we have just made space in our lives for her behavior. It's like having a dog that bites you occasionally, a transgression you forget when the dog curls up next to you. But when that same dog licks your face, the fear comes back that he will bite you again. You fear how quickly affection could turn into pain.

What else could my parents do? I can't imagine what it must be like to have this happen. To have your child behave this way.

That Thanksgiving was the perfect example of how we operated when things were terrible with Tara.

Which they were more often than I wanted them to be.

But we could never identify the root of the problem. We could never get through to my sister. Her behavior was just as mysterious to us then as her death is now.

My plate with its half-eaten slice of pizza comes into focus, and I realize I am no longer at Thanksgiving. I am back in my parents' living room.

I hear, "Jennifer?"

Joanna has returned to my side. I look up and smile at her. I'm glad she's here.

She says, "Everyone is leaving. I'll help you clean up."

I wonder how long I have been distracted. I nod my head and rise to say my goodbyes.

As we're washing dishes, I ask her, "Do you think there's anything we could have done differently?"

She replies, "With Tara? She kept you all so far away from her it would have been impossible to know how she was feeling and what she was thinking."

I say, "I know. My sister was a mystery to me. It's sad, don't you think?"

I am distracted again and rest my hands in the sink. I don't realize how hot the water has become and pull my hands away quickly, waving my swollen red fingers to cool them.

"Jen, if Tara had wanted you to help her, if she had even known what was wrong, it would have been a different story. You can't take this on as your responsibility."

When we finish, I hug Joanna and close the door behind her after she walks out.

My father went to bed a while ago.

As I turn off the lights, I realize that I am now truly alone with my parents. I remember that it was what I wanted when Tara was born. My face feels hot with the memory because I now have received what I had asked for all those years ago.

I also fear that I will always be alone with memories of Tara, which don't allow me to be truly free of the pain she caused while she was alive. Or why she caused it. A solitary traveler along the road to understanding what went wrong—why she didn't love me—waiting patiently for the next rest stop, the next time I can experience my life without relating it to some painful memory she caused. But for now, I am relegated to living with Tara lingering over my every experience, an uninvited companion in death, much as she was in life.

I've had too much wine to drive home, and I can feel my peak of exhaustion coming quickly. I walk toward the guest bedroom where Tara had been staying.

Before I get into bed, I turn on the closet light and reach for the plastic bag I placed on the top shelf when we got home. I haven't had the stomach to open it yet. I'm not sure I do now either. But my curiosity is getting the best of me.

I hold the bag in my hands. It contains papers and a cell phone and car keys from what I can see. All the things I would expect to find. Then, something shiny catches my eye. At the bottom of a bag is a ring. I loosen the drawstring and reach in to grab it. I remember this ring. It's white and yellow gold with a "C" on it. Our grandmother, Anna, gave it to Tara for her college graduation. She wore it all the time.

I place the ring on my finger, and it fits. I don't know why I want to wear it, but I keep it on. I return the bag to the shelf and turn off the light.

I lie in bed and stare at the ceiling. I don't know long I've been lying here.

I wonder if my mother were to look at me right now, my open eyes fixed upward, she would wonder if I too were looking for my sister. As if I, too, thought that Tara would be floating in the air above me.

I feel something similar, but not quite like that.

I am feeling oddly spiritual, feeling the collision of life and death in this house, in this room. I can't help but feel I am occupying the same space as a ghost, that Tara is with me, seeing me, pressing against the boundary of life and death to make herself known to me. It's hard to explain it, but I feel like with her death, she will now be with us even more closely than she was in life, for there are no longer any emotional boundaries to keep us apart. Her very absence from our lives now puts her front and center in them.

The thought terrifies me.

I wonder if it's the room or the ring. I trace the C with my finger to see if it emits a kind of cosmic force. I can feel my fear pulse through my hand. I suppose the ring will hijack my mind with energy from Tara, wherever she is.

I shake it off and tell myself I imagine things.

I can hear my parents talking and crying through the bedroom wall as I lie awake. I fear that my parents will now be prisoners of my sister's death, tethered to her forever, but in a much more complicated way. I worry that they will suffocate under the weight of what they think they did, could have done, and or perhaps didn't do enough. I can hear their conversations, exhausted, broken, and confused.

I place a pillow over my head to drown out their voices because I need to sleep.

If I dream of the ocean tonight, I fear that I will once again save myself, even if it means leaving Tara behind. I worry that I can't save us both.

And given a choice, I don't know that I would try anyway.

Chapter Four

Tara has been gone for three days. I haven't moved the plastic bag from the closet since that first night, and even though I can't see it, I can sense its presence in the house. Like a telltale heart, I can almost feel Tara's possessions pulsing through the wall of the guest bedroom.

When we took the bag home from the police station, my parents were too distracted to ask about what it was. So, I hid it. I don't know the full extent of what's in there. I'm not even sure they're ready for it. I'm not sure I'm prepared for it.

My parents aren't home. They are out running errands, attempting to distract themselves now that we've planned the funeral and made all the arrangements.

I am also distracted, but it's by the feeling of being unsatisfied. I need to know more about how and why my sister died. Perhaps some of those answers lie inside the plastic bag.

But I worry that there will be answers in there I don't want to find. I fear that I will learn more than I wanted to from that bag.

But I have to do it. It's all I have right now.

I retrieve the bag from the closet and place it on the kitchen counter.

Anyone passing it by would likely think nothing of it, a clear bag containing a wallet, a cell phone, some papers. I place the bag under a pile of mail on the counter to cover it, as if I am afraid that it will leap out and attack me. I avoid opening like it is radioactive.

It was the array of items that lay across a hotel room as my sister hung from the back of the hotel door, inanimate witnesses to her final act. It makes me slightly sad that the end of a person's life could be reduced to a disposable bag of random objects. I wonder how random they are.

I pass the bag on the counter every time I refill my cup of coffee, averting my eyes as if they would burn with a simple glance at it. I reorganize my mother's spice rack with my back turned to the bag. I take a quick inventory of the fridge and hide behind the open door, well out of sight of my sister's things. I choreograph chore after chore in a frenetic orbit around the bag, its force keeping me close to it yet unable to touch it.

At least not yet.

These were the final things Tara saw and touched before she died. It's as close as I can be to her physically from now on. I don't know why I feel these things would have almost a magical power as if I would touch them and unwittingly conjure my sister to appear in this kitchen. And I don't know if that is something that would bring me comfort or send me spiraling into an even more bottom-less pit of fear about what has happened to my sister now that she is dead.

I pour a cup of coffee. My parents' house phone rings, and my hand jumps, causing coffee to spill over the side of the mug. I slam it down on the counter, spilling it more.

"Shit—"

I bend down to wipe it up before my parents return. Last night, my father melted down about an overflowing trash can in the guest bathroom, triggered by the slightest infraction of order. My parents have always been adamant about order and cleanliness in their house, and their grief has escalated that insistence into frantic energy, a displaced rage for the shrinking universe of things they can now control. I don't want to throw fuel on the fire in the form of a coffee cup carelessly handled.

After the fourth ring, I answer the phone, and my mother is on the other line. She has already called me two times since they left the house earlier this morning.

"Jennifer? Are you okay?"

"Yes, I'm fine—" I clench the paper towel in my hand, causing it to drip the coffee I just collected back onto the floor. "What's up?"

I grab another paper towel and wipe the floor clean, standing and hurling the damp towel into the trash can.

"I was worried about you. I love you."

"I'm fine, Mom. I love you too."

I place the phone onto the receiver, exhausted by the endless check-ins. I had already texted my mother that I was okay and had given her no reason to think otherwise. My sister's death appears to have created a fear in my mother's mind that I will disappear too. That I will be there one day and gone the next, leaving her and my father desperately alone, the parents who outlived both of their only children.

After I clean up the coffee and wash my cup, I look at the bag.

I feel guilty for getting frustrated, so I text my mother.

`Everything is good here. I love you.`

I have always softened to my parents quickly, even when I was irritated or infuriated by them. One night, years earlier, my parents blamed me for what they had considered me instigating Tara, causing her to storm out of dinner early. I had unleashed on them, furious that they couldn't see it was Tara who had started the problem that night, making some snide comment about what I had been studying in graduate school, the way I did my hair, or the political candidate I supported. My rage had erased the actual root cause of the fight from my memory, but I do remember feeling like defending myself from Tara was a complicated endeavor in front of my parents.

But then I had seen the way they looked at each other after Tara left that night, one daughter gone from the table and the other ready to flee as well. My father's shoulders were crouched, my mother's eyeliner was running along the tear tracks on her face. And so I had apologized, I had relented, I had submitted to the family dynamic that Tara had created. My sympathy for my parents had always outweighed my frustration with them.

And even though I have often felt like the sacrificial lamb at the altar of Tara, I put myself in that position again and again. Because I have been the good daughter, the very role I established in opposition to Tara's behavior. I am steadfast in my belief that I am responsible for making my parents happy when Tara couldn't. Even when it breaks me down, making me feel like an extra in another person's overly dramatic story, rather than placing me on center stage based on my own merits.

Without a comparison to Tara, I wonder if my light will shine as bright as it did when she was alive, simply because it no longer has such darkness to be compared to.

Maybe I am just a secret type of monster. One who hated having my sister around but needed her around to give myself an identity. And now that she's gone, I don't have either. Maybe I can't grieve like I've seen others do because I don't know what I'm grieving for; I don't know if I am sad about Tara dying and whether my sadness would be for her sake or mine.

I need to review the bag's contents before my parents come home. I need to be prepared for what they might find. Perhaps I am also wondering about Tara's things as if touching them might spark some feeling in me, some connection to grief that I haven't yet experienced. That seeing the sheer everydayness of a few items chosen for her final journey will bring me to tears, will make me miss her, will make me feel like a better person.

I have some of my grandma Anna's things on my bedroom dresser. A hair roller, a Greek icon, her watch. Things that make me feel closer to her, things that my grandmother once held in her hands. They are things that someone would pass by and not take notice of, but they are things that make me remember. When I see them and touch them, I can almost smell her kitchen—a combination of coffee, lemon, and sunlight. I can see her standing on a stepstool, stirring an enormous pot of soup on the stove. I can smell the perfume she quickly sprayed when I would catch her sneaking a cigarette in her bedroom. I can feel her touch as she embraces me and tells me that everything will be okay.

So many emotions and memories are tied to everyday items. They are my portal to my grandmother, and they keep me connected to her through all my senses. I prepare myself for what will arise from what Tara has left behind.

I take the bag out to the back patio to smoke a cigarette while I inspect its contents. I light my Marlboro Light and blow a perfect cloud of smoke toward the sky; its light gray veil makes the sun look like it is shining through cobwebs. I flick the ash into a soda can and rest the lit cigarette on the wrought iron fleur-de-lis on the corner of the table. The design makes me think of a trip I took in high school to Quebec, where our band and chorus played in a music festival. There was fleur-de-lis everywhere in Quebec, seemingly planted on every square inch of that city. I remember our choir director helping us pronounce it: "Say it, kids, it's flooooor-deh-leeeeee." Seeing it here on this table makes me think of that trip and how freeing it felt to be away doing the things I liked to do on my terms. It was a taste of freedom achieved

through a distance that I would continue for years after high
school.

I take a breath and loosen the string's knot at the opening of
the bag.

One by one, I place the items on the table. Tara's cell phone.
Tara's laptop. Tara's car keys. Tara's wallet. Tara's notepad and
pen. I had expected to feel some emotional electricity holding
them in my hands. I had expected a revelation. I am embarrassed at
my assumption that they would be supernatural. But, instead,
they are as unremarkable in death as they had been in life, mere
physical objects. The ash from my cigarette falls onto my knee
through the wrought iron, and I slap it away to find a slight burn
left behind. "Shit," I cry out to no one.

I wonder what my sister's last few days and hours were like.
Since she is not here to ask, I must study her primary sources. This
time, instead of scouring political documents to pose theories
about the intent of Madison or Warren, I'm tracing the path of my
sister's plan to die.

I open her laptop and scroll through her emails. I don't see
anything in her Sent folder that catches my eye. Tara sent a few
recipes to my mother. She forwarded a few jokes to friends.
That's it.

I look at her inbox, and once again, there isn't much there.
Some chain emails, some coupons for Bath and Body Works and
Coach. But nothing that would tell me she was thinking of taking
her own life. Nothing out of the ordinary.

I browse her search history. It's been cleared.

I open her cell phone and listen to her voicemails. Her hair-
dresser left a message with an appointment reminder for next
week. There are voicemails from my parents and me, asking Tara
where she is. I can hear the panic in my parents' voices and the irritation in mine. I can't tell if Tara ever listened to them. I don't

know if she was even alive when we left them or if she had already died.

I begin to scroll through her texts. Four days ago, starting at around seven a.m., there were several text exchanges between Tara and numbers I don't recognize. They must be coworkers because they are talking about appointments and reimbursements.

There is a text from Leslie with a picture of the baby asking Tara to call her back.

The morning we went to the police station, there were texts from my parents and me trying to get in touch with her.

There is Pamela's text asking Tara to call us immediately.

They are all unopened. Tara never saw any of them.

I am no closer to learning anything than I was before.

So, I look further back in time to the night before, when she must have still been alive. I see that Tara texted her ex-boyfriend Matt a few times, but none of the texts were returned.

```
Can we talk?
I miss you
I'm not mad anymore
```

Was Tara trying to get back together with Matt? Was she trying to make peace with him knowing that she would die? Why was she mad at Matt? I need to talk to him. They've been broken up for a while, but maybe there is more to it. It nags at me that Matt told me he hadn't heard from Tara, but she texted him the night she died. Why would he lie to me? I make a mental note to call him later today.

As I return the phone to the bag, I notice a smaller plastic bag containing several folded pieces of paper. I take it out and open it. The paper on top has *Mom and Dad* written in Tara's handwriting. I grab the smoldering cigarette from the table and take a long drag. And another.

I can see a second note inside that bag.

I open the bag and pull the second folded paper from it. On it is written, *Jennifer.*

The detective never mentioned that Tara had left suicide notes. Of course, Tara being Tara, it didn't surprise me that she wouldn't have, or even occur to ask if she had.

I flick my butt into a flowerpot and light another. I smoke the entire cigarette and stare at my name. I read my name so many times it almost seems foreign to me, some made-up word that doesn't make any sense. Tara has addressed this letter to me, a final communication from my sister. Before she died, for better or worse, she thought of me. I was significant enough to warrant my own note. It makes me feel morbidly special but also incredibly afraid.

Suicide notes are the stuff of movies, the neat wrap-up on a mess of a situation. But here, on this patio, I didn't expect a clean and tidy ending to a mess of a scenario. Instead, I reek of cigarette smoke and sweat as I come face to face with the final scene of our family movie. The last words my sister wrote, the final monologue delivered before the antagonist exited the stage.

I stand up from the table, gathering all of Tara's things. I press the note addressed to me in the back pocket of my jeans and return my parents' letter to the larger bag. I can't bring myself to open the note right now. I don't know if I ever will. I consider burning it but think twice about it. It scares me. Will it hold words that seek to comfort our wound me?

I have good reason to be afraid.

Over the years, I have endured mocking birthday poems and yearbook graffiti, and insulting notes left on my desk to find after school. As a result, I am skittish about reading any communications from my sister. My anxiety is getting the best of me. I worry that Tara used her final moments to indict me, with broad strokes of blame scrawled across the page. But it makes me wonder if there is a grain of truth in my fears. I fear that I am partially to blame for my sister's death in that I didn't see it coming, or maybe I didn't care to.

I walk back into the house, place the bag on the counter, and make a fresh pot of coffee for my parents while I wait for them to arrive. I wash my hands and spray some Happy on my neckline to displace the smell of smoke. I laugh as I think of my grandmother doing the same and how history so often repeats itself. I fluff the pillows on the couch and neatly place my shoes by the front door. A picture on the wall leans to the right, so I walk over to straighten it. I have done my best to create the order and peace my parents will likely need to hold Tara's cell phone in their hands and read her final texts. To power up her laptop and browse through her emails. To read her suicide note and absorb her last words before she ripped the world as they knew it out from under their feet.

Before greeting my parents at the door, I check my back pocket to ensure my note is still there. It is. I wonder if I can feel the same connection to Tara I do to my grandmother by the note's mere physical presence. But I already can't remember what Tara's voice sounded like; I can't smell her perfume; I can't feel the touch of her skin or picture the way she walked. She has disappeared from my memory so quickly. And now it will be in my control whether she reappears in my mind or a hastily scribbled last communication before her death.

Either way, I am not ready for it.

Chapter Five

TARA

LAST NOVEMBER

I watch the turkey grease congeal on the edge of the platter that sits on the kitchen counter as my family slowly falls apart again in the dining room. I anticipate it will once again be considered my fault. I study the slick brown pools collecting and smothering the ring of violets on the edge of the china that was my grandmother's pride and joy and think of all the times I've heard my sister say, "Tara, you ruin everything."

These greasy remains are the turkey's morning-after hair, the hot mess that shows only a glimpse into how great it was hours before. I poke at the rubbery spots that surround the carcass and think, what an end to the life for this poor turkey. What a fate to be relegated to grease and bones on my aunt's kitchen counter. It's not the first turkey I've seen served on this platter, but I don't remember it having appeared so pathetic, so dead before.

It's Thanksgiving at my Aunt Diane's house. In the world of Hallmark cards and sentimental movies, days like Thanksgiving are festive gatherings swirling with some special magic. But they never quite feel that special to me. In the end, they fall flat and unsatisfying, a stale cracker on your tongue that satisfies your hunger pangs but still leaves you wanting.

We're a small family, especially for Italians in New Jersey. Everything I've ever seen in the movies would place us at a long table, filled with multiple generations, thirty or forty of us, drinking wine, kids running around, women in floral house dresses serving platter after platter of food while cousins and brothers and sisters yell and laugh and argue. We look so different from the family tableaus that contain so much fierce love and enthusiasm you feel like the room could explode. The power of numbers and genetics, and history wrapped into a pulsing bundle of energy.

But not us. We're usually a small group that consists of me, my parents, my aunt and uncle, my cousin Pamela, and my sister Jennifer. Some years, distant cousins and friends attend too, and I always prefer that because it gives me more room to hide. It provides me with more opportunities to deflect, a much-needed buffer between my family and me. My parents alone are generally okay, but things become toxic when we add Jennifer to the mix. And no one understands that.

I can hear Jennifer telling a story about her job in the other room. A colleague said she should write a book about something I can't believe people care about. I can't even follow it; it's so dull. My sister is a professor of political science at Rutgers. And everyone thinks it's the biggest deal on earth, as if she won a Nobel Prize or something. But I know that teaching college kids about the Constitution and how elections work doesn't make you a genius, even though everyone seems to think it does. I can see through it all. She doesn't know anything about my life or what I go through. But Jennifer loves showing how smart she is, especially compared to me. Being a professor is the perfect job for her, as she's spent years trying to teach me what to do and what I need to do better, how I need to be better. As if she's some expert.

I don't like being around her. She's a know-it-all whose shadow I've lived in my entire life. So, when I'm stuck in situations that force me to be around her for any amount of time, I get edgy, preparing for the backhanded comparisons and false attempts to make us bond over cute moments we shared when we were little. As if Jennifer and I can relive them in the present and erase everything that has happened since.

From the start, nothing has worked out between us. Jennifer would say that it's all my fault, but she's not perfect either. She's fucked up as many times as I have, but I'm the one everyone thinks is the problem.

I look at the greasy platter sitting in the sink and think about my grandmother, Sadie. I was so young when she died, but I wonder what she would think about how things have turned out between Jennifer and me. I wonder if she had still been alive, would that have reduced how stressful so many of our Thanksgiving dinners have been.

There was the one year that Jennifer pointed out the new tattoo I had been trying to hide. She asked about it right in front of my parents. She said she didn't mean to, but I know she did. Jen never misses an opportunity to call me out. That same night she went on and on about her new job, always making sure she was in the spotlight, always trying to make me feel like shit. I saw her roll her eyes when I brought up leaving early to go out afterward with my friends. She must think I'm blind and can't see how she judges me. The only thing I was thankful for that Thanksgiving night was getting the hell out of there.

But having my cousin Pamela around makes it easier for me to avoid spending any time with Jennifer. Pamela is my favorite cousin, and she's way better to hang out with than Jennifer. I walk over to the hallway just off the kitchen and look at my favorite photo of us. It hangs on the wall between an old clock and other framed family photos. It was taken on Christmas Eve when I was thirteen or fourteen. Pamela, Jennifer, some other cousins, and I are in it. We are all smiling in the picture, sitting on the edge of my parent's fireplace hearth. I can almost smell the photo: marinara sauce and roasted garlic. I can hear the Christmas music and the sounds of laughter in the background.

Pamela and I look like sisters in the picture, which I always wanted. For as long as I can remember, I have wished that Pamela was my sister instead of Jennifer. I even wrote Pamela a letter about it once. I had just had a massive fight with Jennifer. She claimed I stole her favorite lip gloss and ran right to my parents to tell on me. She was crying, yelling about her privacy being violated, about how she couldn't trust me with anything. My parents took her side—they usually did—and I ended up getting the TV taken away for a week. As my father pulled my TV from my room, yanking the cord from the socket with a heavy sigh, I sat at my desk and thought about what it would be like to be in a different family. One where I would feel like I fit in.

I did take the lip gloss. But I never wanted my parents to know they were right. And I secretly loved creating havoc in the house. It made me feel in control, my ability to force them all to be out of control. It's like I could pour gasoline on a fire that was always smoldering, and with one move, launch the household into a raging inferno. It was my secret power, and I felt it nowhere else in my life. I have always felt like a tattered flag whipped around by the wind, and after years of feeling that way, I decided to become the wind.

I wrote Pamela to tell my side of the story about why I didn't want Jennifer as my sister anymore. How much I wanted Pamela to take Jennifer's place. I folded the letter and placed it in an envelope. I wrote Pamela's name on it and put it in the back of one of my desk drawers. I wouldn't send it to her yet. Instead, I would save it for when I needed it, my lifeline, the fantasy I would latch onto when I needed saving.

So, the letter sat in my drawer for years, holding my hopes quietly in that envelope. And Jennifer would never know my secret. And that fantasy never died; it's just gotten pushed aside by other, more significant dreams. None of which have come true either.

I can see through to the living room, and Pamela cheerfully refills drinks while singing along to Barry Manilow. She is smiling and laughing with everyone as if she doesn't have a care in the world. As if everyone doesn't make her crazy or irritated or sad. I wish I were more like her.

Pamela is the type of person I want to be, effortlessly happy and confident. Beautiful and fun and loved. All the things I am not. She always has a handsome and kind boyfriend who comes to every family party. She has all the things that I want but don't have. And it doesn't make me hate her. Instead, it makes me want to be as close to her as I can, as if her magical powers can rub off on me and make me prettier, funnier, happier.

My phone beeps, and I open it to check it, hoping it's Matt. He was with me last Thanksgiving, and I hoped that our break would be over by now. But I quickly realize it isn't him, and our break isn't over.

It's my best friend, Leslie. I had texted her earlier asking if she wanted to meet up tonight.

```
Hey T I'd love to but Kara is in town and I
wanted to spend some time with her before she
leaves tomorrow. Leggett's tomorrow night?
Your favorite bartender is working haha

    Whatever, loser! Just kidding - talk to you
                tomorrow. Say hi to Kara.
```

Kara is Leslie's older sister. I always wished Kara was my sister too. She was pretty and popular in high school. Kara bought us beer when she turned twenty-one. Kara was everything my sister wasn't. Jennifer didn't care about being popular, so she wasn't. Jennifer could have been pretty if she tried, but she didn't. My sister cared about school and not what other people thought about her, so they just didn't think about her. The opposite of fun. The opposite of my cousin Pamela. The opposite of Kara.

It annoys me that Leslie and I don't have plans later, but I expected it to happen. Leslie's family enjoys spending time together, so Leslie is often booked with family time when I try to make plans with her. Sometimes, I join her, but the feeling of her family is unfamiliar to me. They're like the Bradys. The love I've always seen shown by TV families has been breezy, filled with laughter, only occasionally interrupted by strife. Disagreements ended with fiddle playing and ice cream sundaes. Siblings are best friends. Parents forgive you even when you mess up. But I'm not ridiculous; I don't expect life to mirror television. Leslie's is the closest I've seen to it.

The love I feel from my family is different. It feels forced, full of effort, suffocating. A too-stiff couch that doesn't let you settle into it like you want to. They need to call each other all the time to check in. They plan endless family dinners and insist on involvement in each other's lives. It always felt a little too much for me. But being alone is worse, so I show up most of the time.

I walk back into my aunt's kitchen and see the platter still sitting there. I slide the turkey carcass into the trash and place the plate into the sink. Just like that, it no longer exists.

I think to myself that we all start as turkeys running happily through the yard, and then one day, we're flung into a trash can once the pumpkin pie is served. And that thought doesn't make me feel sad like I'd expect. It will happen to all of us; it's just a question of when. So I control the things I can when I can. It's the only way I can endure my life while I have it.

Control is the one thing I've practiced more than any other. I can push everything that hurts me out of my mind with the proper focus. I've done the self-talk. I have given myself the locker room speech time and again.

Not feeling pretty enough or smart enough or lovable enough today, Tara? Administer tiny doses of love that keep everyone strung out, fearing withdrawal, and wanting more. Pretend to be the person you want to be.

Feeling like you're a worthless piece of shit today, Tara? Get the upper hand in all situations. Plant seeds of doubt to make your position look favorable.

Think your life is out of control, Tara? Reclaim control of the things that hurt you. Know when to arrive and when to leave. Know when to speak and when to remain silent. Know when to offer affection and when to withhold it.

I've done all of it. Not that it's gotten me anywhere. It gives me temporary rushes of satisfaction, pulses of adrenaline that keep me moving forward. However, I still feel like I'm dying a slow, strangling death by disappointment and exclusion.

Even before studying the turkey carcass, death has been on my mind lately, making me think about things differently. I watched a show on TV where the main character died, and everyone felt so bad that they didn't treat her the way she deserved when she was alive. It drew me in. I could relate to it. The thought of people regretting the way they've seen you while you were alive and feeling terrible after you've gone triggered something in me. I can't stop thinking about it. But I keep it to myself.

I've never really feared death; I have always considered it a necessary part of the routines and rhythms of life. It's the exact price we pay for being alive. I don't think it's the scary monster under our beds, the shadows we run from. Death doesn't seem so dire when there are no other satisfying options in sight. When drinking, fighting, or fucking our demons away doesn't make them go or solve our problems, death appears peaceful. It wipes the slate clean, rights the wrongs, pushes the dust under the rug. It cleans up the messes we've made in our lives by simply ending them. It controls the uncontrollable simply by eliminating it.

Out of sight, out of mind.

I'd love to be out of sight for the night and head out to the bar with my friends. But I am reinforced by Chardonnay, sheer will, and the absence of other plans on my social calendar. So when Aunt Diane announces it's time for dessert, I head into the dining room.

Jennifer is talking to my parents when I enter the room. I see them as an army of three, ready to spring into a defensive formation as the enemy approaches. I take a seat next to Pamela and decline dessert when it's offered.

Pamela sees one of the neighbors walk by the front window of the dining room.

"Oh my god, there's Mrs. Moore. Do you remember when I used to babysit the Moores' kids?"

My aunt laughs and says, "I thought your father was going to run over there and kill someone that night."

Pamela laughs too and says, "Those kids were the worst. I hated babysitting for them. One night, they poured chocolate syrup all over the couch, and their parents got mad at me."

My aunt chimes in, gesturing toward the room, "And they paid her less than usual that night! When Pamela came home crying, you completely freaked out, George!"

My uncle laughs with a mouthful of pie, raising and shaking his fist in pretend anger toward the neighbor's house.

We all laugh at my uncle's gesture. He's one of the kindest people I know. So to imagine him threatening the neighbors is unthinkable to me. But defending his family in any way he needs to, that, I can imagine.

Pamela sighs, "It was the worst job, but it paid well. Until that night."

Jennifer says, "We've all had bad jobs, but that is the worst story for sure."

My dad jumps in, "Tara knows about bad jobs!" He turns in my direction, just as animated as my aunt and uncle. "Remember when you got that paycheck for $1.36? I couldn't believe it."

He looks at me, trying to encourage my participation in the story. As if this time will be different. I decline.

He begins to tell the story to the whole room, even though they've all heard it before.

"She tried her best to sell everyone in the family a life insurance policy, and that commission check was way less than she thought. I couldn't believe they gave her a check for that amount. The look on your face, Tara—"

Everyone laughs, but they know I don't think it's funny. I try to deflect.

I say, "Hilarious, everyone. It sucked. I don't know how many times we need to tell this same story." I fold my arms in front of me, stiffening against their laughter.

"Oh, come on, T-Rex. It's all in good fun." My dad smiles at me, calling me by my childhood nickname to soften the moment. I can see that my father wants to connect with me. He always tries to. Something in my mind shuts it down every time. I don't know why.

I say, "Just stop. You don't care what I think." I finish the rest of my drink and stand up from the table.

Jennifer looks ready to speak because she can't just stay out of it.

She can't mind her own business.

She says, "Stop it, Tara. You're being ridiculous. It's a funny story from a long time ago. It doesn't mean anything."

What they don't realize is that every time they shine a light on me like that, for one of my misfortunes or missteps, it puts me even deeper into the dark. There are two different standards for Jennifer and me. According to my family's selective memory, it's as if I've been the sole owner of the low and desperate moments in our household.

Earlier today, my parents were talking about Jennifer's new job and pretending like she never called home crying once a week, needing money to buy books when she was in graduate school. Or how, despite all her education, she made sandwiches at a deli for two years before she "figured everything out." Or how she once dated a guy that she told everyone she'd marry but who broke up with her in a text message on Christmas Eve.

I am tired of it.

I stand up and say, "I've told you; I hate this story, and it pisses me off every time you ignore my wishes."

The table begins to buzz. My aunt and uncle try to get my attention and smooth things over. I walk past them. My parents and Jennifer start to fight. I ignore them.

Walking out has always been my superpower; it declares that I am in control of where I will be, regardless of anyone else's comfort level. I willfully remove myself from situations to make my point: clearly, you don't want me here, so I'm getting the hell out.

I fill my drink, walk out the back door, and light a cigarette. My cousin Pamela walks up next to me.

Pamela asks, "What are you doing?" She grabs my shoulder and squeezes it. "I don't want to go through this again."

I reply, "What are you talking about? They annoy the shit out of me, and Jennifer makes it worse." I'm irritated by Pamela's comments because I want her to be on my side.

"I don't understand it, Tara. Everyone just wants to have a good laugh. I hate this. It always turns out this way. Please come back in when you finish your smoke. Your mother is stressed out, and so is mine." And she leaves me there, under the stars.

I breathe in deeply, filling my lungs with the fireplace and cinnamon signals floating on the slight breeze across broad fenced yards. Even though the temperature has dipped tonight, this fall has brought unseasonably warm weather to central New Jersey. The weather doesn't seem to make sense for the time of year. The last hearty clusters of brown leaves cling to the tips of their branches, attempting to defy destiny for just a few precious moments more. Everything smells clean in the late fall, during the brief respite between much more extreme seasons. Each breath draws in an earthy sense of change, a scent I can almost feel on my skin that signals the beginning of something new.

And I do feel like I'm on the verge of something new. I don't yet know whether it's just a new way of thinking or acting. I do know that I am not the same person I have been. I can't be that person anymore. I can't live the way I have. It hasn't been living; it's been existing. And it's not enough.

I clutch my wine glass and hear my ring clink against it. I look down at my hand and see the ring my grandmother gave me when I graduated college. I miss my grandmother. She made me feel loved when I needed it most.

I've always loved this ring. I trace the letter "C" with my finger and imagine it stands for "Cursed," instead of "Tara." It's what I've always felt myself to be. Even when I had hoped for more.

I always thought Matt would replace this ring with his own one day. I used to joke about it with him. That probably won't happen now. Or maybe it will. I'm tired of the waiting and wondering. I don't let myself think about it anymore because I don't have the energy.

Nothing turns out the way I want it to. And it's not just Matt.

The gap between the life I have and the life I want is too far and deep. Even in the mundane day-to-day tasks of life, I find no peace. The effort of life is more exhausting than the reward. And my fatigue is bringing me to the point of no return.

I walk back into the kitchen to see my mother because my cousin asked me to, not because I want to. My mother is standing there, neatening up the pile of plates and silverware. I can tell when she is upset because she makes herself quietly busy sorting, ordering, and cleaning up.

I know my mother means well most of the time. But I just don't feel like I fit with her. I feel like she fits better with Jennifer, something of which I am always painfully aware. Is it possible that someone can love you and still feel like a stranger to you at the same time?

"Tara," she says as she looks up at me with a concerned smile. "Please go talk to your father. I hate to see you two fighting."

"Mom—" I finish my drink quickly, place the glass on the counter, and reach for the bottle of Chardonnay to drain its last glassful when she reaches for my arm. Carefully, I pull away from her. I've never liked to resolve disagreements with physical comfort. I am not comfortable with affection, especially from my family. I don't know why. I just know that it makes me feel naked and vulnerable. I prefer to keep it at the surface level rather than diving too deep.

"My mother pleads with me, "It's Thanksgiving. Please go talk to him."

"Why? He started it."

My mother becomes more assertive and says, "Tara, he was just trying to have a laugh with you." I sense an irritation growing in her voice.

I walk around to the other side of the kitchen island and lean both hands on the counter. I am trying to ground myself, to establish my position.

"Mom, but Jennifer gets involved too, and I hate it."

Without looking up at me, my mother responds, "Jennifer doesn't mean any harm. She's your sister."

Her comment infuriates me. They're always on Jennifer's side. And the fact that she is my sister means nothing to me. I want to say to her, "I hate myself, so why would I love my sister?"

But I don't.

My mother continues with her task, rinsing spoons and knives, her purple gloves dipping in and out of the soapy water with purpose. As if she can clean everything around her until it is new again. She turns off the faucet and looks at me.

She says, "Please, Tara. I just want all of you to get along. It's all I've ever wanted."

I respond, "But it's not funny. I've told Dad that I hate when he tells anyone that story. It makes me look pathetic."

My frustration isn't just about the story, but I don't know how to tell my mother that.

Even though I have never felt like I'm the daughter my mother hoped for—another Jennifer—I feel for her. I don't know why I am so distant, so very apart from her. From my father. From Jennifer. It's the reason I'm in the kitchen contemplating my exit. But it's too late for me to turn back now. In my mind, it can't be undone.

With each sip of wine, my resolve and my irritation grow stronger.

I can hear Jennifer in the other room, acting as if it never happened. I know she could see how much the joke hurt me, but she doesn't care. Because she believes I don't matter anyway. If she loved me, if they all did, they wouldn't make jokes at my expense.

I can't help myself. So I pick my moment and go back into the dining room. Maybe my family will have a change of heart and beg me to stay. Maybe they'll fall to their knees and repent for being such assholes. Maybe they'll realize that they've underestimated me this whole time. Maybe.

When they see me, all conversation stops mid-sentence. My father is across the room from me, and Jennifer immediately goes to sit by his side. As if she needs to protect him. It's a clear establishment of teams—them versus me. It sends me into a rage.

I don't hear what is said as I slam down my glass and head to the foyer. I don't listen to what is said as I open the front door and shout back to them. I don't think about anything except grabbing my purse and the extra bottle of Chardonnay I brought. I don't think about anything but getting in my car and getting the fuck out of there.

The rest of it is a blur, but once I'm thinking more clearly, I realize that I'm in my car, speeding away from my aunt's house. I control where I will be and where I won't. I will decide when a situation is enough and when I need to make my exit.

Chapter Six

JENNIFER

APRIL

Today is the final day of Tara's wake, and I am running late.

Earlier this morning, my mother set aside a framed photo that she wanted to display during the service. I stayed behind to sneak one last cigarette after my parents left with my aunt and uncle. I then forgot the photo on their kitchen counter, forcing a last-minute return to retrieve it.

The photo was taken on an Easter Sunday, probably twenty-five years ago. In it, Tara and I are standing in the front hallway of our childhood home. We are both in our Sunday best, holding our baskets, smiling for the camera. Both of us have long brown hair with bangs, strong noses, and clumsy overbites. We look like we don't have a care in the world, with our pale-yellow dresses ruffled at the sleeves, with white bonnets on our heads, and sparkling patent leather shoes.

Sometimes I wish I could have frozen myself in time at this

very moment when I was too childlike to realize that despite our physical similarities and my assumed union of sisterhood, our futures would be so drastically different and so challenging. A time when we played games of Uno and Connect Four without incident, and when I felt both of us neatly sewn into our family fabric.

Somewhere in our history, a deterioration began, one that made that type of relationship impossible: a time when we became triggered by each other, combustible. This break came early, and it came forcefully. Neither of us would be able to tell you the date or time of the first cruel word, the first apparent injury, for we can only remember our relationship as it has been since. I know this because there is never that spark of recognition in my sister's eyes or mine, that surfaced memory of a better time that would soften us toward each other. Those early years, the ones that met all our expectations, have dissolved in our memories, displaced by a much more powerful set of realities. Those early memories are not powerful enough to force a change of direction. We are no longer those two girls in the photo.

Memories frozen in time and picture frames.

I am racing to the wake with the forgotten photo now in tow, weaving across this multilane highway. Luckily, I have a cousin's PBA card in my wallet, a talisman against a speeding ticket. Of course, if all else fails, I could also use the "I'm sorry, officer, but my sister is dead, and I'm racing to feel like shit all over again at her wake" approach. But neither is necessary.

Approaching the last stoplight before my turn, I slow to a brake and check the rear-view mirror. Looking at myself, I remember a time as a child I always envisioned what I'd look like as an adult. Would I grow into my nose, or would it still seem too large for my face? Would I wear my hair long or short? I can't remember that vision now, what I had imagined back when I was that girl standing in an Easter dress, not knowing what the future held for Tara or me. I didn't yet know the loneliness I would have to learn to live with.

I look down at the photo on the passenger seat and think that moment in the picture must have been during one of the last years of peace between us when I still felt a connection to my sister.

For me, the following years were filled with my best attempt at compensation, as I tried to submerge my sadness and confusion through sheer activity. I immersed myself in books and music, and school, focusing on anything that would occupy my time and allow me to prove that I was worth something. What I could not know at the time was that the harder I tried to compensate, the more apparent our differences became, forging scar tissue in Tara's mind that would determine our future.

And Tara's future is now permanently secured, earlier than expected, and more tragic than anyone could have anticipated.

I see the funeral home on the left and quickly finish my cigarette. I pull the last drag off my Marlboro Light and flick it out the window, bracing myself against a bitter gust of wind. It's a filthy habit, I know. And it makes no sense given how afraid of dying I've always been. I smoked my first cigarette when I was in my twenties to get a taste of rebellion, to feel more dangerous. And now it's a crutch, soothing me with its physical experience, a repetition that offers comfort when everything around me seems chaotic.

I've been smoking more than usual since Tara died. Its cadence and familiarity are comforting for me. And I need comfort, in whatever form I can get it. I am trying to survive both Tara's death and the very idea of death itself.

I take death very seriously in all its terrifying finality.

My greatest fear has always been of dying, of being alone for eternity, with a silence that never ceases, with not a thing on the horizon but nothing. It is a fear of nothingness: of life going on without me while I just lie there, so to speak, whether in a box or an urn, as time goes by and by and by. Frozen, forgotten, fixed into permanent past tense.

I learned everything I feared about death from going to funerals as a child. Growing up Greek Orthodox, I came face to face with an open casket at each funeral I attended. I remember being terrified that we were expected to go up and kiss the Greek icon that lay on the person's chest in the coffin. I was never able to do that, even as I got older. But I do remember looking at their waxy skin, at their stillness, and thinking, why is their body here if they are not? I wondered where they went, what was happening to them now that they were no longer alive.

I've seen aunts and uncles and distant cousins act as if they have some agency in death's wake as if they could control the uncontrollable. I've witnessed the orchestrated responses to death, the attempts at self-preservation, where people grasp at the familiar phrases and activities they believe can bridge the existential break. The familiar words of comfort, the usual condolences. The linguistic dance of death, where anything that happens in a sign, where everything means something, and everyone becomes a philosopher while standing next to a casket.

At these moments, I've seen people turn to all the habits and vices that get them through their everyday lives—coffee and cigarettes, alcohol, Valium. It has always seemed to me that mourners attach almost supernatural qualities to these habits as if they would grant them control amid the escalating chaos of someone else's demise.

I can picture my Uncle Bob years ago, sitting in his chair in the corner of his living room, circles of smoke swirling around his head as he emptied glass after glass of bourbon the night after my Aunt Connie's funeral. I was just twelve at the time, but I was mesmerized by the repetition of his grieving. Light a cigarette. Smoke. Fill a glass. Drink. Repeat. I remember the large coffee urn sitting on the kitchen counter, the sound of it percolating and waiting for the orange light to appear. My Aunt Susan filled coffee cups and freshened trays of baklava on the coffee table, even though everyone was already filled to near bursting with coffee and pastries and grief. Creature comforts were the tools my aunt used to deal with her sister's death. Over the years, I saw the people I love furiously smoke, drink, and caffeinate to try and drive away their pain. Over the last week, I've tried all three approaches, and nothing has worked yet.

The wind intensifies through my open car window, blowing some loose papers around. I anchor them down on the passenger seat with the photo before rolling up the window and turning up the heat. I've always hated the early spring, with its fluctuation between blustery and vernal, a petulant child who cannot make up its mind. I much prefer fall, which always seemed to be a season much more optimistic, despite knowing that its beauty is fleeting and based on its very decay. But Tara chose last week as her time to die, so here I am now, freezing my ass off even though it should feel like spring.

Tara has always been as temperamental as today's weather, an impetuous child who always did things on her own terms. And here we are, gathering to remember my sister, under remarkably unspectacular conditions. The weather is appropriately somber, with an overcast sky straining to hold up clouds the color of granite. The chill of March still lingers in the air even though it is early April, and the sky seems equally ready to burst with either sleet or snow. Through my windshield, I see a gust of wind sweep in and twirl loose debris into mini cyclones spinning around the parking lot.

The funeral home sits back from the street, a busy throughway with multiple lanes of traffic snarling in every direction. Two colonial pillars frame a circular driveway, home to two stretch limousines and a hearse, gleaming black despite the lack of sunshine. There are beds of shivering violets in late bloom across the broad lawn and polished light posts anchoring each side. The very facade suggests a residence with all the comforts of home—such an appropriate setting for a family's final goodbye. How many family traumas this home must have seen, loved ones gone too soon or not soon enough, long harbored resentments and regrets absorbed into the atoms of its floors and walls, witnesses to family disasters one after another. Ours is simply the next family in line, one chapter out of many in a never-ending book of sad stories.

As I turn into the entrance, I see mourners arriving in groups, wincing as they clutch coat collars and hold down dress hems to protect themselves from both the elements and embarrassment. I see some of my mother's coworkers, fellow accountants at her firm. I see my parents' neighbors, the Millers and the Tuccis. I see a few of Tara's friends from high school. So many different people from all corners of our lives are coming together to mourn for my sister.

I spray myself with perfume to mask the smell of cigarette smoke and step out of the car. I steel myself against the wind, struggling with each step, each gesture performed with a level of frustration far beyond its merit. I drop my keys, and it infuriates me because I am trying to balance the framed photo and my purse while my hair falls across my face and my coat blows open, exposing my skin to the elements through my too-thin dress.

I mutter under my breath, disproportionally angry at myself for my clumsiness. I can't help but notice how the innocuous irritations of daily life become amplified during times of duress. Things that would otherwise seem so trivial become attached to the overarching emotion of the day, becoming players in a much larger struggle.

As I battle the wind, I feel like I'm battling much more than that.

I walk into the funeral home, and the room feels heavy like I'm walking through mud. It's the lingering stench of suicide in the room. The mourners here are as traumatized by Tara's death as her decision. I know this because the news of her death was shocking to everyone I delivered it to, not only because she was so young but because she took her own life.

Suicide.

I think about how many times as a teenager I flippantly proclaimed, "I just wish I was dead," after an embarrassing mistake or a social exclusion. Now, I blush at the thought. On my worst day, I would never take my own life. I wonder what that worst day looked like for Tara and why she didn't ask anyone for help. I don't understand it.

I remember learning about what Tara did from the detective a few days ago. He provided some details but offered nothing to help me understand why Tara did it.

Maybe Tara didn't ask for help so she could have a final rebellion thrown at the world; a checkmate played against all of us. I wonder if her suicide was a final "fuck you" to us, defeated opponents worn down from years of absorbing Tara's fits of violence, both physical and emotional, large and small. But maybe I am placing myself at the center of her intentions when I was not even a part of the formula of her death. Tara always did think that I made everything about me. Maybe she was right.

But I am certainly at the center of the fallout of her death. For good or bad, I am the one who is dealing with our past now that we will have no future. Or at least no future that I can understand right now. With Tara's premature departure from our troubled sisterhood, Tara delivered an unsatisfying type of closure, a painful relief for both of us, two sisters bruised and bloody and scarred from the endless steel-cage match of our unfortunate pairing. Two sisters forced into a not-so-simple sharing of space founded purely on genetic tethering—a relationship that lacked the enthusiasm and conspiratorial intimacy that should have drawn us more closely together.

But few people know this. The friends, family, coworkers, and strangers surrounding us at the funeral home probably see Tara and me as those two girls in the Easter photo. They assume I am heartbroken from the murmurs and snippets of conversation I overhear.

They are wrong.

As I pass through the foyer, I hear a man say, "There's her sister. Poor thing."

A woman responds, "What a tragedy. They are such a nice family."

I move to the main room to avoid conversation. I feel like I'm under a microscope: me, the older sister left behind. I pass the funeral director as he replaces a trash bin overflowing with discarded coffee cups, tissues, and gum wrappers. They are arti- facts of mourning that could just as easily be the remnants of a twelve-step meeting in a basement of a local church, evidence of secondary addictions and emotional catharses. Either way, it is a paper trail of painful struggles that have resulted in some doors closing forever and others that will refuse to, despite the most extraordinary efforts. It is so fitting for this moment, in which I fantasize that I will address everyone in this room and tell them that Tara's behavior has negatively affected my life in the following ways. That this will be the intervention I had always planned in my head, scripted right from the TV show. But we never made it to the hotel conference room, never saw the look on Tara's face when she walked in, surprised that everyone who loved her came together to save her. And instead of forcing Tara into a cathartic rehabilitation, we are witnesses to the result of her finally and permanently hitting rock bottom.

I set the Easter photo down among the items already assembled on a table on the far side of the room. Even from a distance, even with my eyes closed, I would be able to see them, for I have committed these images to my memory, every detail studied over the years. Tara, on her first day of kindergarten. Tara, dressed as a pumpkin on Halloween. she and I with our new Cabbage Patch Kids. Moments in time that captured Tara as we want to remember her. Relics that capture minutes or milliseconds of someone's life propped up as evidence that life did indeed imitate art. That belief that what you saw is what you got, that there was happiness and love and peace in Tara's life.

To me, they are an artifice, presenting Tara and our family as others imagined we were. A collection of moments in time that elicit little sentimentality in me. The photo of us on vacation where Tara became furious when her best friend Leslie wasn't allowed to join. Tara's bib from the New York City marathon, which my parents couldn't see her run in because they had already planned a vacation that week; for that, Tara gave them the silent treatment for weeks. A ceramic Reese's Peanut Butter Cup from Hershey Park that Tara threw at me after a fight about who could use the house phone next, smashing the mirror above my desk. Item after item weaving a messy tapestry of memories that I did not want to revisit.

Every memory I see is tainted. Behind the smiles, I see screaming. Behind the orchestrated poses, I see shattered mirrors. Behind the two sisters, I see strangers.

I walk toward my parents at the front of the room. I feel so alone because I can't relate to their pain. My family's memories and mine are very different, theirs gleaming in a newly fabricated sunshine, mine festering after years in its very real shadow.

I sit between my parents, resetting our family into its new

orbit. Tara has thrown our family's constellation of stars into chaos, and I will be the cosmic force that attempts to realign them. I will once again be the support that holds my parents up when Tara brings them down. I will once again bear witness to their pain and be good enough as if doubling my love and kindness can summon a former sister who was so often absent.

I hang my purse from the back of my chair and pull Tara's funeral card from its side pocket. I've always thought funeral cards were odd. They feel like funeral souvenirs. I look at the card one more time. It's a nice picture of Tara. She was always prettier than she thought she was. Her smile is electric. It's what always won people over. But it feels almost grotesque on this card. It's such a contrast to a suicide.

My mother reaches for my hand and squeezes it. I smile at her and let her know I put the photo she asked for on the table in the back of the room.

My heart breaks for my parents, who I assume are inevitably considering that they could have seen something, done something, anything to have prevented Tara from taking her own life. Perhaps they wonder the same about the way Tara treated us and if there was something they missed or ignored that allowed Tara to grow into her anger, fueling her hostile reaction to any love we showed her.

The wondering is the most painful part—the inevitable calculus of responsibility that follows a suicide. The assignment of blame for things we don't even understand. I certainly can't blame our parents because I love them with a light so bright; I always have. They are kind and generous and have always loved us more than enough. And I have always returned this love, multiplied by two, intended to deliver what my sister could not.

And they have been victims too.

All the parenting and love and comfort could not even begin to compensate for the flawed cosmic decision to place these two tiny Greek-Italian atoms into an existential supercollider. It could not have prevented the meltdown of our nuclear family, with reactions that continue to bear accelerating heat despite all attempts to cool them down. I know love and compassion and caring could not have made it any different simply because they didn't.

I don't know how and when this all started. I don't understand why Tara was the way she was. I wonder if I should have pushed harder to find out.

I can't point the finger at our childhood growing up in central New Jersey: Girl Scout troops and sleepovers at our grandmother's house and the smell of meatballs every Sunday and birthday parties at the Ground Round and summers spent walking the boardwalk in shirts that read *"Jersey Girls Best in the World."* I can't find the answers in my childhood home, with its dusty rose-colored bedrooms that held posters of Michael Jackson and New Kids on the Block taped lovingly across their walls, a rusting but much-beloved swing set in the backyard, a green shag rug that I sunk my toes into as I did homework.

None of it makes sense to me.

I see a long line of people waiting to sign the guest book. They shake their heads in disbelief. As they catch my eye, they wave or nod in my direction as they blow their noses and blot the corners of their eyes.

The room approaches total capacity. I feel like it's becoming too warm in the room as a trickle of sweat runs down the length of my back. I discreetly try to gauge whether I've put on enough deodorant today.

Everyone around me is crying, shaking their heads in disbelief. They cluster and embrace each other; they whisper and share stories about Tara. I feel like I am on display as Tara's sister. I feel like everyone is trying to gauge my level of grief, which I assume they think is unimaginable. But they don't know me, any of them.

I feel the eyes of the room on my back. I can sense their sympathy, their pronounced sadness, for what I must be feeling right now.

None of them know what happened on those days and nights when others weren't looking. They don't know how often I heard that Tara hated me, that I was a loser, that she never loved me. They haven't seen my parents cry at a family dinner gone wrong or another mysterious disappearing act for them to solve. They aren't sitting where I'm sitting, and they haven't sat where I've sat.

I am the only one who has seen it all.

I notice that the podium in front of us is tilted slightly off-center, and I step up to straighten it. My sister, what remains of her, is perched on a marble pedestal nearby, surrounded by a well-arranged field of flowers—yellow, red, and pink carnations fashioned into hearts and crosses—an existentially mismatched pairing of the living and the dead. Among this thriving garden, Tara appears as an unruly metallic weed sprouted up.

I smile to myself as I think that we are two sisters finally standing together in peace, one in a black dress, the other in an urn. Honestly, this is the closest Tara and I have been to each other in some time. Still, it's only a question of physical proximity at this point. And now her death has made our separation clear and final; Tara is inside the urn, and I am once again on the outside.

It's hard to believe that my sister is in there, but not there, a person now reduced to ashes and bone fragments and dust. How easily we transform from living, breathing, warm-blooded creatures to cool piles of cremains only identifiable by etchings on our final resting places: *Tara Ann Rossi, 1977-2009*. She was only thirty-two years old. I run my fingers along her name, tracing the outline of the steel vessel, its surface cool to my touch.

I feel a sense of grotesque power as I stand here.

I am here, and Tara is not.

I look around, paranoid that other people can see into my

thoughts. Can they know about the dream on the beach? What would they think of me?

I hope they don't know that I do not share their version of grief, as I am sure they would not understand mine. That my tears appear out of frustration and not sadness. I regret my entire relationship with Tara, and now I resent everything about her death. Tara has painted me into a corner. There are things she left unsaid and undone. There are answers to questions like, "Why didn't you love me?" that she can no longer provide. But I still feel a kind of liberation with her death, which will remain my secret. Because no one would comprehend how Tara being safely in an urn allows me to feel safe with my thoughts and feelings finally.

For the first time in a very long time, I can take a deep breath. I can simply exist without the worry of stepping over some mysterious boundary, of saying the wrong thing, of fueling resentments and misunderstandings of which I have little awareness. But Tara's death cuts both ways. It gives me anxiety while taking away a sister who did not love me. It makes people mourn for me, even though they mourn for the wrong thing. I don't feel worthy of it. I feel like a fraud.

I wonder where my parents will place Tara in her urn, imagining it nestled safely on the mantle between scented candles and family photos. I wonder what stories will be told within earshot of her final resting place, a recounting of our family history over freshly filled drinks, a trail of memories laid down between bites of Triscuits and pepperoni at the next holiday dinner.

It remains to be seen if these memories will shine through the thick gloss of nostalgia or smolder under a veil of silence intended to keep the suffering contained. If my particular memories, hardened by experience, or theirs, softened by time and absence, will prevail.

I turn back to Tara when I hear the funeral director, Michael, arrive by my side with two late-arriving flower arrangements. He kneels onto the deep wine-colored rug, dressed in a dark suit, placing the new arrivals precisely among the others. Michael's demeanor is gentle but direct, his movements slight but intentional. I glance down onto the top of his head and notice a rebellious cowlick among his thick dark hair, which is only peppered with gray. I remember that Tara also had one section of hair that refused to behave, which is why she wore baseball hats so often. I rarely noticed it, but she acted like it was the end of the world.

I feel for this man, a funeral director who experiences grief every day. I wonder if it makes him perpetually sad or more optimistic about the value of life.

I clear my throat. He turns to look up at me.

He says, "It must be so hard, losing a sister, and so young."

I smile at him.

"Thank you. I appreciate that," I say. Even though he hasn't asked me to, I continue, "We weren't close. We just never really got to a good place, you know?"

I can't find the words to explain. I don't know why I feel the need to explain.

"Anyway. It's over now," I tell him.

I fidget with my rings, twisting them around my fingers, looking past him. I do not look him in the eye, but I can feel him studying me, searching for the right moment to make his exit. I wonder how often suicides transform funeral small talk into uninvited explorations of unspoken family pain. I am economical with my words simply because I don't have many that I feel like sharing. I realize how dry my throat is and excuse myself to get a glass of water.

Before I leave his side, he places his hand softly on the outside of my arm and says, very softly, "I'm very sorry for your loss. She'll always be with you."

I nod quickly, and even though my arm instinctively retracts away from his hand, the reflex is in reaction to his sentiment rather than his touch. His words have injured me in some way, but I don't understand why or how.

I say, "Thank you. I need to go."

I slip past him, stranding him in the field of flowers.

I wonder if he sees in me some sense of loss that I cannot yet feel. I wonder if he realizes that the thought of Tara being with me forever brings me feelings of dread rather than comfort. That her death killed a painful aspect of my life, one to which I do not want to return. Or maybe he's just doing his job, and my story is no different from anyone else's. Perhaps my history has made me overly narcissistic about how central I am to anyone else's story.

Maybe Tara was right about that.

I navigate the sea of people inside the front doorway, stopping briefly to receive awkward half-hugs and sincerely delivered sympathies. Exhausting interactions laced with distant and vague memories. I struggle to escape this room and these people who want to talk to me, see me, touch me. I begin to deflect their gestures because I need to be alone.

My cousin Sarah runs up to me and hugs me hard. Into my ear, she says, "Oh, Jennifer. I am so sorry. You must be so upset. I can't believe Tara did this."

Sarah doesn't know me at all. If she did, she'd know that I am not upset, at least not in the way she assumes I am. I think to myself, if that's the case, then no one here really knows me.

I was never very close to Sarah. She lives about two hours away in Pennsylvania and never knew the Tara I knew. She never saw one of us storming out or crying. She only saw the fun Tara, who sometimes showed up at family reunions, the social butterfly navigating small talk and jokes while sipping Corona Lights. I never told her about the Tara I knew because there was no reason for Sarah to know. It would have opened too many questions and opinions on the situation, and I had all the views I needed. She is a distant cousin who doesn't deserve her memory of Tara to be as weighed down as mine is. It's not worth it. I nod at Sarah, step away from her, and move toward the lobby.

I am stopped again by one of my colleagues, Ryan Willis. He smiles at me, placing his hands on my shoulders.

He says, "Oh, Jennifer. I am so sorry."

"Thank you, Ryan," I reply.

"Your sister seemed like a lovely person. You will always have the memories of her to keep her in your heart."

I can feel my chest tightening. I have that tingly feeling on the side of my head. I wonder if I am going to pass out.

I say, "I have to get a cup of coffee for my mother."

Ryan nods that he understands as I walk away.

I need to get away from everyone. The room feels as if it has less air than moments before, its size smaller, its feeling more intense.

As I pass through the lobby, I see my Aunt Diane and Aunt Susan huddled together, rocking softly on a loveseat, faces frozen in disbelief. I see my cousin Pamela standing with some of Tara's friends, wistfully remembering a Tara I never knew. I pause to listen.

I hear Tara's friend Marisa say, "That time at Martell's was the best. Remember that Tara challenged that guy to arm wrestle?"

Pamela laughs at the memory.

Marisa nods her head feverishly and continues, "And then she kissed him! He was so surprised that he gave up on the arm wrestling, and she won. She was so crazy."

They all laugh, remembering a Tara full of good times and surprises. Someone that I didn't know. I also realize that Pamela was there the night they are talking about and wonder how many times Tara chose to hang out with Pamela and not me. I live minutes from that bar, Martell's, and was not invited. My response is conflicted—I didn't want to spend time with Tara for fear of it unraveling into a fight. Still, I also wanted her to see me as someone she wanted to spend time with.

"Jennifer?"

I hear my name and turn to see a young man in a dark suit.

I say, "Yes?" I try to hide the exhaustion in my voice.

"I'm Alex. I worked with Tara. I'm very sorry," he says.

"Thank you," I reply.

He says, "I can't believe this happened. She seemed so happy, so much fun."

"Yeah," I reply. Another recollection of a sister I didn't know.

He tells me, "At our work holiday party last year, she was just telling us that she was going to get engaged soon. Her boyfriend must be so devastated."

I am confused and reply, "What?" He must be mistaken. Tara and Matt were already close to being broken up by last winter.

"I'm sorry if I upset you. I'll let you be. My sincerest condolences."

I say, "Thank you."

How could Tara have said that? Why would she have lied about Matt?

I think about my text exchange with Matt. He should be here. He was a part of her life, and she was a part of his. His absence is much like Tara's—it's another thing I can't explain. His absence and Tara's lie tell me there is so much more to the story that I don't know.

I turn into a side hallway and lean against the water fountain. I grasp a small paper cup and fill it to the top, finishing it quickly. I am grateful to escape the lack of air, the urn, and the people, the fallout of my sister's death, the trail of emotional remains my dead sister has left behind. I pour a second cup and step back toward the lobby with its view of the memorial we have built to honor Tara.

Everywhere are memories of her—photos, poems, stuffed

animals from her childhood bedroom. The feeling of dread covers me wholly and quickly. I turn around and collapse into the first chair I see, kicking off my shoes. I feel myself begin to sink into the carpet, exhausted. I am finally alone, away from the urn and the photos, memories, and stories.

I wonder if the funeral director is right. What if Tara will be with me forever, a metaphysical attachment that I cannot sever even with the clearest of focus? The thought makes my stomach fall, a wave of nausea rising into my throat. It feels like it could strangle me. Despite the funeral director's sympathetic prophecy, I had assumed that Tara's absence would be permanent and entirely peaceful. I wanted it to be. I had believed that our book was closed and back on the shelf, its spine turned toward the mid-afternoon sunshine that would eventually fade its title from memory.

I was okay with that.

When we parted ways in this life, I didn't expect we would reunite in her death. I would not be able to stand the torment. The ominous words of a funeral director simply doing his job have sentenced me to remain in a sisterhood that I thought I had escaped.

The idea of the dead being with us forever is fine generally, but not in this case. My memories are different from everyone else's. Everyone else remembers a Tara that was fun and funny. Everyone else can remember the kind words she's spoken to them. But it just doesn't line up with my experience. Knowing it aligns with others' experiences with Tara makes it even more painful for me.

I close my eyes for a moment and hear someone calling my name.

"Jennifer?"

I look up, and it's Brian Williamson, one of my oldest friends. We have known each other since the first day of kindergarten until we graduated high school and our lives took us in different directions. We've kept in touch with the occasional Facebook message and have seen each other out at bars here and there, but I haven't talked to him in a few years.

"Hi, Brian." I smile, exhausted before our conversation even begins.

He says, "I am so sorry about Tara. I can't imagine what you're going through."

He's right. He can't.

He perches himself on the couch next to me. I remember him as a little boy. We used to play Star Wars in his backyard, and he always chose me to be Princess Leia. In eighth grade, a man killed Brian's father over a disagreement. I remember how terrifying it was, learning how his father died. It seemed like the world could end at any time if something like that could happen. I wondered what would happen to his family and if they would survive only to be torn apart by it. We sat in this very funeral home, just teenagers, wondering what Brian's future would look like now that his father had died.

Another tragic death, just like Tara's.

I wonder if Brian has the same memory I do right now. He looks uneasy, tentative. He fidgets with his watch and smooths his hair.

I tell him, "Thank you. It's been a tough time. It means a lot that you came."

"Of course. Your family has always been important to me." He places his hand on my arm.

I put my hand on top of his and smile.

"You were always such a good friend, Brian."

"It's hard to believe that Tara did this. She always seemed like she had everything in the world going for her."

I feel myself wince at his observation. I say, "I know. It was such a surprise."

I am not lying. It was a surprise, another piece of the Tara puzzle that will leave me wondering. Another bit of information she withheld from me. Another secret I will never know.

"I just wanted to say hello and let you know I was thinking about you and your parents. Unfortunately, I have to go, but please give them my condolences."

He rises from the couch.

I reply, "I will. Thank you so much."

I nod as I watch him walk away and wonder how much the person I am today matches the person he knew back then. I try to remember if I made it evident to others how I felt about Tara or kept it my secret. I feel bad that I didn't ask Brian about how he's doing, but perhaps he didn't expect me to. I'm sure he wanted to leave as quickly as he could. I'm sure his grief is imprinted on these walls. In this place, he sat for three days looking at his father's dead body, receiving condolences, wondering what would happen next.

I need to get back inside.

I see my parents' neighbor, a priest, walking toward me.

He says, "Hello, Jennifer."

I reply, "Hello, Father."

"I'm glad I found you. I am concerned about you and your parents. But I am also concerned about your sister. So now we must pray for Tara. We must pray with all our might that she can make it to Heaven. I will be praying very hard for her and hope you will do the same."

He smiles at me and walks over to talk to my parents. I see him whisper in their ears and hope his words were more comforting for them than they were for me.

First, the funeral director, now the priest, added additional stress to my situation. I not only have to live with memories of Tara forever, but I also have the responsibility to pray for Tara's soul. I have been unofficially ordained as an answer-seeker, as if I'm even qualified to dissect Tara's mind, to search her pattern of words and behaviors to uncover one clear answer why she hung herself in a hotel room.

I imagine the additions to my to-do list.

Send thank you cards.

Pay for catering.

Clean out storage space.

Pray for Tara's soul.

Figure out why she decided to act against God.

I return to my parents' side and whisper to them, "I know he's your friend, but that priest told me I have to pray for Tara's soul. How the hell does he think that is comforting?"

My parents look at me and shake their heads.

My father responds, "Maybe that is his version of offering comfort. Maybe this is the only way he can understand it. Maybe it's the best he can do. We're all doing the best we can."

They look so tired. They look so sad.

I wanted them to fight back, just like I wanted them to fight back against Tara all those times. But it becomes apparent that they are peacekeepers, not fighters. They are coping with everything the best they can. Things didn't work out the way they wanted, then, or now, and they approach it differently than I do. While I've been fueled by a sense of injustice this whole time, they have quietly resigned themselves to the idea that they cannot change the things they cannot change. And why cause more pain by fighting it all the time?

I've never quite seen them in this light before.

Knowing that rage will be expressed by me alone at this moment, I gesture for them to head back to our seats.

I help my parents from their chairs and guide them toward the door. My father is almost unrecognizable to me, a shrunken version of himself, a sweater left in the dryer too long. I realize that he is not wearing his glasses and wonder how he can see at all. Maybe he doesn't want to.

I place my arm around my mother's shoulders and realize I can't smell her perfume, something she must have forgotten in her daily routine this morning. The small flourish she carried with her every day prior has been relegated to an unnecessary afterthought in her new reality.

As I consider both of my parents and how they are different now, I realize that the small accessories we usually place upon ourselves--whether glasses or perfume--lose more and more value when the fundamentals go missing.

Chapter Seven

LAST DECEMBER

Sometimes I feel like we're all dancing and laughing and talking on the deck of a ship, not knowing that it will soon sink. Living our lives blissfully unaware that everything can go terribly wrong at any time. But I am aware of looming danger, perhaps more so than anything else in my life right now.

I watched *Titanic* last week with Leslie even though I didn't want to. I usually don't enjoy movies, especially romantic ones. They always seem artificial and unrealistic. But Leslie was having a stressful week and wanted to watch it, so I relented. The whole time we watched it, Leslie couldn't stop talking about that kiss on the bow of the ship, but I was more intrigued by the iceberg. It mesmerized me as it tore through the hull of the vessel, doing so much damage for something that appeared so beautiful and perfect from the surface. The danger was lurking there in the dark water the whole time, unknown to the passengers dining and dancing all those decks above. For me, that was the most romantic part of the movie: the fine line we walk between safety and danger, the ever-shifting balance between pleasure and death.

Tonight is my company's holiday party. I work for one of the largest office supply companies in the region, so they can afford to throw a lot of money at us every December with an open bar and catering from a local Italian restaurant.

I walk toward the bartender and order a Chardonnay, making small talk with my coworkers. I smile because I know that they are the unknowing fleet of cruise liners that circle my iceberg. I could never let anyone see that my iceberg exists and is larger and more skillfully hidden than most. That below my surface is a slow-moving but enormous behemoth that has sliced many boats from bow to stern, sending them free-falling into the deep. That I am not the person I present myself to be.

I make the occasional joke and ask about husbands and kids and vacations, keeping it light and focused on topics that lie above the waterline. It wouldn't be fair to them to force them to appreciate my massive frigid underbelly that will never see the sun. My co-workers will never know that as I stand here at our holiday party, I know it will be my last. I have decided that I don't want to do it anymore, the small talk or anything.

It is no longer a question of if but of when.

My thoughts have become too much to tolerate, and my escape routes are limited.

I think, *Tara, why are you so fucked up?*

I think, *Matt, I miss you. Please come back to me.*

I think, *Jennifer, you are right to hate me; I hate me.*

But I am smart enough to know that these are not my friends, and this is not the place or the time for me to bare my soul. The conversation would seem awkwardly out of place if I did so here, among the ugly Christmas sweaters and flashing snowmen ties. In these scenarios, I must be light and fun and just like everybody else. I am shockingly good at being this person: fun Tara, everybody's best friend. And it's easier than getting in too deep with busybodies who want to dissect everyone else's business. People like Jennifer who think they know what's best for me.

As I think about it, I don't get in too deep with anyone. I am alone in how I feel and want to keep it that way. No one would understand.

I thank the bartender for my drink and turn to face the room. Jeff and Mike play music a little too loudly in the corner, trying to get the party started despite the holiday soundtrack piping in on the speakers above them. Jeff tries to wave me over to their side of the room as he turns up the music. I laugh and give him the "just a few minutes" sign.

One of the regional managers strolls through the room, doing the old wink-and-point at some of the people on his team and straightening his snowman tie. He catches my eye, yelling, "Hey, Tara!" as he passes by.

Sarah and Michelle have drawn in a small crowd around their desks, a captive audience for their story about when we went down to Atlantic City and saw one of our customers cheating on his wife at the Tropicana. He mysteriously doubled his order the following week and every week after, a subtle form of hush money. I can hear them include me in that story, catching "Tara," "hilarious," and "can't believe she said that to him."

I walk onto the makeshift dance floor and signal toward Jeff that I'm ready to do this. As Usher starts to play, I begin to dance. I hear a few people whistle, and a small crowd of people quickly surrounds me, wrapped up in a frenzy of pulsating overbites and sweaty limbs with rolled-up sleeves dusting off dance moves from high school. I know I am a good dancer; I spent years in my cousin Pamela's bedroom as a teenager, shadowing her as we listened to HOT103. Pamela always went to clubs and knew all the latest moves, and I wanted to learn every one of them. I drag reluctant partners to the floor to join me; their resistance to my cheerleading quickly fades, intoxicated by weak cosmopolitans and party store strobe lighting.

I'm the constant across the room, and it makes me feel powerful and important. If I were to ask anyone here who the most fun happy person they work with is, I know they would say it was me. Acting breezy and problem-less is what I do best.

I nurture and manicure my relationships like my father does the flowers in his garden. Rather than cloak the latent buds in the darkness of my thoughts and suffocate them all, I shower them with sunlight. I make myself the center of their attention, the one who makes everyone laugh, the one who wears the smile so big people say it can light up a room.

My social talents are what make me so successful in my sales job. Selling is essentially storytelling and understanding what motivates others to make decisions. It's the dirty little secret that no one admits. It doesn't matter what you're selling if you're not someone the customer wants to buy from. I am that person a thousand times over. I have perfected the art of selling myself, of creating a persona that persuades people to join Team Tara. I need people to be on my team.

The song ends, and I high-five everyone on my way off the dance floor. They plead with me to stay, and I promise to return "right after this cigarette." A new song begins, and they begin to dance again.

Everyone is enjoying themselves tonight and I am happy to see that. I will be just like everyone else tonight. I will complain about the new expense reports and sneak out for cigarettes. I will do shots with them and support them when they're having a bad day. I will be my typical social self.

The power of personality can hide our weakest points, masking the uncertainty beneath. My uncertainty is massive and requires a lot of masking. And no one will ever know that.

I assume that no one wants to know about the inner workings

of my mind—the things that keep me awake at night—as much as I don't want to know theirs. I imagine that everyone-- coworkers, friends, and lovers--wants me to appear as they need me to. They want a light and stress-free good time, one that avoids problems that could drag others down. I know that there are rules of engagement. I assume that any conversation that makes others look deep into who they are when no one is looking—the deep dark questions about whether life is worth living—would threaten to rip apart the unspoken agreements we make to be fun and easygoing in social situations.

I try to picture what it would look like, to be honest about how I feel. I smile at the absurdity of the thought of doing karaoke with my colleagues and dedicating my rendition of "Total Eclipse of the Heart" to the universe so that Matt will love me again. I can see myself on the stage, sipping a Corona while leading the room in an epic singalong, and finally understanding that I have no reason to hate myself. In my fantasy, I walk off the stage, fist-bumping everyone in celebration of the existential crisis that I have finally resolved through good times and Bonnie Tyler.

I've never become close enough to anyone to feel like I could be myself. Except for Matt. Since we've been on a break for a while now, I feel less and less like I will ever be with him again. I miss him. I feel lonely without him.

Matt always came with me to parties like this. Even though we'd sometimes bicker because he thought my work friends were obnoxious, I always preferred bringing Matt to attending alone. When you show up with a date, it shows everyone how loved you are.

I push the thought away before it takes me to a dangerous place.

No one needs to know that Matt and I are no longer together. Without Matt here tonight, the truth is what I make it. I always thought that Matt and I would get married. Maybe that's the person I'll be tonight—the soon-to-be-engaged, happy, and fabulous Tara. The story I choose to tell can have a happy ending.

Matt couldn't make it tonight, but he sends his best.

He's so sorry to have missed the party tonight, but he's having dinner with some relatives who are in from out of town.

I've always known he was the one.

He has been waiting to buy the ring because he's looking for the perfect diamond.

The truth is what I make it.

Tonight, I can be the person I've always wanted to be.

I can control the narrative.

I can find where I fit.

But where do I fit? I think it's with Matt, but I haven't heard from him since we went on a break.

I miss him.

I hear someone shout over to me, "Hey, Tara—how the hell are you?"

It is my coworker, Steve. It is clear to everyone that Steve has a crush on me, and I find it flattering and distracting. He joins me near the dance floor. I take inventory of him, appreciating his thick brown hair as he pushes it back from his eyes, his forehead shiny with sweat. It makes every thought of Matt disappear for now. Maybe I'll take Steve into the supply closet later. Even though Matt and I haven't broken up officially, I remind myself that we are on a break. And who knows what he's doing right now.

I can't even think about it.

I refocus on Steve.

I reply, "I'm good, but I can't even believe they made Julie a manager. She's terrible."

I roll my eyes for effect and take another sip of my drink.

He says, "I know. You should be the manager—you're the best

rep we have." He smiles at me, and I can see in his eyes that the supply closet is on his agenda too.

"Oh, Steve, I don't want to have to boss guys like you around," I tease him. He laughs loudly and playfully swipes his hand at my arm. I turn to face the group on the dance floor and shout, "Drinks are on Steve tonight!" as I make my way toward the bar for a refill. I smile at him over my shoulder and see his eyes shine—another victory.

When I return to the floor, we all dance for another song or two, and I take inventory of my coworkers. I can see in their eyes that they want to hold his moment in their minds before they return to their quiet apartments and sleepy suburban split levels. I imagine that they're taking a mental snapshot of this evening, this moment when the drinks flowed and the music played, and they felt fun and free. I wonder if I'll become a part of a memory, a moment they'll keep tucked away, summoning it as needed when they're mowing the lawn, or the kids are screaming, or the toilet overflows.

But what kind of memory will it be once I've done what I plan to do?

I can see them kneeling on their bathroom floors, plunging wads of toilet paper, cursing at the situation when they learn that I have taken my own life—yelling for the kids to go outside and give them some peace when the call comes in, alerting them that I have disappeared. How I will disappear, or where to, I don't know yet. But my co-workers will be shocked because they will not believe that I am a person capable of it. They would not think that I would have any reason to want to do it. They have never seen my broken parts with their jagged edges that rip me apart and bring me to the verge of bleeding to death. They don't know me.

To know me, they would have to creep nearer to the outer limits of my pain, where I would tell them I am waiting for something—that *thing* that I can feel, not on my skin, but in my soul.

Some connection, belonging, placement in the world. Something that would place being here over being gone in my mental calculus.

There are moments when I feel joy and others where I have such gratitude that it takes my breath away. I do. There just aren't enough of them. I can't relive my college graduation party repeatedly to feel how I felt that day—worthy, accomplished, good enough. I can't keep sustaining myself on the excitement of those drunken flirtations at seaside bars, ones that hinted there could be something more than surreptitious glances and slow dancing in our future. I can't go back to the life of child Tara, who thought that something as simple as playing in the first snow of the year with my friends was true happiness, one I would see replicated in my life a thousand times over. So, I cross the conference room floor, angling myself in the sightline of the bartender, and motion for another Chardonnay.

I hear another voice calling me, "Tara Rossi? Is that you?" A woman sees me from the hallway, stopping in the doorway to say hello. I grab my refilled glass and take a long drink.

It's Tina May, a girl I knew from school. I went to a sleepover at her house once when we were thirteen and ate so many Skittles that I threw up in the guest bathroom and had to leave early. After that, I avoided Tina and sleepovers, especially since Jennifer was friends with Tina's older sister. They gave me bags of Skittles as a joke for years.

I was always a joke to Jennifer.

I yell, "Tina? Oh my God, it's you. It's been a long time." I throw my hands in the air and smile widely at her, as the wine makes me more than enthusiastic than I am.

Tina smiles back and moves to hug me. I step toward and back away quickly.

I'm curious why she's here tonight.

I ask her, "Do you work here?"

She replies, "No, my boyfriend Kevin just started a few weeks ago."

She points to a man in the corner. I see him straightening his Santa hat and singing along to "Jingle Bells." He's adorably awkward and perfect for Tina, who I remember being slightly awkward herself. In middle school, she was the boys' soccer team manager. When one of the players took a hit to the crotch, she didn't realize the location of the injury and rushed over to help him with an ace bandage. The jokes told themselves. I smile at the memory of her face at that moment, red hot and glowing from her innocent mistake.

"How's your family doing, Tara?"

I reply, "They're good."

"They were always so nice to me. I remember your mother baking for our class parties. And your sister? Did she ever become a professor?"

I tell her, "She did. Works at Rutgers. Lives in Belmar." I am limited in my responses because even though I know that Tina doesn't know how I feel about Jennifer, I don't want to disrupt the rosy picture she has of our family. It would overexpose me.

Tina smiles and says, "Good for her. I knew she would do something great. She was always so driven at school."

Years later, I still live under the weighty memory of Jennifer. I make way more money than she does, yet I'm sure everyone still sees her as more successful. But I am the more successful one. Yet, my professional life doesn't make me happy. It doesn't make me feel good. It doesn't show me that I am good enough, that I am beautiful, that I am loved. Even though I am selling over my quota and Jennifer is stuck grading awful Political Science 101 papers, it doesn't make me feel any better.

My personal life and attempt to have the fairy tale have always fallen short.

But it doesn't have to fall short tonight.

It can be whatever I want it to be.

I tell Tina, "I'm getting engaged soon."

Her eyes light up. "Oh, congratulations!"

"Thank you. We're very excited."

The lies come so easily.

Tina keeps talking, the words a blur as I lose focus on her.

I think of Matt, and the night we decided to take a break. The look in his eyes was tired and frustrated. I look at my phone, but there are no missed calls or texts. Matt was going to come with me to this party before we separated, but I still held the hope that he would remember the date and reconsider our decision to take some time off. I wanted him to pursue me, to want to be with me.

I am done with the small talk because it has sobered me up, and I no longer want to be a good time. The focus is no longer on me, which leaves me feeling even more alone—no memories I want to revisit, no boyfriend here at the party, and nothing to go home to—and I need to leave.

I check my watch and interrupt Tina's ramblings.

"It's good to see you, Tina. But unfortunately, I have to get home."

We smile at each other, and I offer Tina a half-hearted promise that we'll get together for a drink soon. I typically avoid interactions with anyone that knows my family outside of my carefully curated circle of influence. With friends and colleagues, people close to me who are on my side, and people far enough away that they will believe whatever I tell them, I can also control the narrative about my family. I can campaign for my side of the story, painting them in whatever light I wish them to be. But when I encounter someone from the periphery of my past, someone who knows my family but doesn't know them the way I do, I am forced to listen to their rose-colored recollections.

I wander the perimeter of the room, unable to locate my purse. I feel wobbly, frustrated. The music that initially motivated me is now irritating, background noise that incites a rapid progression toward rage. I see my bag slung on the back of a chair in the corner of the room, then I grab it and push open an exit door. I storm out into the hallway, letting the door slam behind me. In my haste, I trip on the sidewalk, the contents of my bag spilling at my feet. I drop to my knees, tears dripping on the pavement as I gather my things.

I need to get control of myself, of my life. I am tired of the role-playing. I need to control the thoughts that work against me day after day. The negativity, self-doubt, and knowledge that I will never have the life I want. That true happiness will always lie just outside of my reach. I realize that I can't just have the thought of changing it. I need to act. It's the only way I will be able to have peace.

I'm tired—of how I feel, of how I believe I must make others feel. I pull a cigarette from my bag and savor the first inhale. This cigarette, this habit, I think–this, I can control. I study the Marlboro Light, glowing and smoking in my hand, entirely in my control. I can smoke this cigarette sitting here under the light of the parking lot, and when I've had enough, I can snuff it out, smothering the embers under my foot.

I can decide when it is enough.

Chapter Eight

JENNIFER

MAY

The funeral home called this morning because we left behind a box of Tara's funeral cards. The funeral director, Michael, said we could pick them up anytime. I had already promised my parents that I would retrieve everything we left behind after Tara's services. When everything was finally over, my parents and I didn't have the emotional energy to attend to the final administrative details. After saying our goodbyes that rainy afternoon in April, we forgot to take the photo collages, cards, and stuffed animals with us.

I wondered where all of these mementos would go—if they would be placed in the attic to revisit every year on the anniversary of her death or dispersed around my parents' house as a memorial. I had no use for any of it, as I considered the matter closed. If my parents hadn't asked me to pick up the cards, I would have left these memories at the funeral home forever, along with the moments they made me relive, time after time.

I pull up to the funeral home and consider leaving the car

running while I run inside. I don't plan to be here long, but a limousine in the driveway blocked that option and forced me to park. There is another service in progress.

I grab my phone off the seat and see that I've missed a call. I press the voicemail button and place the phone to my ear:

"Hi, Professor Rossi. It's Helen. I spoke to the Dean, and she approved your leave of absence. We are all just so sorry. Let us know if you need anything. Mary will be in touch closer to August to talk to you about the fall courses. Ok. Talk soon."

I feel the relief unwind my entire body. I had requested the leave of absence a few days ago, knowing that my life will likely be a combination of errands and caretaking for the foreseeable future. And I just don't feel ready to go back to work. I don't want to interact with people, grade papers, or prepare lectures right now.

I place my phone in my pocket and tell myself to remember to send Helen a quick email later to thank her for the update. She is one of the program coordinators in the department. When Helen's father passed away last year, our department ordered some flowers for the service and food for the family on behalf of the Political Science faculty. But did I think about how Helen was feeling? Or was I just going through the usual motions of sympathy for her? Did I send food and flowers and say how sorry I was because that is what I felt like I was supposed to do? I wonder how her father's death affected her. But, unfortunately, it's too late to ask her now.

I shake the thought from my mind and refocus on my task.

I walk up to the front doors of the funeral home, greeting the mourners standing outside with slight smiles and nods of my head. I didn't want to intrude.

I walk through the front door. The smell of lilies and the sound of soft music welcomes me. I can see the dark suits and black dresses circling the room, grabbing tissues from thought-

fully placed boxes and refilling their cups at the water cooler—
grief's welcoming committee. People are spilling over from the
main room and pack the length of the hallway. I am compressed
between coats and purses and men in suits with foreheads glis-
tening in sweat. The only clear path goes right by the doorway,
landing my eye-line directly on an open casket. In it, a woman lies
who seems to be in her mid-fifties, but it is difficult to judge in her
current state.

I am suddenly in the middle of the funeral of a stranger. I feel
like a trespasser who has entered a scene where my part was
unscripted, a last-minute addition that doesn't make any sense in
the story. Yet I don't flee from the scene. I stay. There is something
that draws me to it.

A man and a woman stand in front of the casket. They clutch
each other and sob. They hold wadded tissues in their hands and
the veins in their necks strain with the physicality of their grief.

"I can't believe she's gone. I just saw her last week," the
woman says, her voice hoarse and trembling.

"I can't believe it either," the man responds as he wipes his
eyes with a tissue.

The woman can barely pull the words together to express her
grief. She collapses into the chest of the man and sobs, "I will miss
her so much."

He smooths her hair and holds her close to him. They stand
there for another moment, then turn toward the casket, cross
themselves, and say their final goodbyes.

As they move away from the casket and toward seats, I look
away, embarrassed to have witnessed such a private moment. But
there is something else. It's as if their grief is a solar eclipse,
drawing my attention to it as it injures me. I try to put my finger
on what freezes me in the doorway to watch this scene. I don't
know them, but I can feel their sadness. Their mourning is
powerful and precise. I wonder if someone else standing in my

place during Tara's funeral would have felt the same. My stomach turns over when I think they wouldn't have.

The funeral cards on the podium catch my eye. I remember looking at Tara's card and thinking how mismatched her photo seemed with her manner of death. It was as if her funeral card read: "This smiling person killed herself three days ago." It would be much easier if the person's manner of death accompanied funeral cards and obituaries, a little icon of a gun or a rope or a heart that can give the reader more insight about the person's death at a glance. To answer the question that always comes first: "How did they die?" I picture Tara's revised card with a tiny rope icon in the corner. I tell myself, *you are a terrible person* and walk over to take one of the cards.

I read: *Mary Morgan, loving wife, mother, and sister, 1958-2009.* She was only in her fifties. She died suddenly and unexpect-edly—a stroke, from what I'm overhearing—and the sadness permeates every corner of the room. I think, *this is what being sad looks like.* It hangs in the air so heavily that I can almost feel it on my skin.

It is a feeling I didn't have at Tara's funeral.

It unleashed a liberating feeling for me when Tara died, the first turn of a page in a new chapter. But here, in Mary's presence, I feel a sense of actual loss in a room among strangers mourning for someone I never knew. I have no memories of Mary to escape. I have no harbored hostilities to bear. I have no resentments to perpetuate. All I can feel is loss.

I notice two women sitting on my left. One is comforting the other.

One woman asks, "Why can't I cry, Rachel?" She wrings her hands. She looks distraught and tired. "Mary was my best friend."

The other woman, Rachel, replies, "Lisa, maybe it's not the time for you to cry. Don't be so hard on yourself." She smooths Lisa's hair.

Lisa replies, "I don't know what I'm feeling right now. It doesn't feel right."

Rachel holds Lisa's hand and says, "Being sad doesn't always look like you think it should look or feel like you think it should feel."

I can't cry either. Or at least I haven't cried yet. I still don't feel Tara's absence like Lisa feels Mary's. At least not in the same way.

But I am struggling, just like Lisa is.

I think, *I am just as confused as you are, Lisa. I am just as bad at grieving.*

Rachel and Lisa hug for what feels like an eternity and then walk outside. Lisa has told Rachel that she needs to get some air. I want to hear more. I want to ask Lisa so many questions, but I feel a tap on my shoulder.

I see the funeral director, Michael, standing in front of me. He catches me off guard. The surprise makes me drop the funeral card to the floor. Since I arrived, the room has cleared out somewhat, making my presence even more apparent. I wonder how long he's seen me standing there.

He says, "Hello, Jennifer."

I reply, "I came to see you and get the cards and everything else we left behind."

He says, "I figured as much. Here you go. I am very sorry again about your sister." He hands me a box of cards and a large shopping bag.

"Thank you," I tell him as I brush a strand of hair from my face. I'm finding it hard to make eye contact. How long has he seen me watching Rachel and Lisa? Out of the corner of my eye, I can see the dropped funeral card on the floor near my feet.

I am suddenly embarrassed that I have been an intruder at a stranger's wake. But it's more than that. I have felt more grief standing in this foyer than I did when standing before the urn that contained my sister. I remember the moment at Tara's funeral standing before the urn as Michael placed some new flower arrangements on the floor in front of me. I remember thinking that I had to explain why I was so conflicted by Tara's death. Can he see more sadness in me at this moment than he could then?

I fear that he thinks I'm a terrible person, a crazed woman who stands and watches other people's funerals like some people watch movies or sports. A woman who has been brought to the verge of tears by a stranger but remained emotionless at her own sister's wake.

I feel a pain in my stomach. I am suddenly not feeling well and realize that I need to leave. I say goodbye as Michael is pulled into conversation with one of Mary's sisters about the location of one of the floral arrangements. Before leaving, I bend down to pick up the funeral card I dropped, quickly putting it in my pocket. I don't know why I do it, but I need to take it with me. Maybe it's as simple as feeling respect for Mary and not wanting her card to be walked over on the carpet, shoes leaving dust and dirt on her picture. Maybe it's something else.

The air feels colder than before when I walk out the front door, and it has started to rain. I reach into my pocket and make sure the card is there. I can feel the smooth plastic laminate on it, the scratchy edges. I feel like a child making sure the milk money is still in their pocket, fearful of what might happen if they lose it. I don't know what I think will happen if I lose this card, but it feels important to me right now.

I walk to my car, carrying the leftover items from Tara's funeral. I can't help but feel sad that a stranger's death could stir in me more compassion than my own sister's. Today, there was something familiar: a real sense of loss that something beautiful was now missing from the world. I didn't feel that way when Tara died. Instead, I felt like something painful and stressful was now absent from my life. But it has been replaced by a much more troubling feeling—the feeling that I don't have closure. Tara's life and the awful way she ended it are pressing like a vice on my neck. I don't know how to free myself from it.

The box and bag feel heavy in my hand, much like the weight of Tara's death. I toss them onto the rear seat and start the car. My phone rings, and it's Joanna. I silence the call. I don't want to go through the details of how I'm feeling or what I'm doing.

I am tired of people checking up on me. I can take care of everything; I just need to be left alone. I need to be where I am right now. I need to see what other people do when someone dies. I need to see what their grief looks like.

Before I pull away, I can see Lisa standing in the parking lot toward the back of the funeral home. I wonder how she will go on. I wonder how I will go on. Why couldn't she cry? What happened between these friends that prevents Lisa from showing any evidence of being sad? Her mystery is as compelling to me as my own.

I consider getting out of the car to ask her these questions. I want to comfort her, to tell her it's okay, but I don't even know if that's true. It certainly isn't in my case. I envision our conversation, where Lisa tells me that even though Mary was her best friend, they fought a lot of the time, and honestly, she feels like she finally has a break from the stress of their friendship. That a break between them was a long time coming. I picture myself smoothing her hair and telling her that I understand and that sometimes it's okay not to feel sad when someone dies. I want to know if she feels the way I do.

But I am once again putting my own experience onto others. It's much more likely Lynn would respond that she's cried so much there's nothing left except emptiness or something normal like that. And that would make me feel far worse. It would make me feel even more alone in my experience.

I pull away, leaving Mary and Lisa behind.

I try to place myself back at the beach in my dream.

I wonder if my dream about the ocean held a grain of truth, and I have just been misremembering it. I consider that instead of pushing Tara away while she was alive, I might have pushed her away after she was already dead. I now see myself untangling from Tara's grip, but she was not breathing. I heard her crying out because she didn't want to disappear, but her lips weren't moving. Did her cries mean that she feared going deeper into the water or going deeper into my memory? Was she worried that I would forget she was ever alive and that she would die a more horrible type of death the moment we never spoke her name again?

It's all knotted and chaotic in my mind.

But I don't regret pushing Tara away.

It felt like the only way I could survive.

Chapter Nine

I feel so alone. I can't talk to my parents about how I feel because I worry it will break their hearts. I can't tell my friends about it because I'm ashamed, even though they know my history with Tara. And none of them could help me with my quest to understand why Tara died. It's the detail that none of us have. I don't know if we ever will, and it bothers me.

I feel lost without the details. I've always needed all the information about a situation laid out before me. I have spent countless hours of my life studying, analyzing, and breaking apart problems to understand their hidden truths. I reread emails multiple times to understand the sender's intent before responding. I dig into family stories about long-held grudges to see who was really at fault. I analyze every gesture and word spoken on a first date to predict if we will fall in love or if there are warning signs I can read in how my date cuts his meat or speaks to the server. I can't tell whether I had this compulsion before I realized my relationship with Tara was fucked up or whether it resulted from it being so.

The divide that separates my sister from me grows wider every day. She intentionally separated herself from me my entire life, and then she chose to die alone. But she lived with Matt for over a year; he must have some insight into her thinking. Or maybe Tara lived with Matt but remained separate from him too.

I searched what I could and found nothing that gave me any answers. I studied Tara's emails, texts, and call history. The only thing I saw was a few texts Tara sent to Matt the day before she died. I had texted Matt and asked him to call me. It's been a few weeks, and I haven't heard back yet. I had hoped that he would tell me something to help me understand. But he may be just as in the dark as I am.

Could they have broken up over infidelity? A fight? I'm sure Tara was upset she and Matt broke up, and she was back living with our parents, but was that enough to trigger her suicide?

I have pulled apart the few pieces I have and put them back together differently. I have dissected the minimal evidence I've collected with the hope of uncovering my sister's root cause of death. I am the coroner standing over my sister's body, poking and prodding at it to reveal its mysteries. But the mystery was in her mind, and I couldn't access that.

Tara took her reasons to the hotel room that night. And they disappeared with her. So, I need to try another way. The detective must have more information to share. My parents and I were so stunned the day we learned Tara had died that I fear we didn't ask all of the questions we should have.

I called the police department this morning to speak to Detective Marshall again. They told me I could stop by to see him at noon. As I drive to the station, I think of what information I'm seeking. Do I want to know the chain of events that lead up to Tara's death? Do I need more specific details about how she died?

I'll take whatever I can get. I had so little insight into my sister's life when she was alive. I don't want to feel that way anymore.

I pull out of my parking spot just as Nirvana's "Smells Like

Teen Spirit" comes on the radio. I loved this song from the minute I first heard it. I turn it up louder.

I am immediately back sitting in my college dorm room, playing the CD repeatedly. I had listened to it nonstop for months until it disappeared when I was home visiting my parents on a break.

I knew Tara took it.

Tara always made beautiful and special things disappear. They'd end up destroyed or gone forever. Often, she would do it out of carelessness or malice, which one it was at any one time didn't matter to me. One of the benefits of going away to college was that my stuff was always left alone; I didn't need to worry about my roommate going through my stuff or destroying anything. I didn't have to be constantly on edge about protecting myself or my space.

Once I was at college, I drank in my freedom like a hiker lost in the woods who encounters a stream after days spent dying of thirst. I could finally stop shielding those things I wanted to protect, like a collector who submerged their treasures in amber to preserve them. I no longer had to slip sentimental postcards and photos between the pages of Jane Austen novels or stuff CDs into half-empty boxes of tampons to protect them from vandalism or theft. I was in control of my environment for the first time in my life, and I never wanted to go back to the way it used to be. But I was always aware that it could change at any time.

I was back in New Jersey for a few days on spring break. I remember that Tara wasn't at home when I realized the CD was missing. My parents were both working, and the house was quiet. It was a rare event, and I loved having the house peacefully to myself. When that happened, I could easily search for my missing property. And sometimes, I would just take advantage of the situation and walk into Tara's bedroom to look around. It was the only time I ever physically had access to her space. It gave me a rush, like a trespasser in enemy territory. It exhilarated me because I was the one finally in control, and there was nothing she could do about it. I could search behind every book, look in every corner to find her secrets as she did mine.

If only Detective Marshall knew how much detective work I've always had to do with my sister. If only he knew how many searches I've conducted and how many pieces of evidence I've analyzed.

That afternoon, I walked into Tara's room and could smell her body spray lingering in the air: Bath and Body Works Freesia. Looking around, I couldn't help but think that I was looking at the inside of Tara's mind: messy, careless, juvenile. There were piles of laundry scattered across the floor, a trash can overflowing with tissues and soda cans, a thin gray line of dust across her vanity mirror.

I saw a pile of CDs on her desk and began to sort through them. Michael Jackson, Janet Jackson, Bon Jovi, Whitney Houston. It's funny how alike our musical tastes were despite all our differences. I began to open her drawers, thinking she might have hidden the CD. As I rifled through her bottom drawer, I saw an envelope addressed to "Pamela." I guessed it was our cousin because I didn't know any other Pamela.

I picked up the envelope. It was unsealed. As I opened the letter, I skimmed over most of it—it was mostly updating Pamela on friends and school and asking how Christmas was. Then I got to the end.

Write me back soon! I wish you were my sister instead of Jennifer. I don't want her as my sister anymore. I hate her.

I reread the last lines, breathless, as I saw Tara's rejection of me so clearly spelled out in words. Seeing it made it real. My eyes stung with tears, blurring my vision as I tried to picture Pamela and see all the things that would make her a better sister than me. I suddenly became exhausted. Yet, my fatigue was more than physical. It dragged down my mind as well. All the things that I had always believed about Tara were true. She wished me away, wanted me to be somewhere else—someone else.

Her words crawled under my skin, scraping painful grooves along my bones and threatening to slice open my arteries, spilling my soul and blood all over its pages. I hated her, but I also hated that I desperately wanted her to love me. I stuffed the letter back into the envelope, almost tearing it. My hands began to shake as I threw it into the drawer and slammed it.

I wanted Tara to suffer badly. And if I couldn't show it to her face at that moment, I would take it out on her things. I saw each necklace and photo and trinket in her room as a piece of her, and I wanted to destroy them all. I wanted her to hurt as much as I did. So I opened every CD case and broke the discs in half, dumped out her body spray into the sink, knocked over her framed photos, ripped pages out of books, took every dollar bill I saw. I wanted her to feel violated and broken. I was frantic, upending anything that was in order.

I slammed the door behind me and ran into my room. No matter what I tried to do, how many second chances I gave her, Tara hated me. I bet she doesn't remember any of those times that I tried. Years later, when she went to college, I tried to be the cool older sister and bought her a few boxes of condoms that I placed in a paper bag under her bed. I told her to try to make good decisions and be responsible. I coached her to not let anyone force her to do anything that she didn't want to, and always to be safe. I was hoping that Tara's college experience would change her for the better. I wanted to show her that I cared. Instead, she told me to mind my own fucking business and what would I know about sex anyway because I never even had a boyfriend. My attempt to bond with her got me nowhere. It just put me even more sharply in her crosshairs.

I know she doesn't remember the night I drove her home from

our cousin's bridal shower. She was drunk and sloppy and in no condition to drive a car. Even though I didn't have to bring her home that day, I offered to because she was my sister. I have conditioned myself to help her, even when I don't think she deserves it. Like the child who doesn't learn by touching the hot stove, I keep reaching for the glowing coil even though I know how much it will hurt.

I think about the letter again. Tara hated everything about me. She hated me so much that she wanted to give me away and make someone else her sister. I felt betrayed, embarrassed. I wondered if Tara ever shared her thoughts with anyone else. If she painted horrible pictures of me to everyone she knew, forcing them to smile at my face but sneer behind my back—me, the unknowing and unwanted loser, just waiting to be replaced in my sister's mind. My frustration exploded as rage overwhelmed me, and I began to cry violent sobs that took control of me.

I so clearly remember that afternoon searching for my CD. I remember wanting Tara to disappear from my life forever. At that moment, I hated Tara. I hated her so much that I wished she would die. This memory is part of why I haven't read Tara's suicide note yet. I fear seeing Tara's feelings about me written down on paper. It makes those words permanent, especially since she is no longer here to rewrite them. But, given our history, I don't anticipate the note saying much. Still, it scares me.

I turn the radio off. I need to focus on what I want from the detective. It could be my last chance to get more information, so I need to make it count.

An officer escorts me to the detective's office—the same cramped room with mismatched furniture and harsh fluorescent lighting. I find it depressing that Detective Marshall sits in it to deliver the saddest and most tragic news of people's lives, day after day, week after week. The same room where I learned that my sister took her own life.

I wonder how he does it.

"Hello, Detective," I say as I enter the room. He is wiping a ring of coffee his mug left on the desk.

He looks up and replies, "How are you, Jennifer? How are your parents doing?"

"We're doing okay. I mean, as okay as you can expect," I say because it's mostly true. Although I am not sure I am truly okay. I feel very far from it.

The detective flings the paper towel into his trash can. He motions for me to sit and asks, "What can I help you with?"

I ask him, "Is there anything else you can tell me about Tara? About the day she died—or the days before?"

He smiles at me as he absentmindedly shuffles some paperwork. I'm sure Tara's story is one of many sad stories that pass over his desk. So many secrets lie within those piles. I wonder what might be in Tara's file that I don't yet know about.

He pulls a folder from his desk drawer and opens it.

He asks, "What do you want to know?"

I think *I want to know everything.*

I say, "I know she hung herself in a hotel room, and that's about it. Were there drugs or alcohol in her system?"

As far as I know, Tara never did drugs or took pills, but I had to ask. But I didn't know her that well. So, maybe she did. But perhaps it's just that I can't imagine doing what she did unless I had some chemical assistance.

"Her lab reports just came in; they were clean. And we saw no evidence of any medications in her personal effects," the detective replies. I don't know if it makes me feel better or worse that Tara was sober the night she died. She always softened the jagged edges in her life with alcohol. Maybe she didn't perceive dying as a rough edge?

I ask, "What about her phone calls? Did she call anyone from the hotel room? Did anyone call her?"

He responds, "No, there were no calls to or from the room. The phone was off the hook when the police arrived on the scene. We didn't see any outgoing calls from her cell phone, either, during the time we estimate she died."

I ask, "What time do you think it happened?"

He consults the report. He says, "The coroner estimates that Tara passed between nine and eleven p.m. the night before she was found."

I think about what I was doing that night. I was watching reruns of *Seinfeld* and doing a crossword puzzle. I was doing nothing consequential while my sister was preparing to die, the most significant decision she ever made. I try to remember if I felt anything unusual that night. I try to remember if my body could sense that something was awry and that, twenty miles away in a hotel room on Route 70, my sister was dying.

I am running out of questions. But I persist and ask, "Did anyone visit her room?"

"There were no visitors to her room. The hotel lobby camera captured her checking in around seven p.m. She was alone. The camera in the hallway shows her going into her room about ten minutes later. She was still alone. Her hotel room door stayed closed until the next morning when the housekeeper opened it."

"What room was she in?"

He looks down at the file and responds, "702."

I briefly imagine Tara walking down the hall to room 702, knowing this would be the last time she'd be on that side of the door. I wonder if she had been scared or relieved it would soon be over. I feel a pang of sadness for her. I've never put myself inside Tara's head before. I've never really had to. But since she is no longer here to tell the story from her perspective, it is one of my only remaining options.

I try to think about more specific questions, but I can't. So I ask, "Is there anything else you found you can tell me about?"

"We did find a receipt for the rope in the trunk of her car. She purchased it two weeks before she died," he replies.

I am stunned by this detail and say, "What?"

My parents and I had met Tara for dinner a few nights before she went to the hotel. We had a few laughs. We had made it through the evening without any fighting. I find it hard to believe that Tara had already known what she would do when we saw her that night. I can't comprehend how she could order shrimp scampi when she knew she would hang herself in only a few days. It shocks me that she had planned to end her life and still ordered a cannoli for dessert. I found it hard to comprehend that someone could live day to day knowing their days were numbered, and that number was a product of their own decision.

And then it hits me. It went so well that night because she *did* know. There was no longer any need for anything but pleasantries because she no longer had any reason to fight against us. Instead, she was trying to enjoy our company.

For the last time.

I think of my sister smiling across the table to me that night at dinner—the last time I saw her—and feeling like I was duped. I don't understand how someone can plan to put a noose around their neck soon and still have a smile on their face.

It is one more way I feel distant from Tara.

I can't help but feel betrayed by our last night together. I feel foolish for thinking that we could have had a pleasant night for any other reason other than my sister had decided to die soon afterward and didn't care to fight anymore. Thinking back to that night, I should have known that it wasn't real.

I need to see it for myself. I need to see the proof that Tara planned this weeks before.

I ask the detective, "Can I see the receipt, please?"

He hands me a piece of paper. I look at the details. Tara went to the Home Depot in Toms River at 1:17 on March 27th. It was a

Saturday. She purchased a length of Marina rope, some batteries, a pack of gum, and a soda.

He must see the puzzled look on my face, feel the buzz of my mind.

"This must be so hard," he says.

It is.

I can feel the rhythm of his foot tapping the floor across from me. As he said those words—*this must be so hard*—I think of the housekeeper who found my sister. The one who had to push hard on the door, probably imagining that the door was broken that afternoon, not that someone was hanging behind it.

That woman's life was probably forever changed.

I ask him my final question, "Can you give me the name of the housekeeper who found Tara?"

He is visibly surprised by this question. Maybe I am, too.

The detective looks at me with something like pity. Or is it compassion? I don't know. I can't read the softening of his eyes, the downturn of his mouth. Does he think I am a sister obsessed with her sibling's death out of a torrent of love and grief? Could he guess that I am instead a sister obsessed with finding grief? With finding the emotions I am supposed to feel?

He replies, "I can't do that, Jennifer. I need to respect her privacy."

"Okay. One more question, then. Does the housekeeper still work at the hotel?"

He looks at me knowingly. He nods his head and says, "As far as I know, she does."

"Thank you."

"Jennifer?"

"Yes?"

He says, "Be 100% certain you want to find what you're looking for. Sometimes it's better to live with just not knowing."

I walk out of his office and head to my car. I think, *Fuck you,*

Detective Marshall. You have no idea what I'm looking for and why I need to know.

I think about finding the housekeeper and seeing what she can tell me. Yet, I worry that it will be like my parents hearing me tell others about Tara's death. That she dies again every time I speak the words. I don't want to do that to the housekeeper. I don't want to make her remember that day. I don't want her opening that hotel room door over and over again.

But I need to.

I need to feel what she felt and see what she saw. I need to track her last few weeks and see what I find. I can't explain it, even to myself.

I start the car, closing my eyes and thinking of Tara standing in line at Home Depot, a length of rope in her hand. I can see her considering which soda to buy and which pack of gum she wanted. As if it were any other day.

Other shoppers would have seen her purchases and not thought a thing of them, yet Tara must have looked at the rope and felt something I couldn't comprehend. I wonder why she decided to hang herself. It seems so violent to me. She had previously limited her violence to her thoughts and words. She had reserved it for her relationships. Now, it was central to her manner of death. The very idea of it scares me.

I am hurt, and I am angry. It's not just that I am left behind to eventually clean out Tara's storage space, manage my parents' grief, and tie up loose ends on her paperwork. It's that she lied to us. A lie of exclusion. A secret that would change us all forever.

My phone buzzes, and I look to see I finally have a response from Matt.

```
I still can't believe this happened. I am so
sorry Jen.
```

```
              Did you talk to her before she died? I know
                                        she texted you.
```

```
I didn't. I was busy with a few things and
didn't get a chance to text her back.
```

```
          I didn't see you at the funeral home. I'd
                                love to talk to you.
```

```
I don't think it's a good idea. Send my love
to your family.
```

I wonder what Tara did to Matt that was so bad he didn't come to her services. I was hoping to learn what it was, thinking it would help me understand her behavior in the months and weeks leading up to her death. Matt was the most significant missing piece for Tara when she died. At least from what I can tell.

And now she has.

I worry that I am focusing on the wrong things. I'm worried about what I might find as I search for more information.

That day, so many years ago, my need to find my CD led me to learn things I didn't want to know. It confronted me with words that wounded me, with the truth that my sister did not want me or love me.

I worry that my new line of investigation will once again take me somewhere I don't want to go.

But I can't stop.

Chapter Ten

I don't know if my dreams represent my fears or my conscience.

Tara died a month ago. Mary Morgan's funeral was last week. Death swirls around my head day and night.

Tara comes to me while I sleep. Sometimes she is alive when I see her, but most times, she isn't. I dream about dumping my sister's ashes onto a table, sifting through bone fragments to try and piece her back together. I can taste her ashes on my tongue, dusty and dry. I can feel her coating my fingers and stinging my eyes.

There are other dreams where I am chasing Tara down a long dark hallway. I yell for her, but she does not answer. I reach for her, but she is too far away. I lose her in the darkness as I become breathless and need to stop running. I am left alone in the hallway, and I am afraid I can no longer tell from which direction I came or how to escape. I can hear Tara's footsteps continue to put distance between us, but I am disoriented and can't tell in which direction she is heading.

Some dreams are memories, where I am back again on a

Christmas morning many years ago, hearing Tara complain about her gifts—not enough of them, and not the right ones—and it makes my mother cry quietly over the kitchen sink. But in the dream, my mother's tears flood the sink, spilling over onto the floor, soaking everything as it rises fast around my mother's ankles. In this dream, my mother calls out to me. I think it's to save her from drowning, but she says she doesn't want me to push her under the water as I did with Tara.

The worst dreams have been about dying itself.

I dream about people hanging themselves. I see them perched lifeless from the back of doors, suspended from chandeliers and staircase railings. I don't recognize most of their faces, distorted and lifeless, their necks unnaturally angled. I see Tara among them, her face purplish-blue, her features slack. I walk up to touch her, and she is cold. I can smell that she soiled herself once her body released into lifelessness. This rancid sweetness competes with her perfume, which has more floral notes. The rope is deep into her skin, and I can see bruising around its edges. She is before me, hanging from the hotel room door, blocking my exit. I frantically try to pull the door open, but it slams into Tara each time, spinning her slightly and making the door creak under her weight. I wake up before I can escape the room and be free of the sight of Tara—sweating, my heart racing each time.

That was my dream last night.

I throw my blankets off to release their weight and get some air. I am exhausted. The freedom I initially felt when Tara died has transformed into a feeling of being trapped. Her death has held a mirror up against my soul, and I want to shatter the mirror rather than see the person reflected in it. It forces me to face myself and all the ugliness I feel. I don't know how to fix it. I don't know how to fix myself. And without Tara here for me to confront, I feel like I'm chasing a ghost, trying to get her to love me, trying to change our history.

I am dying for a cigarette. I shake my head at the thought that I could be "dying for" something. I wonder what Tara died for. I remember the day Tara and I discovered that we both smoked. I remember thinking, *what a thing for us to have in common.*

I walk into the kitchen and rifle through the junk drawer, searching for a pack hidden among the tape and scissors and expired coupons. I make a mental note that I should reorganize this drawer because if my father saw it like this, he'd take it upon himself to reorganize it and find the cigarettes I try so skillfully to hide. We Rossis have a way of finding things we don't want to see, primarily when our incessant urges to get to the bottom of things and bring order to chaos take over.

I'm living proof of that right now.

Under a deck of playing cards, I see an old Save the Date I should have thrown away months ago. It is for Tara's friend Kim and her fiancée Jason. I've known Kim since she and Tara were in the fifth grade, but I didn't know her very well. So I was surprised that she invited me, but Tara told me that Kim had included our whole family. Kim and Tara were in one of their high points then, and so Kim thought it would be nice to ask all of us.

On the Save the Date, Kim and Jason pose on the beach. The water looks peaceful behind them, almost like a sheet of glass reflecting the sun. "K + J" is written in the sand, surrounded by seashells. I'm sure they posed for the photos somewhere nearby since they live in Bradley Beach, only about two miles away from where I live. But it looks like a completely different ocean to me. It seems like a universe away. Different from the sea of my dream, which swirled with a furious force. The one that swallowed up my sister.

I throw the Save the Date into the trash and slam the drawer shut. I remember putting a pack of cigarettes in my desk drawer. I open the top left drawer and see Mary Morgan's funeral card. I look at her picture; she was a quietly pretty woman with short dark hair and a wide smile. So different from the state I saw her in last week at the funeral home.

I haven't looked at the card since I brought it home and tucked it into my desk drawer. It has sat in there since then, a talisman of grief that I have not been ready to touch again. I can't throw it out; I'm too superstitious about the dead. My grandmother had a drawer bursting with funeral cards, and when I asked her why she kept them, she told me that it helped her remember. I never understood why she needed cards to remember the dead. I am collecting them anyway, just like she did.

With each one comes a memory.

After Tara came Mary. I remember the man and woman who had been standing before Mary's casket, with their grief so visceral and raw. I did not feel the same thing standing before Tara. Her death was jarring to me for sure, but my tears were angrier, more frustrated than sad.

I remember Mary's best friend Lisa and her inability to cry, to show others that she was appropriately sad. To me, that was the most tragic moment of Mary's service. And the more familiar moment for me.

I need to distract myself, so I grab the newspaper from the front porch.

There is a canvas bag hanging from the doorknob. I open it, and there is a bottle of red wine with a card that reads: *When you're ready for this, we're here to drink it with you. – J & B.* I think how sweet the sentiment is. Joanna and our friend Becky must have left this last night. I feel bad that I haven't seen my friends since Tara's funeral. I'm just not up to it.

I feel unresolved, unsteady.

I feel more focused on death than on life, at least for now.

I grab the bag and today's paper and head back inside.

It's *The Star-Ledger,* the newspaper my father used to work for. Seeing it reminds me of so many cold winter mornings when I was younger. Whenever one of the drivers of his team called in sick, I would take a ride with him to help deliver newspapers. Whenever we watch *The Sopranos*, my father loves seeing a copy of *The Star-Ledger* sitting in Tony's driveway. It has been our remote connection to those characters on-screen—men and women who resemble people we know, aunts and uncles and friends who go to pork stores and Italian restaurants and the Jersey Shore. Flawed characters who work through the struggles of daily life, keeping some things hidden and wearing others on their sleeves. This familiarity has always drawn me to the show: how suffering and conflict can become normalized and routine. It's how I felt for years, living only one doorway away from Tara.

As I turn to the Monmouth County section of the paper, a headline catches my eye: "Local Woman Dies Suddenly on Belmar Boardwalk." I live right across from the Belmar boardwalk and am curious if I know who this woman is. I read the article. Laurie Phelps was out on a training run yesterday and collapsed on the boardwalk near 13th Street, only a few blocks from where I live. I wonder if she was one of the runners I could see outside my window every morning, these supernaturally motivated athletes who defied snow and rain, dodging seagulls and baby strollers as they trained for the next 5K or half marathon. I remember watching Tara run the New York City Marathon years ago, and how much her determination impressed me that day.

I try to remember if I ever told Tara that.

I read about the parents, two sisters, and a brother Laurie left behind. I read that she was a graduate student at Rutgers, working toward a master's degree in early childhood education. I teach at Rutgers and wonder if our paths have ever crossed while grabbing iced coffees or walking across campus. I learn that Laurie ran the New York City Marathon a few years back, and I try to remember if it was the year Tara ran it. I wonder if Laurie ran by me while I scoured the packs of runners looking for Tara, desperate to catch a picture to send to my parents.

I walk into the kitchen and refill my coffee. I can't stop thinking about what Laurie's family and friends must be feeling. I don't know why her story speaks to me so much. I think it probably has something to do with my fear of an untimely death, a life ended too soon before I'm able to reap all the rewards of my hard work. So a young woman who drops dead on the boardwalk while she's training for a big race cuts a little too close to home in my psyche.

And I need to get my head straight because I am falling apart. I am tense and short-tempered about everything. I am careless and sloppy with chores. I am creating more chaos in my life by not being more in control of my thoughts or actions.

I am taking everything as a sign. There are signs everywhere that tell me I deserve to be punished.

The glass that suddenly slips from my hand and shatters on the tile floor, spreading shards that escape the broom and puncture my feet days later. The howling of the wind during a spring rainstorm that leaves piles of branches and debris scattered across my patio and cracks the glass tabletop. The dishwasher that shorts out mid-cycle and leaves swampy water and dirty plates that fester until I open the door. I face a seemingly endless mosaic of mishaps and frustrations that feel like my own fault; little micro-punishments inflicted on me because I am not a good person.

I need to learn more about Laurie. I need to see how her friends and family react to her death. I need to feel sad for her. I don't know why. But I put aside the questions I have for myself because I'm not ready to face the rotten underbelly of my emotions, to overturn those rocks and see the worms and spiders escaping from their deep burrows under the ground upon their reveal.

I grab my laptop and walk out to my back deck, immediately

opening my browser to Facebook. I search "Laurie Phelps" and see a profile picture of a woman holding a medal after a race. It must be her. After clicking on her profile, I see the messages posted on her wall.

Mike Miller: I don't know how we will live without you, Laurie.

Tina Murphy: I can't believe it, RIP my dear friend!

Natalie DeStasio: The world has lost one of the best — I'll never forget our days at St. Rose and how you made me laugh every morning in English class. I'm praying for your family.

Rita Phelps: My dear niece Laurie, your light shined so bright. You will be forever missed.

There are so many testaments to Laurie. Friends, family, coworkers, and classmates are devastated that Laurie is gone from this earth and their lives. All aware that memories are now all they have. There are photos of Christmas trees, her dog, her sorority.

One photo strikes me. Laurie was at the beach; the sun was shining so brightly on her face she needed to shield her eyes with her hands. She was laughing at something beyond the camera. Her hair blew across her forehead. Laurie was so alive. And now she is not.

I scroll back up to the top of the page and see a new comment that has Laurie's sister, Amy, posted:

Amy Phelps: My dear sister, my best friend. I can't even begin to believe that you are gone. You have left a hole in my heart that will never be filled. I will love you forever.

Her words are unfamiliar to me. The thought of sisters

viewing each other as best friends is unsettling and strange. Yet it is what I always wanted from my sister. I think that deep down, I am just as fragile as Tara sometimes appeared to be. And while my sister's fragility always shot her into extended periods of detachment and frequent fits of rage, mine has created the need for acceptance and reassurance.

I think I've always felt that love from my sister would be validating in some way. If I could make her love me, I would have won. As if love is a battle for the upper hand.

I reread the post that Laurie's sister wrote. Maybe I'm punishing myself by forcing myself to read all of this, seeing genuine grief stated before me. Perhaps I deserve to see all these other words written, words I never felt for Tara. Yet, I don't turn away because I need to feel something. And if that's only sadness for what I don't feel right now, I'll take it.

I find myself once again entangled in one of these moments intended for others to share, not me. I am once again an intruder in the fallout of someone else's death—first Mary's at the funeral home, and now Laurie's online. The first was by accident, the second by design. I stumbled upon Mary's. I am pursuing Laurie's.

I dig myself deeper and deeper into Laurie's life, scrolling through her posts, spying on her history. From what I've read in the newspaper, Laurie died from a cardiac incident. I find it ironic that the heart is the symbol of life, of love, and yet it is what failed Laurie in the end. I sense that there was so much life left for her to live. I can almost feel the hole in the universe left by Laurie's departure from it.

I see the date on the obituary and realize that the paper is a few days old and that Laurie's funeral will take place today. I tear the death notice and the article from the newspaper. I'm not sure why I do it, but I don't think twice about it. I don't question myself on the whys right now. I quickly fold up the clipping as if it can conceal the fact that I've saved it. Nobody would understand if I told them.

I place the newspaper clipping in the drawer with Mary's funeral card, the drawer quickly becoming a makeshift repository of grief. Nevertheless, it feels right to keep it all for now. I close the drawer and turn off the light.

I need some fresh air, so I head inside to brush my teeth, toss my hair into a bun, and head to the boardwalk. It's a beautiful morning, one where you can feel how warm it will be soon, but with a breeze that is taking the edge off and cleaning away the humidity. I've always loved the boardwalk, the smell of saltwater and driftwood, the sound of the ocean, the feel of the wooden boards creaking under my feet. I wonder if Laurie felt the same connection to it and if that's what drew her here to run.

I walk toward 13th Street, the spot where Laurie collapsed. You would never know anything tragic happened here—it is quiet and empty and free of police tape or people hovering to catch a glimpse. I wonder who or what decides I can stand here without incident, yet someone else took their last breath in the same place. I certainly don't deserve to be the survivor of the two. Laurie was so good, and I am a person who does not even feel sad that her sister died.

Why am I the sister who thought life was worth living, and Tara did not?

I couldn't see Tara's death coming, and I couldn't stop it. I worry that I have been so focused on those things that put me in opposition to Tara that I lost sight of the things that might have brought us closer together. Not just that we shared the same bad habit, but some common ground that might have given me the relationship with my sister I always wanted. That maybe I didn't try hard enough before she died, and now, I am not trying hard enough after.

I walk for another hour as the sun rises in the sky. I remember taking walks with my mother along the boardwalk when I was in high school, just the two of us. I could forget that Tara existed just for a short time and feel free on these walks. I could be myself, and my mother could feel at ease with only the random scavenging of seagulls threatening our peace. I remember sharing buckets of french fries with my mother on these walks, marveling at how much malt vinegar she drenched over them, making them soggy and crunchy, starchy, and tart at the same time. It is one of the taste memories of my childhood. I can hear the bells of the boardwalk games as we walked by, wiping the grease from our fingers: the popping of water balloons, the clanging of bells, the crashing of Skee-Ball pins.

I remember how my mother laughed at the people carrying enormous stuffed animals down the boardwalk. She'd look at those prizes that were almost the size of an adult and ask me, "Now, where are they going to be able to put that?" I wonder when I'll hear her laugh again. I wonder if she'll ever be able to be happy like that again.

When I see that it's almost eight a.m., I head back to my house. Laurie's funeral starts in a few hours. My mind oscillates back and forth between curiosity and a real need to see Laurie's family, especially Amy. The sister-best friend who so beautifully remembered Laurie on Facebook. The sister-best friend who feels lost without Laurie. The sister-best friend who grieves.

I think about Laurie's family. I wonder what their grief will look like and how it will feel. I wonder how they would speak of Laurie and how closely it will match their private moments with her, how aligned the memory and the reality will be. Whether the memories will be rosy and glossed over or scrutinized under a microscope, each piece dissected and picked apart until they become unrecognizable and chaotic. I think that no other family must have gone through our unique chaos and assume that everyone in Laurie's family will be honestly and truly sad that she is gone. I need to see it for myself. I need to feel it.

So, I decide to go to the funeral.

I walk into my closet and see the clothes I wore to Tara's funeral: a black dress and a black jacket. They're hanging like a museum installation. Like a costume to wear during a performance of grief. I figure that they are the most appropriate thing to wear, and perhaps they will help me grieve better this time. People always say, "The clothes make the man." Let's see if it works this time.

Three hours later, I am parked outside the church, waiting for the Phelps family to exit. My phone rings. It's Joanna. I silence it. I need privacy right now because I am in a place that I can't share with anyone else I know. I can't fathom managing my friendships when I have much more important things to figure out. So right now, I am relying on strangers alone.

When the family finally exits the church, they blot tears from their ruddy and red-streaked cheeks. They grasp their hands in support and stare blankly at the pallbearers that carry Laurie's casket out of the church. I think, *there she is*. It's as if I know the characters in this play like I've studied them, trying to access them without talking to them; being a part of their mourning without being able to express why Laurie's death makes me so sad. I don't know why it does, and I don't know if my sadness is about Laurie or me.

I have never come so close to feeling that another person's death—Tara's, specifically—has so changed me. How much it eventually will, I don't know yet. But I know that I've never watched someone's funeral, especially not the funeral of a stranger. And this is the second time it's happened. I can't stop it and am not sure I would if I could. I watch them slowly place Laurie's casket in the hearse and carefully arrange the flowers that will soon surround her.

I follow the caravan of cars and limousines to the cemetery, noting what a beautiful last ride Laurie has. The towns of the upper Jersey Shore are quaint and charming and not at all like they're often portrayed to be. My favorite house in this neighborhood is a comfortable beach cottage with a massive wraparound porch. It's close to the town green, home to my favorite candy shop from my childhood.

I remember how Tara and I ran around the store, jumping from case to case, leaving handprints on the glass as we pointed out which candies we wanted. On summer nights, we would share bags of chocolate-covered pretzels as our parents took us for drives through neighborhoods like this one. They were moments I would hold onto, hoping they would last forever.

When we got older and things changed between Tara and me, I would take a similar drive by myself. I would look in the windows of each house and take mental snapshots of the people inside. There are sisters laughing at the dinner table. There are sisters getting ready to take the dog for a walk. There are sisters reading a magazine together.

How could I ever know that I'd be driving this route for this reason?

The trip to the cemetery takes about twenty minutes, and now the sun is shining more brightly as if it's putting on a show for Laurie's last day in its face. I flip down my visor to block the sun as we enter the cemetery gates and drive around the main road until I see the white tent set up to my left. I walk to the gravesite and sit in the back row.

Amy is sitting in the front row of the section across from me. Her brother and sister are next to her, all of them beside Laurie's parents. Amy holds her younger sister's hand; they are both crying. Amy's blonde hair spills across her face as she sobs, and she struggles to smooth it. She lifts her sunglasses to wipe her eyes and looks tired. I wonder if she also has terrifying dreams. I wonder if she must chase Laurie in some of her dreams, and in others, she can't escape from her. I wonder if she dreams about reaching into Laurie's chest to restart her heart. I wonder if her dreams about Laurie are nightmares in which she feels like she's forced to deal with her sister for eternity in an endlessly troubling way.

The priest begins to speak.

"Laurie filled the world with so much love. She was a gentle soul who wanted to make other people's lives better. She had big dreams for her life. Today we mourn her passing but let us not forget the determination and love with which Laurie chose to fill her life. Let's follow her lead. Let us not forget how full of life she was. As we live our lives every day, let us be grateful we knew Laurie."

Laurie wanted to live. Her death was an unforeseen and mysterious event that occurred while doing something important to her. It was a tragic surprise, an abrupt finish to work in progress. Laurie Phelps died doing something she loved. Laurie Phelps probably wanted to live and assumed she would.

The priest continues, "How precious is life. Laurie lived her life to the fullest, something we can all aspire to."

I think about Tara and her death, which was purposeful and intentional. Her death was the planned outcome, the goal, the desired ending. It was a choice against living. It was the unexpected coda on an unfinished song, one that was disharmonious and amelodic. Tara's death was not sandwiched between joy and the pursuit of happiness; it was the sad ending of a tumultuous existence in a Ramada Inn.

Tara didn't think life was precious. Or maybe she thought it was, just not her experience of it. The thought makes me feel something like grief. Still, perhaps it's for the loss of any opportunity for Tara to enjoy being alive. Maybe that is the real tragedy of her death.

The priest continues.

"I look around at Laurie's family and see nothing but love. What a beautiful relationship they had. I know you will all miss her terribly, but she will always be alive in your hearts."

Tara didn't want to be alive. We will never have the chance to have what Amy and Laurie had. I'll never know what it's like to have that kind of sisterhood. Then I think better of it; I couldn't change what we were like when Tara was alive, so how can I change now that she is dead? I feel like I'm playing catch-up, chasing something that will elude me forever.

"May we live with the same smiles on our faces as Laurie. May we appreciate life as much as she did. May her soul rest in peace, and may our love for her rest in our hearts forever. Amen."

Laurie's casket is lowered into the ground. Amy is reaching for her, not yet ready to let her go. Her parents try to pull Amy back to her seat, and she resists them, pushing their hands away. She finally collapses onto her knees and is helped to her chair by her brother. My hand covers my mouth to silence a moan; I physically feel Amy's pain. I am also feeling my pain, my shame at the kind of sister I am. And the kind of sister I was.

It takes me a moment to realize that tears are running down my face, and I grab a tissue from my purse.

I can't be here anymore. I rise and head to my car.

As I pull away, both the glare of the sun and the view of Laurie's family are now in my rear-view mirror. I press down the gas pedal, lurching the car forward, trying to put even more distance between myself and Amy. I make it to the cemetery's exit and am gasping for air. I roll down both front windows, gulping the sea air as I drive away. It's salty and warm in my lungs.

I have seen what genuine grief looks like; it is being starved of the person who has died like I am starving for air. It is turning to face the sun and having it burn your eyes because the one you love will never see it again. It is wanting to follow someone down into a cold pit of dirt, thinking it preferable to live in darkness than never see that person again.

It can't end here. As I pass through the cemetery exit, I don't feel smarter or better than when I got here. I haven't gotten any magical answer that can put whatever I'm feeling to rest. Instead, I feel more unsettled than when I came, my brain filled with thoughts of Tara, Mary, Laurie. I am carrying the dead with me, lying alongside their bones and ashes in my mind. I need to bury them properly before my thoughts bury me.

Chapter Eleven

TARA

JANUARY

I look down at the Save the Date. It's for my friend Kim's wedding this fall. She and her fiancée Jason are posed on the beach, making hearts with their hands. It makes me want to puke. Kim is one of my on-and-off friends who comes in and out of my life all the time. We have an erratic friendship that can go from hot to cold instantly. I don't have the energy for it anymore.

I toss the invitation into the trash and return to folding laundry.

I have decided that love is generally a disappointment anyway, so I will not be saving the date. Love makes me compromise—I've never been good at that. It makes me vulnerable, and I hate feeling helpless. Love forces me to look at myself as someone else sees me. I never believe what they say because they sometimes paint me in so beautiful a light that I don't recognize myself.

I'm not naturally good at love. It scares me. It reveals who you are, the person you become when no one is looking. And I have always felt that person I am is not good enough. So, love hasn't come easy for me. I've learned that to be lovable, I need to push my boundaries, change my thinking, be someone different. It's impossible to do that forever.

This is how I've ended up alone again. I'm alone only in the sense that I am not in a romantic relationship because my social life is just fine. But I am in my mid-thirties, and while all my friends are getting married and having kids, I am staying with Leslie and her family in their condo. Matt and I are on a break, a pause in our relationship that has lasted longer than I thought it would. It was only last year that Matt and I invited my friends over to our house for dinner and drinks, feeling like a real adult. And now I'm answering questions from Leslie about if I'll be home for dinner or if I've taken my laundry out of the dryer yet.

I pull a T-shirt out of my laundry basket. It's a Yankees shirt that I stole from Matt when we first started dating. I pull it to my face and smell it. It doesn't smell like him anymore. Another way he's gone from my life.

It seemed like it happened so fast, the collapse of our relationship. Matt and I were together for almost three years. It was the longest relationship I had ever been in. It was the first time I lived with someone. I thought we would get married someday and have children. It is what I had always wanted for myself, someone to love me the best, to believe I was lovable.

Matt and I have known each other for years and traveled in some of the same social circles. One night we were at the Headliner bar seeing a band, and I don't remember how it happened exactly, but we started talking. I had always thought he was handsome. His sandy blonde hair was always slightly messy, and I thought it was cute. We went out on a date the next day and ended up being together for three years. I moved into his house a little over a year ago and was happier than I had been in a long time. We cooked dinner together, picked out curtains, planned vacations. I felt settled, stable, content.

I remember the first time I brought Matt to meet my family. I was nervous because I didn't want them to embarrass me with some story that would make him see me differently. I didn't want them surfacing some anecdote they thought was funny that would make me look foolish. They love to tell people about when we were on vacation, and I ordered the Truckers' Special at breakfast on the drive down to the Outer Banks. I was only six, and the waitress laughed at my order, which would have been far too much food for someone my age, so she told my parents. They made me order something else, to which I responded, "What is this, a diet vacation?"

They insist on telling that story. I don't know why I hate hearing it so much. Maybe it's because I think they've always second-guessed my decisions, even something as simple as a break-fast order. Perhaps it's because I always feel like the butt of a joke. Maybe it's because I don't remember that time in my life, a simpler time when our disagreements were only about ordering too much food.

But the first meeting went well. My parents liked Matt. He came to family dinners and holidays, laughed at my father's jokes, complimented my mother's cooking. Sometimes I even think they liked him better than me. I didn't typically participate in so much together time with my family if I could avoid it, but I wanted to feel normal. I wanted Matt to think that everything was fine between us all, that my piece fit perfectly into our family puzzle. Maybe I feared that he would see it all from their perspective and blame me. I couldn't let that happen.

Matt even got along with Jennifer, which I don't think is easy to do. As our relationship went on, some of the cracks in our foundation would begin to show. I became less afraid because it gave me time to stitch together the version of the relationships and events as I understood them. It gave me time to tell my side of the story.

It would drive me crazy when Jennifer talked to Matt about work, the news, or the weather. He didn't understand why she and I didn't get along. But he didn't know our whole story, how she was the older sister I could never keep up with, that I didn't want to keep up with. How I always felt like my family blamed me for everything that went wrong.

I once vented to him that my parents got upset with me when I was a teenager because I racked up huge phone bills on their house phone, calling my friend who was studying abroad. I said that they were mean and overly critical of me. He told me that I was crazy and that any parents would react to such an overstep, but I would never surrender to that. I was too far down the road of feeling out of place in their presence and refused this outsider's view.

I knew no one would ever understand how I felt. Everyone would dismiss how I often felt inadequate, separate, misunderstood. No one would ever validate those dark places my mind would go and how difficult it was to bring myself back to the light. So when I would hear other people defend my parents or my sister or call me out for something I said or did, I have always pushed back. I have always chalked it up to misreading something they know nothing about.

And my parents were always pleasant with Matt, which was a relief. However, it was Jennifer that made me nervous.

My parents would tell funny stories that embarrassed me, but Jennifer herself embarrassed me. My whole life has been an attempt to distance myself from her because I don't understand her. When I was in high school, Jennifer was home from college and volunteering for some political campaign. She and some of her other nerd friends thought it was a good idea to walk through the bleachers and hand out flyers during the game. People were mocking her, telling her to sit down.

I was so mortified when my friends realized it was her. It was bad enough that stories about Jennifer's successes followed me from grade to grade, showing me all the different ways that I was not her. But at that moment, she had purposely walked right into my high school life and taken it over. Again, Jennifer was the center of the universe, and I was simply a bystander, powerless in the face of her actions.

I worried that I wasn't good enough or powerful enough to compensate for any embarrassment she would attach to me. Jennifer was always smart enough that people almost expected her to lack social graces. Me, I didn't have the pedigree to afford social missteps. So I generally avoided being anywhere near her to save myself from others' comparisons and my low self-esteem.

I hear the front door close and yell, "Hello?"

Leslie yells up to me. "Hey, girl—I'm home. What can I make for dinner later?"

I shout back, "You're pregnant, and you've let me stay here for months. So I will order food, and you will sit on the couch and relax, you psycho."

I hear her laugh as she shuffles around the kitchen.

I quickly put the rest of the laundry away.

As I put the Yankees T-shirt in the drawer, I remember how great things were with Matt, at least at the start.

Until they weren't.

We had settled into domestic life and into all the usual nitpicking and frustrations we thought love could conquer until we got too comfortable. Our interactions became like sandpaper rubbed across a fresh sunburn. At first, Matt and I traded little jabs about coffee cups left in the sink or whose turn it was to take out the trash. Then it became fights about not wanting to go to dinner with friends and accusations of not listening. It finally escalated to questions about commitment and wanting to make this work for a future vision we both shared. My future vision includes getting married and having kids; his doesn't. I had assumed it did, and I wanted it to exist for him, too, because *I* wanted it. I never considered what Matt wanted and thought that being in love meant being on the same page.

Last summer, it escalated, and we began to scream at each other, and each threatened to leave. We both needed to take a break. We needed some time apart to reset. I temporarily moved out of his house and came to stay with Leslie and her husband, Dave. But I always feel like a third wheel. Leslie has a four-year-old daughter and is pregnant, so I need to decide on Plan B. I am not going to bother looking for a place of my own because I still hold out hope of returning to Matt soon.

I have spent these last few months swinging back and forth between extreme optimism and dissecting my every word and every move during our time together, worried that his perception of me now matched my own. Wondering what I had done or not done to make him not love me anymore. Wondering how he would tell me he wanted me back. I would beat myself up day after day but would then remember how he phrased it as wanting to "take a break" instead of "break up," and the semantics seem enchanted. As if Matt's choice of words would guarantee the arrival of the outcome I wished for every day and night. I assumed I would be back with Matt once he realized that he could love me again, that we could move past our differences.

I had tried so hard to be different this time.

I had tried so hard to be lovable.

I wanted to change my luck with relationships. One of my old boyfriends—Michael, who I dated for a few years after college— told me I didn't love well enough. He said those words. He said that when he hugged me, I didn't hug back. When he looked at me, I didn't look back at him with love. I was fun and funny but not compassionate and engaged. We were more like roommates than lovers. During one of our fights, he called me "emotionally anemic."

Michael also hated the relationship I had with my family. He dared to say that I was the cause of most of it and that he was tired of the drama. He thought my family dynamic was weird. He didn't understand my perspective on it, and it made him uncomfortable to be around us, just waiting for the next meltdown. Maybe the reason Matt hasn't said the same to me about my family is that he had an awful childhood with an abusive dynamic that our family could never match, even on our worst day. We probably looked like the Brady family to Matt.

Michael and I broke up. I threw every piece of evidence of our two years together in the trash, told him to rot in hell, and deleted his number from my phone. I didn't need him to tell me I wasn't good enough. I'd had enough of that my whole life, especially from myself.

I tried to do it differently with Matt. When we first met, I tried to be romantic, attentive, and vulnerable. I clutched him close to me as if holding onto him for dear life.

Instead of pushing Matt away, I pulled him closer and closer to me. Instead of being distant, I immersed myself in every facet of his life. Instead of being a roommate, I gave him anything and everything I physically could to keep him happy. Instead of keeping him away from my family, I tried to bring them together as much as possible. Just to prove that I could do it.

I felt like I was changing my DNA in the process. I sensed I was morphing into a new form of my being. I have always met people easily no matter where I went, but I have long struggled with the day after. After the first date or first kiss or first night together, I usually lost interest in the more mundane parts of love, the quieter, softer moments of baring your soul to another person. The complex parts, the messy parts.

But I knew that the person I was would never be good enough to keep someone, so I had to become someone else. I needed to show everyone that I could be just like them. I could have the life I wanted to have. I could be the person I wanted to be. And so, I became someone else for Matt. Love and marriage were happening all around me—I was in three wedding parties the summer we started dating—and I wanted it to happen for me.

But it wasn't real.

It wasn't like Leslie and her husband Dave, who I can hear talking to each other downstairs. I wonder if they're talking about me, about my situation. I wonder if they pity me, the woman who has no love in her life and very few prospects for getting it back. I wonder if there are discussing how to get me the hell out of their house.

I lean into the hallway, and I can hear their words more clearly now—it is a conversation about the color of the nursery—and I realize that I've let my mind wander too far about my friends and their motives. I've assumed that I am the focus of their attention, that I am a spectacle for others to marvel at: "Hey kids, look at the crazy woman living in Leslie's guest room. She yells at the drop of a hat, constantly fights with her family, and will probably be alone forever! Isn't she scary?"

It's not funny, but I laugh to myself anyway.

I've always assumed that I am the moral of the story, the butt of the joke, the topic of debate. It's a habit I can't break.

But the sentiment about love still rings true in my mind.

What I thought was love eventually became exhausting for me and suffocating for Matt. But I did love him. I *do* love him. But we needed some time to reset. Even though I loved him and needed him, I knew it was the right thing. We both needed some space to breathe, and I figured it would only be a few weeks before we were back together.

I've now lived through Labor Day, Halloween, Thanksgiving, Christmas, and New Year's Eve without him. I've gone solo to parties and dinners. I've answered all the questions about where Matt was and how I am doing.

As I put the last of the laundry away, my phone dings, and it's a text from Matt. I feel electric, as if it's a sign.

> Hey — can we talk? I'm home if you want to come by.

I text back immediately. `Sure! Be there in 20.`

I quickly pull my hair into a bun and apply eyeliner. Satisfied that I don't look terrible, I head down the stairs to leave. I haven't seen Matt in a while, and I want to look good, but not like I'm trying too hard.

In the weeks and months since we last spoke, we have been texting from time to time. It's my birthday soon, and Matt's texts have become more frequent, more playful in the last few weeks. And today, he wants to talk. It must be a sign.

I'm sure he wants to try again. We had so many good times. I think about a weekend we spent in Cape May and had dinner on the water. I made him laugh so hard that night. I had ordered the whole fish and had to put a napkin over the fish head on my plate because I thought it was staring at me. After dinner, we held hands and walked down Washington Street, and I felt like everyone must have noticed how happy we were. How in love we looked. How good a person I must be to have someone love me like that.

I shout out to Leslie and Dave, "Hey, I need to run out for a little bit. I'll order some food on the way home."

The door shuts behind me, and I feel a sense of optimism. I am hopeful that Matt will want to get back together, which will mean that I am lovable. It will mean that all the pain that I go through—that I've gone through—doesn't define me and that I am wanted and needed. Maybe it's not even about Matt; it's about someone choosing me. And it's about me choosing a life I want to live and being able to have it, whether it's with Matt or someone else.

But Matt has been my best shot at getting it so far.

I pull into the driveway, anticipating I will feel at home. But everything looks like it has died. Everything I see looks like a tired version of itself. I can see the curtains I hung in the front window when I first moved in. They are faded across the middle where the sun has shone on the fabric all day. I can hear the wind chimes we bought in Cape May struggle against icicles to sound in the frigid evening air. I see the planters I bought last summer still sitting on the front porch in small snowbanks, filled with dead geraniums and dried-out soil. I notice that bags of recycling are piling up by the garage.

I think that Matt must have fallen apart without me. He cannot do simple things to make the house feel cozy and presentable. It must be a sign that he wants me back. That he needs me back.

I pull up the collar of my coat against the cold air and knock on the front door. I smile at Matt when he answers.

I speak first and say, "Hey."

He motions for me to come in with, "Hey."

He doesn't move to touch me and instead gestures to sit down. There are two beers on the table, one in front of each of us. He sits across from me. He seems uncomfortable, nervous.

A song from the Allman Brothers plays in the background. Matt used to change the words of the song "Melissa" to "Tara" and sing it to me. I wonder if it's another sign.

I want to grab onto him to bring him back to me, but I wait. I've felt so alone, so rejected. I think that if I hold onto him hard enough, it will somehow make us unbreakable, inseparable. I speak instead.

I ask him, "How have you been?"

"Good. A lot has been going on," he replies.

He takes a long drink of his beer, wiping his mouth with the back of his hand. I take a drink of mine. It's Sam Adams Summer Ale, the same beer we used to drink at his tiki bar in the backyard. I smile at the memory of singalongs and barbecues and corn hole. It's way out of season, but it tastes like summer. I can almost feel the sunshine on my face, and it's giving me a light buzz.

Matt picks at his cuticles. He doesn't look up at me as he says, "We have to talk about something."

His finger is bleeding, and he wipes it on his jeans.

I say, "Okay."

My stomach tightens. I take another sip of my beer.

He continues, "So, you know I love you, right?"

Matt begins to peel the label off his beer bottle. I watch as he builds a pile of damp, curled paper on the coffee table. He can't seem to keep his hands still, and I wonder what he is thinking.

I tell him, "I love you too, Matt, and I—"

He interrupts me, "Tara, wait."

I feel it in the pit of my stomach. I don't know what it will be, but it's coming.

"I'm just going to say it. I know we were on a break. But I've been thinking about us a lot. I love you, but it's not going to work," he says as he continues peeling his cuticles.

He still hasn't looked at me.

I reply, "Wait—what are you saying?"

I can feel my hands clenching at my sides. I bite my lower lip.

He says, "It's just that. . .we were broken up. And I missed you. I had too many drinks one night, and—"

"And what, Matt?"

He says, "I saw Stacey. We had a few drinks. I was so torn up about you."

Stacey is his ex, some trashy girl he dated right before me. I used to see them together when I first met Matt out at the bar. So I know where this is going.

I say, "What the fuck."

"Tara—"

I yell, "Are you fucking serious?"

He says, "Tara. Stop, she's pregnant, okay? I didn't mean for it to happen. But it did."

There it is.

The nuclear bomb I always feared has now been dropped on my head.

After years and months of practicing duck-and-cover to shield myself from annihilation, it came for me anyway.

I feel wobbly.

Matt appears smaller to me, far away. I lose track of time and place, momentarily blinded by rage. I slam my beer on the table, forcing foam to shoot up and run over its mouth onto the coffee table.

I ask him, "You brought me here for this? Are you fucking serious?"

I realize that I am screaming at him.

I can't see Matt; my eyes have glazed over. I feel a heat radiating from my neck up to the top of my head. I stand up, and the room is spinning. I feel ridiculous for interpreting coincidences as signs. I feel foolish for thinking I'd ever be worthy of something that doesn't get totally fucked up. My mind clicks through the slideshow of memories we share, conversations we had about our future, and I feel foolish. I feel like I am just not meant to be happy, ever.

Matt has made me a fool.

She is having his baby.

I think about Stacey and how it's my baby, my life she's taking. It was supposed to be mine, and now it will be hers.

He says, softly, "I wanted to tell you to your face. I'm not happy about it either, but it happened."

He looks up at me and says, "I'm sorry, Tara. But I didn't want you to find out from someone else."

"I thought you didn't want kids, Matt. That's what you told me."

"Tara, I don't know what to do."

I stand up and begin to pace next to the coffee table. I tell him, "Stacey could have an abortion. Or you could just not help her if she wants to have it. There are a lot of options, Matt."

"I can't do that. Stacey wants to have the baby, and I need to support her."

There it is. It's not that Matt didn't want to have kids. He just didn't want to have them with me. At the very least, Matt is doing what Stacey wants—even if it's not what he truly wants—which is something he never did with me.

I feel my face become hot with rage. My hands are shaking.

I've long thought love is a disappointment, and now I know it's true. I will never open myself up to feeling this way again. I will never allow myself to feel so strongly about someone because it only rips you apart eventually. One day you're at Bed Bath and Beyond, happily buying throw pillows with the person you love, and a few years later, you want to throw that person through a fucking window.

"I hate you!" I scream at him as I pull a framed photo of us off the coffee table. I look at myself in the picture, the person I tried so hard to be to win and keep his love, a person that no longer exists.

I tried everything to be different this time, and it still wasn't enough.

I hurl the photo across the room, hearing the glass shatter on the living room floor. I grab everything in my reach and begin to throw it out the front door onto the lawn. I walk up to Matt, and he still can't look at me. A tear spills out from his left eye, sitting like a raindrop on his lashes. Those long lashes that I used to love looking at while he slept. I pull at his T-shirt until I tear it. I punch him in the chest until I'm exhausted.

"I'm sorry," he whispers as he tries to hug me. I push him away.

Nothing ever stays in place for me. Nothing ever works. And now, the person I loved will be living my life with someone else. She will be having his baby. She will be with him forever.

I order him, "Box up anything else of mine that's still here and leave it on the porch. I'll have Marisa come pick it up."

On my way out, I see a wooden dog statue that I have always hated. It's staring at me like it knows I have failed once again. I kick it so hard the head breaks off and slams against the wall behind it.

"Fuck you too," I say as I open the front door.

I walk to my car and feel like I want to kill Matt, burn his house down, slash his tires, carry his head around the town square by his long hair. I don't need Matt; I don't need anybody. I stop and turn around. He is standing on the front porch like a wounded animal. I walk a few steps back toward the porch and point at him, "You are dead to me. *We* are dead to me."

I realize that I am now dead to me too. Matt is not the reason for that; he is just the latest item on a long list of things that haven't worked out for me. I want to feel bad for him because it will be inevitable that one day, he will think he was the reason why I did what I'm going to do.

But I am the only reason why.

As I drive away, I know I'll never see him again. I drive away from Matt, from his house, and from the life I will never have. I don't know what to do now. I don't want anyone to know what has happened because it's too embarrassing. I'm ashamed that Matt will have a baby, just not with me. I'm embarrassed that I thought we would get back together, some overly dramatic reunion like in the movies.

And it is like the movies in a way. This time, Matt is the iceberg, and I am the ship. I feel like fate steered me toward his sharp edges, even though I saw signs of the dangerous crest raised through the water. Maybe I did this to myself and hadn't realized it. Perhaps I knew it would end this way and pressed on anyway, another piece of evidence to prove to myself that even when I try my best, it won't be enough.

I decide that I am no longer going to try.

Chapter Twelve

JENNIFER

MAY

Detective Marshall told me that Tara had purchased the rope a few weeks before she died.

I wonder what it felt like. To prepare to die.

I'll never really know, but I can try to grasp as much of it as I can.

Texts, emails, voicemails, internet searches, police reports, and receipts. All dead ends.

I walk through the front doors of Home Depot, straight through a wall of air conditioning. It's hot and humid for late May, and the cold air inside gives me the chills. It is the same Home Depot Tara went to. I wonder if that's also why I'm shivering. As if I can feel the memory of her being here on my skin. As if my body knows what she came here to do.

I walk from aisle to aisle, searching for rope. I take my time because I am in no rush. I pass aisles piled high with cleaning supplies and lighting fixtures. I see employees helping customers with paint choices and floor tile. I keep my eyes down. I don't want to speak to anyone. I can picture the absurd exchange in my head now.

An assistant would smooth his orange apron and ask me, "Can I help you?"

I would smile and reply, "Yes, I'm looking for the same rope my sister hung herself with. She bought it here, do you remember her?"

He would freeze, not sure if I was serious or telling the worst kind of joke.

I would laugh and say, "That's okay. I'll find it. I just want to hold it in my hands and see how it makes me feel. Thank you!"

I smile to myself, thinking about how absurd such a scene would be. It's the kind of humor Tara would have appreciated. If she were still alive to hear it.

I find the rope in Aisle 22. I pull the receipt out of my pocket and look for the same rope Tara purchased. It's called Manila rope. I find it on the second shelf. It feels scratchy and rough on my skin.

Did Tara know which rope to get when she came here? When she stood where I'm standing now, did she have a specific type of rope in mind? Or did she see the Manila rope and think, *that one would work*.

I take a small length of the rope and put it in my basket.

I remember that Tara made a few other purchases that day. As I walk up to the register, I pull a Diet Coke from the case. I browse the gum selection and choose a pack of Juicy Fruit. I throw a package of AA batteries into the basket.

As I begin to check out, I have this absurd vision that my specific selection of things will trigger an alarm at the register that says, "This is what people buy when they are going to kill themselves!"—much like a person buying a pressure cooker and nails can almost definitely be flagged for planning to build a bomb.

If only it were that easy.

I complete my purchase and walk to my car.

I touch the rope inside the bag as if I'm rubbing a lamp, expecting a genie to grant me my three wishes.

But nothing happens.

It's another failed connection with my sister.

Chapter Thirteen

Over the last few days and weeks, I have started my daily routine with the same thing: the newspaper. I seek stories of death. I search for funerals. I wait for the newspaper every morning to read the obituaries. Today, I hear it drop to the porch with a promise, its thud calling me to the front door.

I look at the pictures to feel connected to the dead. I read their stories to learn more about their lives. Maybe I am a glutton for punishment. Perhaps I am just not good at feeling sad and need these stories to spark something in me that isn't there. At least not yet.

Every day, I hope to find the answer on these pages. What that answer looks like, I don't know yet. I try to think about it academically, which is my comfort zone. I compare it to what Supreme Court Justice Potter once said about obscenity: "I'll know it when I see it." I think about how much Tara would hate that analogy. She would roll her eyes when I would cite a date from history or some random political fact. I laugh as I picture myself sitting in front of the Supreme Court, arguing Rossi v. Rossi. Arguing both sides against themselves. But in this scenario, it's just me against myself.

I study the stories—poignant and regretful descriptions of lives well-lived that have been cut short by bad luck or error or intent—as if I am trying to decipher a code that will reveal all with its unlocking. I wonder what secrets might lie behind these obituaries. The more I've read them, and seen the exact phrases, the customary remembrances of life, I think that perhaps all of them hide something.

Do we use these memorials to be honest or be kind? You just can't write "Sharon died, leaving behind a husband, two sons, and an army of enemies because she was an asshole most of the time," or "We won't miss George, because he was a lousy father who used to take his kids to the bar and leave them in the car while he downed whiskey sours and smoked Lucky Strikes." It seems that our need to be respectful of the dead requires us to be less than truly honest some of the time. This is why I didn't write Tara's with the headline "Local Woman Does Not Mourn Death of Her Sister; Deceased Was an Absolute Bitch to Her a Lot of the Time."

Because honesty is not always kind. From what I've seen, the rituals of mourning require much greater decorum than honesty will allow.

Kindness doesn't feel right either. I am so conflicted.

Is it my fear of death that makes me reject the kind words spoken about the dead? I worry that I have been so traumatized by my experiences with Tara that I believe death is the perfect time to air grievances, to be truly honest about the dead's impact on the living. When Tara died, I questioned how the people left behind remember the person who has passed, pushing away anything that doesn't fit the story they want—or need—to tell. It doesn't feel honest to me. But I have kept that to myself.

Jennifer and Tara loved each other so much; just look at the photos of them.

How happy they must have been.
How much Jennifer must miss her sister.

The truth would devastate everyone I know, just as it devastates me. It's the reason I don't display photos of Tara in my own house, because to look at them is to remember. And I don't want to remember.

Why are you such a loser, Jennifer?
Tara, don't talk to your sister like that.
Happy fucking Thanksgiving. I hate all of you.

I turn back to today's paper. One of the death notices catches my eye because the photo looks just like my grandmother, Anna. As I read about Ruth Edwards, she sounds just like my grandmother too.

Ruth lived a long life. She left behind two children and five grandchildren when she died at eighty-six. She enjoyed cooking, scrapbooking, and gardening. She is also survived by two younger brothers.

I was devastated when Grandma Anna died. It was over five years ago, but I remember how it felt. I remember crying. I remember being sad she was gone.

I think that Ruth's funeral could be the answer, so I will go to it.

Something pulls me there, and I don't know what I expect to see or feel. But I go anyway.

When I arrive in the lobby of the funeral home, it feels familiar. The storyline is the same today as when my grandmother passed away. Sad, but filled with stories of a long life. People gathered to remember Ruth and how she touched their lives. A sadness that doesn't feel bitter.

I look down at Ruth's funeral card in my hand before slipping it into my pocket. It will sit alongside Mary's, Laurie's, and Tara's in my desk drawer. It is my new collection of memories, the evidence of my study of what it feels like to lose someone and miss them.

I walk past a table of photos, seeing Ruth on vacation in Mexico, her wedding photos, sitting on the sidelines of her granddaughter's soccer game. All the moments in life that show what a person did, not necessarily who they were. I pick up a picture of Ruth and study it. She's a child—ten years old, maybe—standing in a kitchen with what I assume are her two brothers. The photo is in black and white, and Ruth has on a white dress with a dark satin ribbon around her waist, her hair is curled, and she is leaning against the kitchen counter. She is standing slightly apart from her brothers as if she doesn't want to get too close. Her Brothers are smiling wide, clowning for the camera, physically taking up space as Ruth leans away from them, making herself smaller. She is smiling, but her eyes appear to portray something else. I wonder what it is. Shyness? Irritation at her brothers?

Or maybe I am more self-centered and pessimistic than I ever imagined. Every photo I see doesn't hide some family trauma. My specific experiences are not everyone's experiences.

I brush it off and assume I am simply imagining I can see something in the eyes of an old photo of a person I don't know. I place it back down on the table and make my way toward the seats at the back of the room.

But the picture stays in my mind. I remember that my father once told me that when he was a boy, he thought it was always cloudy out "in the old days" because he couldn't see the sunlight in black and white pictures. I often feel the same about how people appear in old photos. These two-dimensional images lack color and light, with flattened expressions and dulled emotions. I assume they hold secrets about the past that I will never understand. I wonder if my father thought that when he saw black and white photos as a child.

I wonder if my father reads as much into photos now as he did then. I wonder what he thinks when he looks at pictures of my sister. How do they make him feel? Do they make him cry because he's sad that she is dead? Or do they make him smile because he chooses to remember a happy time they had together?

I've rarely seen my father cry. One of the only times it happened was when his mother, my grandmother Stella, died. I was seven, and Tara was four. As my mother drove the car home, my father sobbed in the passenger seat, asking my mother to go around the block just one more time. I feel like my father thought that if he returned home and resumed his life, it would make it more painful. To go back to his regular rhythms of life, now without his mother, would make it even harder to lose her. Sitting in the grief of the missing piece someone leaves can make a person sad. Looking at the whole of a life with a missing piece cut out of it makes that missing piece feel even more evident and absent.

I bring myself back to this room, the smell of the flowers, the conversations that pivot between tears and laughter. The mood here is one of mournful acceptance. Ruth did not die suddenly, but instead peacefully of natural causes.

I think about how someone dies and if that changes the nature of the grief that follows. I think it does.

The room isn't as full for Ruth as it was at the other funerals, but I assume that is a product of her age. I can't decide if it's sadder to have more or fewer people at your funeral—to leave behind so many people that the room feels suffocating, or to outlive them all, a small existential victory.

I guess it all depends on the type of grief you imagine your death will surface. I remember Mary and Laurie—stroke victim and the runner who died while training—and think how different this funeral feels. The other women died younger than expected, tragic endings to lives cut short. They left behind large networks of people that filled rooms like this, spilling out into the hallways and anterooms. Ruth died with a limited social circle, a longer trail of memories. Is one of them sadder than the other? I don't know.

But the timing of a person's death seems to change the way people mourn. Ruth's mourners are looking back, remembering their time with her. At Laurie and Mary's funerals, the guests instead lamented over the futures they lost. They are not sure how they will go on without them. Laurie's mother, grieving and devastated that she would never have her own family. Mary's best friend, suffering and knowing she will never go on a vacation with her again.

I wonder what Tara's future would have been.

Tara will never get married. I've always been worried that I wouldn't be chosen as the maid of honor when the time came. It sounds crazy that I would want that from Tara, but I always felt like it was my duty—my right—to have that place at her wedding. Now, I won't. It's a relief because I won't have to face the possibility that she would have chosen someone other than her only sister to assume that role.

Tara will never have kids. I know she wanted them. She was always so good with her friends' kids.

I pictured all of this as her future with Matt. I always thought they would work out whatever they were going through. But they didn't. I still don't know why. Maybe Tara was just too much for him to take anymore.

Tara told several people that she and Matt would get engaged, even though they had broken up. Did she believe that? Or did she need to protect herself with that lie, a shield against the truth that she was alone and likely to end up that way?

The room quiets as one of Ruth's brothers steps up to the podium. He unfolds a piece of paper and flattens it with care.

"My sister was a beautiful person. She lived a long life."

His name is William. His eulogy travels from their childhood in New York City to their migration to New Jersey in the fifties.

Memories of the family's struggles—the Great Depression, multiple wars, fears of nuclear annihilation. A story ripped from the history books, weaving Ruth's life into larger events that influenced her outlook, the way she raised her family, the way she lived her life.

"Ruth loved to spend time doing the things she loved. But, the most important was being with her family."

He looks at the front row before him and smiles. He points to Ruth's grandchildren.

"She loved you all the most. And now you'll have memories of her to carry with you forever. Your grandmother—my sister—will be with you forever."

I wonder how her memory will be held and if it will be clung to like a souvenir, bringing them back to a particular time in their lives. I wonder what that is like, the feeling that memories are something to rest on to give us a taste of a time we miss. I have that in other areas of my life, but I don't feel that with Tara.

I remember one picture that sits on my parents' bookshelf. In it, Tara and I are probably nine and twelve years old. We're each holding Cabbage Patch Kids on Christmas morning, still in disbelief that Santa was able to bring them. We look so happy, as if life could not get any better than that. And at that point in our lives, it couldn't. But it never lasted.

I wonder if, lying deep under William's words, there are lingering resentments, spoken or unspoken, that frame how he remembers his sister. I think about the black and white photo of them as children in their kitchen and what I thought I saw between them, assuming that there is always more to the story being told. A counterpoint that fades in the background once a person has died, as if death acts like sandpaper, erasing a rough spot before we cut ourselves on it.

I resist the urge to run up to William and ask him about the photo. I hold myself back from insisting that he tell me what is going on between them in it. Were they fighting? Did they get along? I need not to feel so alone. I need to know that other people have felt what I've felt.

I see William wipe tears from his eyes and fold up his paper, gently tucking it into his pocket, and I can feel that he genuinely grieves for Ruth. My cheeks flash hot because I have judged the veracity of his grief, the truthfulness of his parting words. I have inflicted my own interpretations on his mourning. And I feel worse than ever. Not only because I have cast my own sister away, even after her death, but also because I am so consumed with Tara that I read her into every situation I encounter.

I hate myself for it. I often wanted to avoid Tara in life, and now I bring her into everything I think about.

A voice says to me, "Hello there, dear."

I turn and see a woman sit down next to me. She looks to be about the same age Ruth was. She seems so alive, so vibrant, wearing a red hat with a large rose on the side of it. She has lipstick on. It's the same color as her hat. Firetruck red. I like her already.

I say, "Hello."

She asks, "Are you one of the girls from the nursing home?"

I am not, but it's a perfectly acceptable reason to be here. So, I go with it.

I reply, "Yes. It's very sad about Ruth."

"It is. But I mean, she was a real pain in the ass. I'm sure you know that if you work at the home," she says and laughs.

I try to mask my shock. It's the first unflattering but truthful thing I've heard at a funeral. It makes me feel better about all the unflattering things I thought during Tara's funeral. I turn to look at her, my eyes wide.

"She would never let me forget the day I lost her favorite hair-clip when we were kids. She was always trying to get over on me because of it. Who holds onto a grudge that long?"

She doesn't know me, hasn't even introduced herself, but she continues.

"I mean, who cares if her garden always looked better than mine? I made better baked ziti. She thought everything she did was better. She thinks that grandson of hers is going to be a Nobel Prize winner someday." She leans in closer to me and finishes her thought, "But I think he's got a better chance of going to jail."

She throws her head back and laughs.

I say, confused, "But—you're here."

"Of course, I'm here, sweetie. I've known Ruth for almost eighty years. I loved her. There's no need to hold onto all that now."

"That's very kind of you," I tell her.

She replies, "Look, it has nothing to do with kindness. It has to do with loving someone. They are not the same."

I think about Tara and how we were rarely kind to each other. I had always taken that as a sign that love was missing between us.

"I've never thought about it that way," I say and smile as my mind races to reframe my relationship with Tara through this new perspective.

"Well, Ruth didn't have an easy life. Even from the time she was young. Despite having a good family, straight A's, and a bone structure to die for, she was always a little bit unhappy. Always a little bit unsettled. But I always saw the good in her. So, I loved her even when she drove me crazy. Even though I never walked in her shoes."

To me, Ruth sounds a little bit like Tara. And I think about the idea of walking in her shoes. I imagine experiencing life from her perspective. I wonder what it was like. I assume it would be incomprehensible to me because it was a life she decided she wanted to end. And I can't understand that. I need to learn how to understand that.

I've gone to the same Home Depot and bought the same rope, but it just isn't the same as walking in her shoes.

I tell her, "You have such a beautiful perspective on life."

She says, "In every relationship—in every life—there are the good parts and the bad parts. I'm letting the bad parts die with her. It's the only way to move on."

I nod at her and grab my purse before heading for the exit.

I say, "I have to go. I'm late."

She nods her head and smiles.

It was right in front of me all this time, and I didn't see it.

Is it possible that people can die in pieces? I never thought about it that way before. I've allowed the bad parts to live on even though Tara has died. I wonder if the day will come that I will throw my head back and laugh when thinking about my sister.

I wonder if I'll ever have that kind of forgiveness.

I wonder what walking in Tara's shoes would feel like.

Especially for the last few days of her life.

Chapter Fourteen

What does it mean to walk in someone else's shoes?

I bought the rope. I want to see the room where it happened. I want to see what Tara saw before she died. I want to find the housekeeper who found my sister's body to learn what she saw after Tara died.

Detective Marshall wouldn't tell me the housekeeper's name who found Tara in the hotel room. Since then, I've been thinking about it, wondering what I would say to the person who discovered my sister's body. How could I possibly connect to a person who was just doing her job and stumbled upon a crime scene? An innocent bystander who I imagine suffers nightmares of bodies hanging in hotel rooms, with death lurking behind every door.

I have had concerns about reopening a door this woman wanted closed. But I am getting closer to Tara's death. I need to know the details from the housekeeper: what she saw, what state the room was in, what she did after finding Tara. Without Tara here to answer my questions, I need to piece together the details of that day on my own.

I can't explain why Tara was the way she was or why she did

what she did, but I'll take anything I can get right now. I feel like so many things are mysterious that I want to remove the mystery from the things I can.

I walk into the hotel. I wonder what Tara felt as she did the same. Was she nervous, relieved, scared?

I approach the front desk. A young woman smiles broadly at me.

She says, "Good afternoon! How can I help you?"

I am confident she does not anticipate helping me with what I need.

I respond, "Hello. I was wondering if anyone was currently in Room 702."

"May I ask why?"

"My sister—she died in that room a few months ago," I say.

The look on her face tells me she knows who my sister is. Her face turns red, and she becomes flustered, furiously tapping away at her keyboard.

She says, "Oh. I'm so sorry. Let me look."

I tell her, "I just want to go in the room for a minute if I can."

She looks up from her keyboard, and I can't tell if she is sympathetic to or disgusted by my request.

"I have to check with my manager," she says.

She walks over to another woman at the end of the counter. I can hear the murmur of their voices. They glance back at me.

She returns to the desk and activates a room key for me.

She tells me, "We typically don't do this, but you can go up for a few minutes."

She hands me the key.

"Thank you," I reply and turn toward the elevators.

I unlock the door to Room 702. I take a deep breath before opening it. The room is cold; someone must have turned the air conditioning down. I start to shiver immediately. The door swings shut behind me, and I turn to face it. This is where Tara died. I am standing in the same spot where my sister hung, lifeless and alone. I press my cheek against the door. I close my eyes and say, "Why did you do this?"

I don't expect to hear an answer. But I am startled by a knock on the door across the hall. As a longtime believer in signs, the knock makes me wonder if Tara is there in the room with me. If she is trying to reach me. I don't know how long I've been standing there when I decide I've had enough.

I leave the room and see a housekeeping cart down the hallway. I walk toward it.

A door to one of the rooms is open. I look in and see a woman stripping the queen bed. I knock softly on the opened door.

I call out, "Hello?"

The woman turns around and asks me, "Do you need something?"

This woman appears to me years older than me, and I know she can't be the one who found Tara. From what I remember the detective telling me, the housekeeper who found my sister was "a young woman."

I say, "I was hoping you could help me. My sister died in Room 702 a few months ago—"

Her face falls. She knows who my sister is too.

I continue, "I wanted to speak to the person who found her. Is she here today?"

The woman looks worried, as if she's keeping a secret she promised never to reveal.

I try to reassure her and say, "I just want to make sure she's okay."

She walks over to her cart and throws the sheets into a bag.

She tells me, "She had a tough time after finding the—um—your sister."

I respond, "I'm sure she did. I feel terrible about it."

She looks down each length of the hallway to make sure we're alone.

She tells me, "Her name is Gina Minuto. She's down on the fourth floor now."

I respond, "Thank you so much."

I return to the elevators and press 4.

As I exit the elevator, I look down the hallway and see a cart to my left. I walk toward it as a young woman leaves a room at the end of the hallway. Her hair is up in a bun, and she has small gold hoops in her ears.

As I get closer to her, I see that her nametag says, "Gina."

I need to talk to her.

"Excuse me."

She looks up at me, smiles, and says, "Hi, how can I help you?"

I feel bad for what I'm about to do to her.

I say, "I'm sorry to bother you. My name is Jennifer Rossi. I understand that you're the one who found my sister Tara here in April?"

Her face turns white. Tears well up in her eyes.

I feel terrible. I try to comfort her and say, "Oh, Gina—"

She wipes away a tear. She shakes her head and says, "It's okay. I am just so sad about it."

I say, "I am too."

And I realize that I am.

I say, "Gina, I just wanted to make sure you're okay."

She says, "Thank you. I'm getting there. How about you—are you okay?"

"It's hard, but we're getting through it," I respond.

Gina smiles at me and says, "Your sister seemed like a special person from everything I read in the online guest book."

I ask her, "What was I like to find her like that?"

A tear runs down her cheek. She responds, "It was the saddest thing I have ever seen."

I tell her, "I can't imagine."

She pauses for a moment and says, "Once I saw her there on the back of the door, she seemed so alone. And---"

She begins to cry harder.

"What is it?" I ask her.

"Her things were laid out so nearly on the desk and bed. The TV was on. It was the mirror that was the saddest part."

I say, "The mirror?"

She takes hold of my hand and says, "There was a towel over the mirror. I think she didn't want to watch herself die."

My hands tremble and slip from her grasp. I can't do this. I can't hear any more details. I say, "I'm sorry to bother you, Gina. Thank you for talking to me."

She reaches to touch my arm and squeezes it before turning back to her work.

I walk into the elevator and hit the ground floor button repeatedly. When the doors open to the ground floor, I walk out the front door fast. I can't spend another minute in this hotel.

I'll never be able to recreate that last day of Tara's. Having details like a covered mirror won't help me. It only makes things worse. I no longer imagine that any of this will bring me peace. I just need to move on.

I think about Gina. We are now united through my sister; we both have been responsible for cleaning up someone else's mess, whether wittingly or by surprise. Gina cleans up for strangers, while I have cleaned up for my sister, the one who time and again ripped our world apart to her liking, dousing us in fuel that could be ignited by the tiniest spark and burn us all to dust.

But I don't even feel angry at Tara about that anymore.

I feel sad that she died alone in a hotel room.

I feel sad that she covered the mirror.

I feel sad that she thought life wasn't worth living.

I feel sad, and I think, *Tara deserves this from me.*

Chapter Fifteen

I have shifted my mindset about my sister, even if only slightly.

Going to the hotel made me sad. It made me sad to stand in the space where she took her last breath. It made me sad to speak to the first person to know my sister was dead.

But I still feel like I'm failing at writing my story of grief.

So I continue to pursue others' stories.

Today, I see an obituary for Beth Williams, a young woman who died after a long illness. She was forty-two, from Spring Lake, an accountant, like my mother. Beth's parents had died years ago, and Beth was an only child.

I open Facebook and look at Beth's profile. You can see the progression of her illness over the last year. Early photos show her vibrant and athletic. In recent photos, she is gaunt, visibly weaker. Facebook posts on her wall show an outpouring of support over the last year:

```
The best friend there was.
A kind and generous soul.
Always had a smile on her face.
```

Loved her family more than anything.
She didn't deserve this.

To know you're dying, that you will not outlast your illness, must be terrifying. How scared Beth must have been to see herself wasting away physically, unable to reverse course despite the best efforts. There is no one to blame but fate, but God. There is no one to tell you that it is your fault. There is only the feeling that you did not deserve the ending you got.

But what happens when there aren't any physical signs of deterioration? How can you know that there is something tearing someone apart?

I clip the obituary from the paper and place it in my desk drawer.

Two days later, I walk into the funeral home and toward the side that says "Williams" on the sign. I haven't been to this funeral home yet. I'm trying to move around so I don't see the same funeral director twice. I won't return to the funeral home that held Tara's service. The funeral director would immediately realize it.

Even though I'm in a new environment, the sensory landscape is the same. I walk into the main room; I can hear the murmurs about Beth's death not being fair, about what a tragedy it is. I can feel this in my body, the raw emotion of it, like scalding water on my skin. It's like my body knows how to feel grief even as my mind hasn't fully caught up. The repetition of this ritual is not just emotional. It's a physical ache that exhausts me. I clutch my purse closer to me and take a seat toward the back.

My phone vibrates, and I pull it out from my purse. My mother has texted me again. I'm supposed to meet her at Tara's storage unit to begin to clean out what remains of Tara—yearbooks, stuffed animals, photos, souvenir pint glasses. The physical evidence that Tara was here and that she lived a life. Years of things have accumulated into a collection from which we will hope to piece together her story. A family archaeological dig to interpret what was important to Tara, what she got value from, what we will assign value to, and what will be destined for the trash pile.

I text my mother that I am running late and will meet her and my father at the storage space in an hour. I have put off going to the storage space for weeks, as I am not ready. I don't have the energy for it, another cleanup effort Tara left behind. Another quite literal mess for me to sort out with my parents. I have yet to get mentally organized about Tara's death. I have yet to clean up my disposition toward it. I have yet to understand the contents of a chapter so suddenly and chaotically closed. I cannot envision attaching meaning to a faded concert ticket buried in a box when I still can't bring myself to miss Tara. But I will do it because my parents need guidance and some objective counsel to prevent them from attributing meaning to every item, memorializing Tara with a haphazard museum of things. So I will sort, evaluate, and purge with them.

While I respond to my mother, a text from Becky comes in:

Hey J. Mark and I want to have you over for dinner next weekend. Joanna's free too. Can you make it? Thinking of you xo

I text her back: Thank you. I'll let you know. Xo

I'll be ready to see them again soon. But not right now. I need to be alone with my search for meaning in my sister's death.

I watch people moving about the room and recognize some of Beth's cousins from her Facebook page. She was about ten years older than me and from a different town, so I didn't expect anyone I knew well to be among the mourners. But this part of New Jersey can sometimes feel very small. I am prepared, having created a story about why I am there and how I knew Beth just in case I get drawn into conversation.

I read on Beth's Facebook page that she used to work at Martell's. It was one of the many bars I frequented when I would make my way from one end to the other of the Point Pleasant Boardwalk, doing shots of SoCo and lime, downing Coronas, and chain-smoking Parliaments. So it's not totally a lie because I am sure that our paths crossed, even if I didn't know it at the time.

It's my cover story, my reason to explain being there. But I don't want to lie to anyone if I don't have to. It feels like it will bring me to a new level of deception that just doesn't feel like I'm being myself. I've never pretended to be someone else. I've always known who I was and have been comfortable with that. The fact that I'm even here makes me wonder if I've been someone else my entire life. What kind of person goes to the funerals of strangers? If you asked anyone that question, they would probably say it's someone who is falling apart. Someone who has lost her moral compass and is scrambling to find it. Or maybe they would say I'm a terrible person, taking advantage of others' grief just to figure out my shit.

I feel worse than ever.

I look up and see an old acquaintance on the other side of the room. At first, I panic. Bill was my manager at the boardwalk arcade during my college summers. Every night we'd stand there, waiting for hordes of kids to walk up to the counter to redeem millions of tickets for some plastic toy that would inevitably break on the way home. I worry he will recognize me and wonder how I knew Beth. It's too close for my comfort. I imagined lying to deflect conversation with strangers. I didn't expect to have to lie to someone who might be able to poke holes in the story simply because he knows who I am.

I should have been more careful. I should have known that different circles of my life could reconnect like this. That death could reweave connections that have frayed and loosened.

I need to leave.

As I walk toward the door, I hear him call my name, "Jennifer? How are you?"

"Bill, wow. What has it been, fifteen years?"

He says, "No, it can't be."

"Yes, it's crazy." I shake my head and say, "It's so sad about Beth."

I nod quickly. "Yes, it is."

Bill says, "I heard about your sister. I'm so sorry."

I had forgotten that Bill knew Tara. She would come to the boardwalk with her friends from time to time. They would stop into the arcade—sometimes Tara would ask me to buy them some pizza, sometimes she wanted to borrow a few dollars to play some games. She knew that I would never turn her down, especially in front of her friends. I had forgotten about that.

Bill says, "I remember the time your sister came into the arcade and won that enormous stuffed elephant. Watching her carry that all over the arcade was hilarious."

I laugh at the memory. I had forgotten about that too.

That night, Tara and her friends had played Skee-Ball for a few hours, and Tara walked up to the counter with armfuls of tickets. This enormous stuffed elephant was propped up on top of the Ms. Pac-Man machine, and Tara insisted she wanted it. She mentioned something about a joke with her best friend, Leslie. I had told her it was too big for her to carry, but she insisted she could. With the enormous elephant slung onto her back, she could barely see. She kept walking into the pinball machines. I watched her navigate her way through the aisles. She would make elephant noises and talk to me while pretending she was speaking through the trunk as if an elephant was asking me to buy her pizza.

Her friends laughed, and so did I. Tara could be funny in an effortless way. She was able to wear situations well that would usually embarrass other people. I can't believe I had forgotten about that night at the arcade.

It makes me wonder what else I have forgotten about.

I quickly change the subject. "How did you know Beth?"

His face suddenly changes.

Bill says, "We dated a few years back. It didn't work out because I was traveling all the time. We kept in touch, had dinner occasionally. Until she got sick."

"I'm so sorry, Bill," I say.

I squeeze his shoulder, wanting him to feel my sympathy, which is real.

He says, "Thank you. How did you know Beth?"

I had prepared for this moment.

"I used to talk to her when she was a bartender at Martell's. I would go there for happy hour all the time, and she was great to talk to."

He says, "Yes, she was. I wish I could have done something to save her."

I can't help but think of my sister. Is there something I could have done to save her?

Bill wipes a tear away as he's pulled into another conversation. I pat him lightly on the back and return to my seat.

I look at Beth's face on her funeral card as I walk out of the funeral home. Bill wishes he could have done something to save Beth. I didn't know my sister needed saving. I had no warning that she was on a rapid descent. No diagnosis told us, "Here are the things you need to do right away to make sure she stays alive." We had no treatment regimen because we didn't know there was something to treat.

But I do remember that I often thought life would be easier without Tara. I just never thought it would happen. It makes me feel so much worse. I wanted my sister to go away, and now that she has, I am failing at being left behind. I am failing at being human.

I think about Tara that night at the arcade. It wasn't all bad between us. I remember when Tara used to call me "Jennie" when she was around four or five. She would stroke my hair and say, "It's okay, Jennie. I love you," if I got hurt. She would ask to put Band-Aids on my cuts, offer to bring me a glass of water when I had a cold.

I was the world to her at one point in our lives, and then things disintegrated before my eyes. I turned her away because it just became too hard. But maybe I was too sensitive, too easily triggered by Tara. Perhaps I should have been more forceful, more persistent in my attempts to win her over. Maybe I should have forced her to lay her cards on the table and tell us why she behaved the way she did. What did she feel that made her want us to feel bad too? Maybe I could have tried harder to recapture moments like that night in the arcade.

But I am trying too hard to rewrite history. A few laughs about a stuffed elephant can't erase everything else that happened between us.

Still, it makes me think.

I remember Mary's funeral and the friend who couldn't cry for her.

I remember Laurie's funeral and the sister who felt like she couldn't live without her.

I remember Ruth's funeral and the friend who allowed the bad parts to die with her.

All these people – alive and dead - are strangers to me. Yet I feel a connection to them. They have stayed with me since I encountered them.

I haven't been able to get the woman from Ruth's funeral out of my head. I can still see her in the red hat with the rose, talking to me about kindness and love and letting go. I had focused on only the bad parts with Tara. What would we have looked like if I had chosen to embrace the good parts? Or if I had walked in Tara's shoes to understand better what she was going through?

Perhaps I am being too literal about walking in Tara's shoes. I consider that her troubles may have been deeper than simple unhappiness or frustration. I worry they were related to something else. Was there an illness festering inside of Tara I didn't see? We try to save people who have diseases every day. Like Beth. We fight for their lives. I had always chalked up Tara's behavior as her being difficult, moody, easily triggered.

But was there something more I missed?

Could I have fought for her life? Would I even have wanted to?

Oh God, I think.

Rather than trying to break down the wall between us, I assumed it was permanent. And maybe that is part of the problem. Perhaps I was part of the problem.

I can't stop thinking that I should have thrown a lifeline over to my sister. But as I envision that, the lifeline looks like the rope she hung herself with. And instead of preventing her death, I enabled it.

But this is no time to fall apart entirely. I have a storage space to empty.

Chapter Sixteen

The metal door rises above us like the blade of a guillotine, perched in midair, waiting for its next victim. Each corrugated band of steel clangs as my father pulls the chain.

My parents and I are at Tara's storage space. The short-term lease is up, and we are here to clean it out and decide what is worth keeping and what we will toss. When Tara moved out of Matt's house and back in with my parents, she left everything here—lamps, pillows, and rugs. The space is filled with items once carefully chosen to decorate her home, now junk to be donated. It heightens my fears about death because it just illustrates our transience, our brief impermanence. So many of the things we place so much value on eventually become irrelevant and forgotten. With her breakup from Matt, these objects became unnecessary items, now sitting positioned clumsily among boxes of books and papers and winter clothes.

I don't want to do this. I feel like going through Tara's property is an invasion of her privacy. But the lesser part of me thinks that it's my chance to finally get back at Tara, to go through her things with reckless abandon. To make a mess, to destroy things. But it doesn't feel right to me. I dread sifting through a collection of another person's stuff, their gathered objects that hold meaning I may never understand.

My mother has picked up a box that contains photos. She wears sunglasses to hide her eyes; she doesn't want my father or me to see her cry as she reviews the snapshots of Tara's life: her third birthday party, her college graduation, her Labor Day party at Matt's house. All moments in Tara's life where anything seemed possible. Now they sit as artifacts of a time that seems forever ago —the time when Tara was still as alive as she looked in those photos. I wonder if my mother thinks of my sister's death when she sees those photos. It's more likely that she remembers her daughter as I imagine a mother would: with kindness and generosity. Using a mental buffer to smooth out the rougher spots, she doesn't cut herself to the bone every time she thinks about Tara.

I'm concerned about my mother. She's already so small, so delicate. I am afraid that her grief will turn her to dust, and she'll evaporate into the air, chasing Tara's ghost. That she will tie herself into knots trying to avoid the details of Tara's death. That she will dry up from the inside out from crying.

"Are you sure you want to do this?" I ask her as I move to embrace her. I can feel the tears on her cheek as I draw her close.

She says, "I have to, Jennifer. She was my baby."

"I know," I say.

She tells me, "You'll understand one day when you have kids of your own. No matter what happens, you can't give up on them, and they never stop being your babies. Ever."

I see my mother in a slightly different light. She is not as resigned as I thought she was. She was just quietly fighting for her daughter all this time, rather than fighting with her.

She releases from my hug and continues with her task, sorting photos into piles.

My father is moving the larger items into the back of a truck headed for the Salvation Army. He shouts out things he thinks I might want, but I don't.

"Jennifer, what about this lamp?"

I do not need a lamp from Tara. I tell him, "No, thank you—it's not my style."

"Do you need another stand mixer?"

I do not. I tell him, "No, you and Mom got me one for Christmas a few years ago, remember?"

"Didn't you always want this painting from our old house?"

I never liked it; Tara did. I tell him, "I like the other one with the trees."

I do not need Tara's things, or at least not these specifically. I don't need reminders of her in plain sight all the time. I prefer my mementos hidden away so I can be the one to decide when it's time to look at them.

As I open boxes and sort through kitchen towels and Christmas decorations, I become afraid of something else. With each pile I organize, I am worried I'll find something that tells me she had thought about suicide before—a note, a journal entry, anything that could have been the sign that something was wrong. The evidence in a mounting case against us is that we saw a troublemaker when we should have seen someone planning to die.

But I keep opening boxes.

I collect a thing or two here and there, slipping her New York City Marathon bib, a Christmas plaque I made for her in third grade, and a Smurf pillowcase into a small bag. I'm not sure why these things speak to me so strongly, but I want to hold onto them.

After a few hours, we have made good progress on the pile. I've carried box after box of clothes and photos to my parents' car. I can tell that the day has worn my mother out, so I encourage her to leave.

I ask her, "Why don't you go home? I can finish up."

She has taken off her sunglasses. Her eyes remain raw and tired. She asks, "Are you sure?"

I nod. "Dad's about to head to the Salvation Army, and there are only a few boxes left."

I smile at her to let her know it's okay.

"Thank you," she says as she slowly walks to the car and leaves.

I wave goodbye to my father and focus on the few remaining boxes.

I open the lid to one of them and find a jumbled mess of things in it; Tara must have hastily thrown everything in here, rushing to get everything boxed up and out of Matt's house. My fear about what I might find remains strong, but I can't help myself. I leaf through the box and find her diploma, baby book, and random concert tickets. I dig deeper and find a souvenir cup from Atlantic City and some Mardi Gras beads. At the bottom of the box is a bulky envelope sealed shut.

It's warm out today, and I'm feeling the effects of hours in the storage space. I grab the envelope and sit down on a folding chair to catch my breath and drink some water. I feel like I am wearing Tara's history on my skin, the layer of dust released from years of things thrown together in boxes. The smells of old photos, of weathered paper, permeate my senses.

I open the envelope and pull out its contents: a stack of cards and letters and postcards. It takes me a moment to realize that they are all from me. My pulse quickens as I sort through the pile. The postcard I sent Tara when I went to Italy a few years back, telling her about the men who flirted with me as they kissed their girlfriends. A letter I wrote her when she went away to college, warning her to please be careful and not be afraid to say no to certain situations. A card I gave her for her fifth birthday that read, "There is no love greater than a sister." I signed it "Jennie" because that is what she used to call me.

There are so many souvenirs here—I don't even remember writing her this many notes, cards, and letters. She must have saved them all. I always imagined that I was secondary in her life. That she did not care about me. But as I continue to leaf through the envelope's contents, I wonder if they made her feel something at one time. I convince myself that they must have. I wonder why they weren't enough to make her love me while she was alive. Is it love that made her keep them? Or was it to make her remember that there was a time when she did love me and make her wish she could recapture it?

I wonder if Tara was just as sad and confused about us as I was. I wonder if she looked at these mementos from time to time to feel something like love for me.

I place the fifth birthday card on the top when the words become blurry. I wonder if I'm imagining it, having a harder and harder time focusing on the letters. I touch the paper, and it's wet; I realize that my tears are washing over it, wiping away the words I once wrote to Tara. Wiping our slate clean so I can perhaps see Tara a new way in death that I was never able to in life.

Chapter Seventeen

TARA

FEBRUARY

Leslie had her baby last night. She texted me a photo this morning to give me the news. The baby girl, named Kaitlyn, has enormous brown eyes and a patch of soft, curled hair.

Kaitlyn came early, so I haven't had a chance to buy a gift yet. After rushing over to the hospital, I head straight into the gift shop before going up to Leslie's room. I stroll past arrangements of flowers and ceramic vases displaying messages like "It's a Boy!" and "Get Well Soon." It smells like coffee and lilies in here; it's a weird thought, but it reminds me of a funeral home. I come across a pile of stuffed animals. They are all shapes and sizes, with different colored hats and bows. I notice an elephant, and it immediately catches my eye.

Leslie and I met in third grade. Our class was doing an art project where we each had to pair up with someone to make a paper-mache animal. Leslie chose an elephant as her animal, and I watched her look around the room as our classmates paired off to make other animals they thought were more interesting—lions, tigers, zebras, penguins. I didn't care which animal I made, so I told Leslie I'd make an elephant with her. She said that elephants symbolized good luck in some parts of the world. So I told her it was her good luck that I didn't prefer lions, and she laughed. Ever since that day, we've been best friends.

I pick up the stuffed elephant and clutch it under my arm. Its soft, gray fur makes my skin tingle. I smooth its pink satin bow as I head toward the elevators. When the elevator opens on the seventh floor, I walk to Leslie's room. The room is filled with flowers and balloons. Leslie and the baby are glowing, bathed in sunlight. As I enter, I cry out, "Congratulations! Let me see that baby!"

Leslie and Dave look up and smile at me with exhilarated exhaustion.

Dave says, "Thanks, Tara. We're so glad you came."

Dave hugs me in an awkward embrace. I've never liked hugging other people. It has always felt stiff and artificial. It has always felt like the grasp of a vise rather than a warm embrace. Like I could be trapped by it. But I try to relax into his hug, to be more open to physical contact.

I whisper in his ear, "Stop knocking my friend up, okay?" He throws his head back and laughs while he pulls away. I always deflect tender moments with jokes. It makes me more at ease. I knock him on the head with the elephant and turn to Leslie, who laughs at our interaction.

I've always been envious of Leslie because her life with Dave seems effortless. Mine with Matt always required so much effort from me. I don't know why it always felt like so much work. My problem has often been that I work better on my own even though being alone frightens me the most. So, I either end up contorting myself into a better version to make the other person happy and keep them, or I don't, and they become unhappy, and I lose them. Regardless of which option I choose, it always ends up the same.

I remember that Leslie and I have always had similar visions of happiness—husbands, kids, soccer games, and weekends at the Shore. We would talk about the houses we pictured ourselves in one day. Leslie dreamed of a colonial in Spring Lake. I always imagined myself in one of those colorful Victorians in Asbury Park. During sleepovers, we would doodle hearts around the names of our crushes while listening to Mariah Carey. In our dreams, we would drive the kids to the boardwalk and laugh together as they played games and ate ice cream.

Those childhood dreams seem so far away from me now.

"Here she is!" Leslie beams as she hands Kaitlyn over to me.

Kaitlyn is so tiny; an enormous headband covers her entire forehead, its large bow hangs over her eyes.

I love my friends' children. I'm a godmother to three of them. Always there—birthdays, communions, graduations—and always in the family photos. Since I don't have a family of my own, I jump from picture frame to picture frame in their lives, an extra in everyone else's happy story.

I love being with them. My friends, their kids. But seeing the fullness of their lives makes me feel even more empty. Their presence highlights the absences in my own life. But I never let them see that. Instead, I smile and hold the babies and let them take the pictures.

I smell Kaitlyn's skin, so clean and new. I take her little hand in mine and can't believe that we all began like this. So innocent and helpless, no thoughts to trouble us and no perceived danger afoot. I wish I could remember myself at that time in my life, but I know it's impossible. I wish I could hit a reset and start over, give myself another chance to find the life I want. Take what I know now and do it over.

"She is beautiful, you guys," I say. I smile as Kaitlyn yawns, her lips contorting into a twist, her eyes opening for the first time.

The baby looks at me, and I wish I could see myself as she does —a blank slate, no history, no assumptions. I wish I could have my own child who would see me in this way.

Dave walks over and kisses Leslie on the top of her head. He refills her water. Matt and I have broken up. I'm in my mid-thirties with no kids, no house of my own, no one to love me the way Dave loves Leslie.

Leslie is my oldest friend, the one I turn to with every problem. When Eric Barnes stood me up for the eighth-grade dance, Leslie told him off and took me back to her house for a sleepover. We ate ice cream and watched movies, and I forgot about Eric by the time we went from *Ferris Bueller's Day Off* to *The Breakfast Club*. When I left college after my first year, Leslie came to help me move out of my dorm and plan what I would do next. That was one of the worst times in my life.

Leslie has always been my problem solver, believing there is always a solution, always a way out of trouble. But some problems are more significant than others. Some issues can't be solved with Ben and Jerry's or a motivational talk. Instead, they brew below the surface for years, hidden from view, and then rise and clutch you around the neck. They claw at your skin, ripping open old wounds and stealing your breath.

I am alone with my problem, and there is no way out. At least not one that I can see. My problem is me, which seems to be the most challenging one to solve. I am just realizing that everything can't be everyone else's fault all the time. I am the common denominator. It's not an easy realization to have.

The door opens, and Leslie's parents enter with her older daughter, Robin.

"Auntie Tara! I have a baby sister!" She looks up at me and

tugs on my jacket. I place my arm around her shoulders and echo her enthusiasm. "I know. And what a good big sister you'll be."

"I am going to show her everything. I am going to teach her to color and play puzzles." Robin is beaming, excited about her new role in the family.

I remember Jennifer taking care of me when I was little. I haven't thought of that in a long time. I don't think about the times before everything fell apart.

"I know you are, sweet girl." I smooth her hair.

Leslie's parents come over to greet me. "Good to see you, Tara. Please send our best to your parents."

I smile at them.

I hand Kaitlyn back to Leslie. The thoughts are coming to me again. I know that I will never have this—the love, the ease of being together, the hope. I've never had it, never been truly comfortable around other people. Never felt like there was anything on my horizon but compromise, situations that would dissatisfy me. The only time I've felt peaceful is when I've thought about not living anymore. It has crossed my mind more and more often lately. I feel grotesque for thinking about it while celebrating a new life, but it makes perfect sense. Unless I thought there was a way for me to feel how this room feels, have this kind of life—true love, my own family, belonging—I would feel differently.

I don't know when it will happen. I don't even know that it will happen at all. But knowing the option exists calms me down. It makes me feel in control.

I hug Leslie and say my goodbyes. I need to get to work. I want to tell Leslie how I feel, but it's too late, and I don't even know if Leslie would be able to help me. She has her own life to manage and doesn't need me messing that up. But the thought crosses my mind.

As I turn to walk out the door, I look back one last time so that I can remember this moment. A new life, a clean slate perched on her mother's chest, wrapped in a hospital blanket. A family that is now complete. I memorize every aspect of it. I will use this moment time and again to calm me down. I fantasize about replacing Leslie's face with mine and Dave's with Matt's. Looking at our baby. Beginning our life together.

I turn away before they can see the tears welling up in my eyes.

I could never let anyone know about the thoughts I'm having. I don't want them to think I'm weak. I don't want to interrupt their happy lives with my unhappiness.

And so, they will remember me today, in this hospital room, smiling because of real happiness for my friends. I need to find time to spend with my parents and sister so they can remember me in the same way. Whether I choose to disappear, in name or permanently, I don't want to leave them all with a bitter taste in their mouths. I will be emotionally generous for once. I will act differently than I feel for just a little while until I decide what I will do.

It's the least I can do.

Chapter Eighteen

I look around the storage space and think, *look at what your life has become.* Plastic totes of clothes and hastily filled boxes with all my stuff surround me. Until today, everything was scattered—some things were still at Matt's, others were in my parents' attic, the rest in Leslie's garage. I am dropping off some final boxes today.

It's late winter, and it's cold enough that I can see my breath. Or maybe it's the cigarette smoke. I can't tell.

Everything I own is in here because Matt and I are over. I stayed with Leslie and her husband Dave at their condo, but they just had a baby and already have a two-year-old. They are now a family of four, and I felt like I would no longer belong there. Before Leslie was due, they told me that I could stay longer if I wanted, but I didn't want to. They were preparing for the next chapter of their life, and they didn't need me there, taking up the guest bedroom, crying quietly into my pillow at night. They don't need me to need them, just because I can't seem to catch a fucking break.

So, I left.

I am leaving all my things here because I don't need them anymore. They are evidence of a life that is no longer one I want. Or one that I think I can have. So I will leave everything here for now and not think about how, when, or why I will ever need them again. What do all of the things you collect in your life eventually mean, especially when your life no longer means anything?

I pick up an envelope of letters and cards I've saved over the years. When I open the clasp, there's a birthday card on top. Jennifer gave it to me for my fifth birthday. There are other cards and letters from her in there. At first, it's easy to think that I don't know why I saved them all. But the truth is, I think I've spent a lot of my life trying to reconnect to something I can't even explain. I am sentimental for things I can't even define. As my own life has fallen apart, day after day and year after year, I clutch to certain things to give my life meaning.

I've often wondered if Jennifer would understand if I explained it to her the right way. If I could explain it to myself. If I could show her this envelope of cards and letters and say, "See, this means something for us, right? This is a sign of something, right, Jen?"

My cheeks flash hot at the thought. I'm sure Jen wouldn't think anything of them if I told her. But it's too late for that.

I place the envelope in the bottom of a tote, covering it with Mardi Gras beads and other things I no longer need.

I push the tote to the back of the storage space.

I don't know what I will do, but I consider flying somewhere and starting a new life. Jennifer has always talked about Italy and how it's her favorite place. She seems like she was so happy there. It crosses my mind that maybe I could be happy there too.

I consider cutting everyone off and changing my name. Maybe if I make myself someone else, I would be happier. I could become Melissa or Tiffany or Donna. I could be anyone I want to be, with any backstory. I could be a young widow looking for a fresh start. I could tell stories about my late husband and how in love we were. People would feel sorry for me, but at least I would feel seen.

I have considered a lot of things but haven't decided yet. But things can't stay the way they are.

I unpack the final boxes from my car and realize that I'm freezing. The temperature has dropped today, making me shiver even though my forehead is damp with sweat. I used to love the winter when I was a little girl when the snow made everything around me feel magical and new. Now, I resent the gusts of wind sweeping through the aisles of storage spaces whipping up the edge of my coat. I hate the way the snow looks on the road after a few days, chalky and gray. I have splatter marks on the back of my coat from walking in it. My boots are caked with salt. I lick my fingers and try to wipe them off. I am trying so hard to be positive, but it seems like everything in the world has been arranged and rearranged to frustrate me right now.

My phone buzzes—it's a text from my mother.

```
Hi baby. We can't wait to see you later.
    There is some lasagna in the fridge.
```

I am staying at my parents' house for a little while. I had to call them and ask to stay with them while I figured out my next move. They agreed right away, which made me even more frustrated for some reason. We have battled my whole life, and I don't understand how they could so easily allow me to come back home. There are so many moments when my parents don't live down to my meager expectations of them. And that makes me feel worse. It makes me rethink everything I've thought for so long.

I've always placed so much blame for how I feel about myself on them. I've always assumed that you could plot a direct line from the thoughts in my head back to certain things they did or said in my childhood. Sometimes it feels like I've built my life on a story that isn't true. It's like when you watch a movie and are convinced that one character is the bad guy when it's the good guy in disguise. I think about Matt, about previous boyfriends, about friendships that have ended abruptly, and worry there is a pattern I haven't seen.

I shake off the thought because it would make me wrong. It would make me the problem. And I can't be the problem; it doesn't fit with the way I've always felt. I can't be both the bad guy and pretend to be the good guy. I want to be good. I need to be good. So any other option being valid means I've sabotaged my whole life. That I have been my own worst enemy. And that makes me feel even worse. It makes me feel even more like I can't continue this way.

I browse the boxes one last time and see my Kitchen Aid stand mixer. I remember buying it at Macy's and feeling so grown up that I had a kitchen appliance like that. I notice that its stainless-steel base has a few dried splatters of cake batter on it. I remember baking cakes on my kitchen counter and feeling like an adult when I used it. For me, it was a status symbol of domestic life, one of the touchpoints of adulthood: having the right appliances in your kitchen for the job at hand.

Leaving it in here while I move in with my parents makes me feel like my adulthood has been stripped from me temporarily. It made me feel vulnerable to ask my parents this favor, and I didn't want them to feel bad for me. I didn't want to live there again, like someone who couldn't make her way. An adult now reduced to a child once again, living under the same roof as her parents. It makes me feel like a failure. But to get my own place right now just doesn't feel right. It would tell the world that I've moved on, and I haven't. It would make the breakup with Matt feel even more permanent.

I haven't told Jennifer yet.

I don't want her feedback on my situation. I don't want her

judgment or her attempt at comforting me. I'll never let her see me like this, broken and vulnerable. I never want anyone to see me at my worst because I don't wear my worst very well. It doesn't fit me right, makes me even more on edge than usual, and catapults my self-doubt into the stratosphere. And it will only prove to Jennifer what I know she has thought all along: that I am unlovable.

The one thing I always had on Jennifer was that I was able to be in relationships more often; while she was alone most of her life, a bookish snob who always cared more about school or whatever cause she was supporting, I was always able to find someone who wanted me. I was the one who was special. The fun sister, the one people wanted to be around. It was my secret source of pride, bringing a boyfriend to a family party while she sat by herself. It also made a statement to everyone in the room: Tara is good enough. It was an energy I fed off, even when I didn't feel good enough. I would stay close to my boyfriend while Jennifer mingled around the room, stopping to talk to our elderly aunts in the corner and refill their drinks. Jennifer seemed to be perfectly happy with the life she had, but it seemed miserable to me.

I can't believe that you could be happy like that, with no one around you to prop you up, to make you feel better about yourself than you feel. That Jennifer can summon happiness—or at least not summon self-hatred—from within herself is just another way I don't understand her.

To be alone with yourself and be content. That thought always terrified me. I always hated being alone. It leaves too much room for the doubting voices in my head that appear in my quiet moments. It forces me to face myself, to see myself, and I have never liked what I saw,

I much prefer superficial affection, even if I know it's not real. It still makes me feel good.

I quickly search for my high school yearbooks. I pull them out from time to time and read all the comments. I find the one from my senior year. I'm greeted with photos from the cafeteria, football games, and science class as I open it. I turn the pages, and each one is filled with notes like "Best Friends Forever" and "I'll Miss you C" and "Keep in touch!" Tons of words written about me, for me. But so many of them didn't know me. They loved the crazy pranks I would pull—like the time I smeared shaving cream on all the windows of the Spanish teacher's car—and the jokes I would tell. They loved that I hosted house parties when my parents were away. I was always fun, but looking back on it now, it seems like all anyone knew about me was that I was a good time. They only skimmed the surface of me. I wonder if they would have missed me or wanted to keep in touch if they knew the real me. I slip the yearbook back into the box.

I decide that yearbooks are stupid and meaningless and no accurate indicator of anything. I don't want to remember any of those things or most of those people anyway. But Jennifer finds her yearbooks to be highly sentimental. To her, they were essential mementos that highlighted her accomplishments—a time capsule for her hard work in high school. I don't think I realized what they represented to her back then, but I did know they were precious to her.

I remember years ago seeing Jennifer's high school yearbooks on the shelf and not being able to resist looking at them. Jennifer was at work that day. She had just gotten promoted to manager at one of the boardwalk arcades. She took Skee-Ball and the redemption of game tokens as seriously as she did everything else, which was too serious. In a few months, she would be leaving for college, and I would be free of her. I would be free of her condescension and criticism. But I most wanted to be free from the comparisons to her. The best piece of news I had gotten in a while is that Jennifer chose to attend a college in Ohio that would take her 505 miles away from us for almost four whole years.

I knew the distance because I checked.

And I never told anyone this, but I hoped she was alone and afraid there. I wanted her to feel like an outsider. I wanted her to feel like I've always felt.

Her bedroom was familiar, yet I felt like an intruder in a foreign place. Over the years, I had to walk by her room on the way to mine, glancing in over her shoulder as she shut the door to me time and time again. Yet I've rarely been inside it. I remember it smelling like her perfume—citrusy and bright—called "Happy," which always struck me as funny. I never really saw Jennifer happy, at least when I was around.

Jennifer was always organized and neat, with memorabilia carefully placed around her bookshelf. Her room was filled with remnants of her childhood: trophies filled the shelves, posters covered the walls, and photos were tucked into the mirror over her desk. Plaques for this accomplishment or that rested against the weathered spines that lined her bookshelves. Thinking about it now, Jennifer has always collected memories, as if clutching to a flotation device that would help keep her head above water, safe from the undertow of forgetting. She would clip things that interested her from the newspaper and save every birthday card she ever received.

I remember seeing the yearbooks there on her bookshelves. Four years of high school memories, four years of activities, and accolades. Four years of "and the award goes to Jennifer Rossi." Four years of hearing stories about band camp and the school newspaper and science fairs. Within the pages of those yearbooks lay the evidence of all the ways she needed to be perfect all the time. I think I hated that more than anything.

For years, I had to ride in her wake, substitute teachers who remembered her, principals who referred to me as "Jennifer Rossi's little sister," awards in the school trophy chest with her name on them. For years, she shone so clear a mirror on me and everything that she was and I was not.

I pulled the first one off the shelf and opened it. It was Jennifer's senior yearbook, with her name chosen for "Most Likely to Succeed" and "Most Musical." I flipped to the band page, and there she is as the drum major. The Latin Club. The school newspaper. The National Honor Society. She collected experiences and achievements like others collected comic books or baseball cards. No matter how I tried, I could never imitate her, never take the world in my hands and set it on fire. I have always thought of myself as kind of smart but never wanted it to define me like Jennifer has. I never wanted my achievements to be my identity. Because that involves risk. The day you're not the smartest one in the room, everyone forgets about you. The day you're not the fastest, your trophy doesn't go in the case.

I found it easier to try to be everything I felt Jennifer wasn't: funny, adventurous, fun. It was the way I would survive the endless comparisons.

In the margins of the yearbook, I saw notes from her friends and teachers, all of them wishing her well and knowing all the great things she would do. Always the chosen one, the golden child, the only child. If only they could have seen how she treated me, they could only know that I was the sister she never wanted. If only they could have heard her tell me she hated me, that she wished I was born into a different family, that I was a monster for the way I acted and what I said.

My rage increased with every page turn. The train was already speeding down the tracks, and I couldn't stop it. I searched her desk for a pen and found a black Sharpie—with it, I documented my hatred across every page. Hatred for Jennifer, but also for the ways that I could never be her. I crossed out the faces of her friends, drew pictures of penises surrounding Jennifer's head in any photo of her, making it impossible for her to look back on these memories without seeing my additions to them. I wanted her to hurt like I did, to feel that nothing was safe or sacred. I wanted her to know what I felt. To even feel it herself. I kept thinking, *now YOU are the one who doesn't belong. YOU are the one who feels small and foolish.*

I did know that someday Jennifer would open these books and cry; she would be confused while she expected nothing less from me. And through the tears and the yelling and the misunderstanding, I knew that there was no way I could ever say to her that I didn't know how to be any different.

But it's so clear to me now.

When you don't know who you are, it's easiest to live up to everyone else's expectations. I fit myself into the role of a problem child and leveraged it as best I could to defend myself against all the things that hurt me.

I hear the honk of a horn and realize that my car is blocking the lane outside. I quickly close the steel gate and lock it. I wave to the car behind me to acknowledge that I am leaving. I rearrange a few suitcases in my trunk, the only things I will need while deciding what I'm going to do. As soon as I start the car and pull away, I don't even think about the things I'm leaving behind. They are meaningless, just things. They don't make me happy. Nothing makes me happy anymore, and I consider never returning to the storage space and just letting it all go. My furniture, my memories, all of it.

I still have a key, so I let myself in when I arrive at my parents' house. Both are at work, and I am grateful not to have to see them as I drag my suitcases down the hallway and back into my childhood bedroom. I open the door to my room, and even though it no longer contains the evidence that I once lived there, it is familiar to me.

I bring my toiletries into the bathroom and remember how upset I got when my parents renovated it. I don't like change. It's funny, I was rarely happy living here, but I have always wanted the house to remain as it was my whole childhood. We had a big fight about it, and my parents told me I was being ridiculous. That it was their house and they wanted to do it. I don't know why it affected me so much. Maybe I thought my childhood home would become unrecognizable to me with too many changes. That I would lose my memories, and if I had no memories, I could no longer define myself in opposition to them. I could no longer be the outcast I imagined myself to be.

And then who would I be anymore?

I'm tired and want to unpack so I can lie down. I remember how it felt to live in this room, feeling like I was a guest in a rooming house as if I didn't fit in my family. This room was my safe zone, and behind its closed door, I lived my life close to, but not with, Jennifer and my parents. It wasn't always that way, but I felt that way most of the time. I don't remember when things changed, but I feel it again immediately as I begin to hang my clothes in the closet.

I place my makeup case on the desk and sit down on the worn wicker chair. Looking at myself in the mirror, I remember that Jennifer and I used to talk about what we thought we'd look like when we grew up. We were young, maybe five and nine, and being grown up seemed so far away.

As a child, I thought I would change, become better, become happier one day. But, as I sit here looking at myself in the mirror, the sunlight streaking across my face, carrying a light misting of dust in the air, I realize that I am once again the child I was then: lost, distant, frustrated.

I place bottles of moisturizer and perfume on the desk's glass top. I used to have photos arranged under the glass, pictures of friends, our dog Rex, my cousin Pamela. Things that made me happy. I would sit at this desk and look at the images as if I could conjure up confidence through them—here are the things I love, here are the people who love me.

I think about the letter I wrote to Pamela about wanting her to be my sister and wonder if my theory was correct; if I were to magically change families, I would change. I would be happier, as if my feelings were solely the product of my environment. I push away the thought because if that were not true, it would just be additional confirmation that the problem has always laid within me, not within these walls.

The thought fatigues me. I lie down on the bed and close my eyes. I used to play a game every night when I'd go to sleep in this very room. I would imagine that I was a doll, and in my mind, I would try on different clothes and accessories and looks to see what I would be like as a different person. I would change my hair from long to short, brown to blonde. I would have blue eyes instead of brown. I would ride in a car sometimes and sometimes in a camper. I would be a doctor or an actress, or a librarian. I would cycle through endless combinations to see which one fit. I always fell asleep before I decided.

No matter how many times I arranged and rearranged my hair and clothes and identity, it never felt right.

Now, I try a different game with my eyes closed and begging for rest. I imagine what it would look like to be happy. I run through scenarios that include Matt and don't include him. I imagine myself as a mother. I imagine that Jennifer and I are best friends. I imagine that I live to be a hundred and live in a house filled with cats who watch me while I knit scarves for my grandchildren. I imagine having dinner with my parents and laughing at my dad's jokes. I imagine getting an illness and feeling everyone's pity as my body wastes away. I imagine that I have died, and everyone is standing over my casket. I imagine they weep for me and regret every angry word spoken between us.

I feel myself falling into a deep sleep before deciding what happiness looks like.

Chapter Nineteen

JENNIFER

JUNE

Four funerals have come and gone. Five, if I include Tara's. It is getting me nowhere, but I'm not ready to stop yet.

I pull the newspaper clipping from my purse. It's weathered from repeated folding and unfolding, wrinkled, and tattered to the point where it no longer leaves behind ink stains on my fingers. I read that Ellen died in a car accident and was a popular student at one of the local high schools. I learned that she has a small family, like me. She has one sister who remains, like me. I glance at the obituary one more time.

Services for Ellen Sawyer will be held on Saturday, June 13, 2009, at noon at the Wilson Funeral Home in Freehold, NJ.

I am sitting in the Wilson Funeral Home parking lot, waiting for a break in the rain. I am thinking about obituaries, trying to figure out what draws me to them. It's not like they tell the whole story. That is not their purpose.

There are so many private moments and details that aren't

shared—that are impossible to share—when someone dies. Just like obituaries only skim the surface, I, too, have not gone deep enough to understand. And I realize that it's just not possible.

I think of Tara, and the final days of her life, the days I've tried to recreate. I read the emails and texts. I bought the rope. I went to the hotel. I spoke to the housekeeper. I realize that none of it will tell me anything.

What I've been looking for has eluded me.

I have been looking for direction, instructions on how to live with death. I thought wanted a recipe for appropriate mourning, a guidebook that could walk me through how I should feel or think or behave. It is now over two months since Tara died. I am still trying to navigate my way between heartbreak and acceptance, continually seeking a way to live with her death in a way that I can live with myself. I just don't know how to resolve the tension between grief and relief, between liberation and suffering, that still lies within me.

I walk toward the funeral home entrance—different from Tara's but with the same look and feel. There are stained glass windows, large columns out front, the perfume of flowers as soon as I pull open the heavy wooden door. The hallway is filled with people. They sign the guest book and huddle in small groups of conversation, waiting in line to view Ellen and pay their final respects. I immediately walk to the back of the main room and take a seat, keeping my head down and avoiding eye contact. Even though I have attended a stranger's funeral before, I still feel like an emotional voyeur, an imposter. But the sadness I feel is authentic, and it is a sadness that I need to feel.

I have memorized the lines and rehearsed the scenes. Still, I am waiting for the emotional muse to spark the feeling required to convince myself and my audience of my authenticity. I am trying on different types of grief to see which one will ultimately fit.

Feeling sad will make me feel less guilty, more human. I'm

doing everything I can to see how others mourn in the face of their losses; I need to read the words and hear the eulogies and see people clutch onto each other at gravesites. Since Tara died, I've been to several funerals and clipped twenty or thirty obituaries. I've read online guest books, searched Facebook for online memorials. I have become a student of death. I hope it will release what is blocking me emotionally, unleashing a wave of grief and sadness for Tara that sits lodged behind a dam of memories in my mind. It will make me feel less like a monster.

I see Ellen in the casket at the front of the room, young and beautiful and peaceful and still. She is here, but not here. Clusters of mourners wait in line to see her up close, kneel before her, and send her into the afterlife with their thoughts and prayers. She is the reason everyone is here, and the tragedy of her death cannot be denied when you see her youth frozen forever in time in a perpetual stillness.

I look down at the funeral card in my hand and take another look at Ellen's photo. Ellen was only seventeen at the time of the car accident, her chestnut hair shining from the sun, face tanned, dark brown eyes still bright with youth and optimism. I have pieced together Ellen's story from overheard conversations and her obituary, the weathered totem that is tucked neatly in my purse. From what I now know, Ellen was a well-liked and vibrant person, one of those people who constantly exuded love and happiness. I wonder if Ellen had another side to her, one not shown in funeral cards or obituaries, guest books, or Easter photos. I wonder if someone in the room feels like I did.

I can't project my history onto others and rewrite theirs. But I do wonder about the pain that others have felt. The pain that they feel now. If it makes them feel like I do.

Ellen is the elephant in the room, larger than life but no longer alive. But I can't look at her for more than a few moments. I have never been comfortable around the deceased, for they are no longer who they were. Without their animation, expressions, and essence, they are a mere collection of cells and tissue soon to decompose until nothing is left.

I did not see Tara after she died, did not go to the funeral home with my parents for a final glimpse at the physical body that no longer housed her soul. It's not only because I have an extremely uneasy relationship with death but also because I searched online for "death by hanging" that first night and the images were terrifying. I didn't want to see my sister like that. I feared that I would only remember her looking like these images did every time I thought of her. Whatever way I chose to remember her, I wanted my memories to be physically intact, even if they were emotionally broken. We cremated my sister rather than placing her in a casket, so her mourners paid their respects to an urn. We mourned her as pagans would, worshipping an idol, attaching power and meaning to a physical object that represented a higher power—kneeling before an urn that held Tara but was not Tara.

I review my surroundings, looking at everything except the casket because I need to return to the present. I need to feel a part of what is happening around me.

Despite housing such solemn affairs, funeral homes bring me such strange comfort—the warmth of the room, the soft lighting, the floral notes in the air, the arrangement of chairs and boxes of tissues all specifically and predictably set up to allow us to mourn. It's as if they elicit grieving, a Pavlovian stage where we can all live our own senses of loss. Here, it is possible for both the display of histrionics and quietly sitting in sadness to coexist. Here, I can sit among strangers who don't know I am trying to mourn for someone else.

I see a yearbook propped open on one of the tables to the side. I want to go up and leaf through the pages. I threw my yearbooks away years ago. It was too hard to look at them after what Tara did.

It was a few weeks before I was going to leave for college. There was a lot to do, and since I wasn't staying local, I needed to get everything together that I would need until my first visit back for Thanksgiving. For me, this meant only the gathering of my things but also my thoughts. I needed a clean break from Tara; things had gotten just too hard. She now ate dinner in her room alone every night, refusing to join us at the table. Being the kind of child I had learned to be, I tried to compensate for Tara that summer by being two daughters in one, spending every waking moment with my parents when I wasn't working. I accepted every dinner invite, I stopped home to see them every night after work.

It's not that I didn't want to spend time with my parents; it's that Tara's rejection of them drove me to overdo it, almost being frantically in their company as if that could make them forget Tara's absence.

But then it was time to leave.

When I finally had the chance to escape to a college in Ohio— hundreds of miles away from New Jersey—far away from Tara and how she made me feel, I took it and did not look back. At the same time, I felt like the misunderstood protagonist in a movie, saving herself and leaving behind those who couldn't escape, my parents. Yet I had hoped that taking myself out of the familial equation would ease my parents' burden, with Tara now being the only child in the house. I had hoped that my absence would make her even more present in our family.

As I was deciding what to pack, I scanned my childhood bedroom. It was so familiar to me, but at that moment, it felt like a museum of things detached from my experiences with them. I was ready for a fresh start. I had to make some hard decisions about what to take and what to leave behind. I walked over the bookshelf, dropping some of my favorite novels into a box: *The Bluest*

Eye, To Kill a Mockingbird, Are You There God? It's Me, Margaret.

I pulled my senior yearbook off the shelf, a time capsule of the not-so-distant past. I had always assumed my yearbooks would travel with me, for they were time capsules that would help me remember. The senior who DJ'd at our pep rallies never gave freshman me a second look—I can still remember his varsity jacket and the smell of his cologne as he passed me in the hallway. My favorite history teacher, who had our class study every person and event Billy Joel sang about in "We Didn't Start the Fire" and encouraged my love of historical fiction. My crew of friends at band camp, kindred spirits having the time of their lives in the Poconos, far away from the judgmental eyes that might mock us.

I already felt different than I did at graduation, only a few months before. I felt optimistic, like better things were on the horizon. But, as I turned the pages, it looked different. There were devil horns and X's drawn on some of my friends' faces. There were comments about sexual things I wanted to do with some of my former classmates. Every photo of me had "Loser" written on it with an arrow pointing to the top of my head. In one image, my clarinet was transformed into a penis. In another, "Most Likely to Succeed" was changed to "Most Likely to Have No Friends." I knew that it was Tara. It was the punishment she inflicted on me because I committed the grave misstep of being good, of being driven, of being successful. As if it was a crime not to be a total fucking loser.

I pulled every year off the shelf and saw the same vandalism of my life, page after page. I began to cry—and not quiet, defeated tears. My body shook, and I felt that my anger could have given me the strength to split these yearbooks apart at the spine. The strength to pull my bookshelf from the wall and break it in half. The rage of years of insults and emotional injury encapsulated in this one act of cruelty. One final act of sisterly revenge to see me out the door to college.

I kept thinking, *I hate you, Tara. I hate you. You ruin everything. I wish you weren't my sister. You're a monster.* I began to cry as I envisioned all kinds of tragedies confronting Tara—her falling off a cliff, swerving off the side of the road into a ditch, plunging down an elevator shaft. In each of these fantasies, I didn't try to save her. Each time, I smiled and walked away instead. I wanted her to feel as betrayed by me as I did her. I wanted her to hurt.

I grabbed the yearbooks and stormed into Tara's room, throwing them at her one by one. I told her I hated her. I told her I hoped I would never see her again. I asked her why she would do this. And she just sat there, calmly perched on the edge of her bed, staring at me with self-satisfaction. Her silence infuriated me even more that I fantasized about slamming one of the yearbooks into her bedroom mirror on my way out, spraying shards of glass everywhere.

Instead, I turned around and said words to her that I had never spoken before or again. I said, "I hope you die, Tara."

She replied, "Fuck you, Jennifer."

She spit those words at my back as I walked out of her room, shoving me so hard I slammed into the wall across from her door.

Looking back, I regret saying that. It wasn't in my character. I was a generally kind and considerate person brought to the edge by years of rage. After replaying this day in my head hundreds of times, I've come to realize that Tara has always believed that our family hated her and took every opportunity to elicit evidence of that in us. Inciting us to scream, to fight back, to say horrible things. When she elicited a response like I had that day in her bedroom, it only supported her theory that we were always against her.

I never told my parents about the yearbook. It would have been too embarrassing for them to see those images, read those words. I never wanted my mother to know I said that to Tara. It would have broken her heart.

I see Ellen's mother at the front of the room. I know what she looks like from Ellen's Facebook page. I watch her wrestle with the rawness of her emotion and the pure physicality of her grief. She appears broken while family members hold her up with cradled arms and words of comfort. She is sobbing into her hands, thrashing from their grasps. I remember my mother's reaction when we learned of Tara's death. I remember a vulnerability in her so raw it made me uncomfortable, like the entire foundation of my life could be ripped from under my feet.

The room is now bursting at its seams with maybe three or four hundred people. It looks a lot like the room on the day of Tara's funeral. I wonder how many other similarities there are here to that day. I look around and wonder if they will leave here and return to their daily lives or if they too will end up like me, triggered into a light type of fugue state where they take on a new identity, become a new kind of person who does things that would have seemed outrageous to the person I was before.

A gradual hush indicates that they will begin the service momentarily and solemnity settles in. A man steps up to the podium, tall but shrunken by grief, young but aged prematurely by tragedy. He takes a moment to compose himself, smoothing his beard that is only slightly peppered by gray. His blue eyes are bloodshot and watery. I consider this man for a moment; he reminds me of my uncle John. They have the same slight creases around their eyes, the same gentle gestures. I was always fond of Uncle John and the way he would tell stories after Thanksgiving, captivating his audience with his dry, understated humor while sipping his scotch. There is enough resemblance to fix the image of familiarity in my memory. Yet, I wonder what this man looked like before he was broken, before the circumstances set in, anchoring him to the deep.

After taking a measured pause, the man speaks.

"My name is Dennis Sawyer, and I was Ellen's father."

Another pause.

"I mean," he whispers.

Even more quietly, he says, "*Dammit*," before restating, "I *am* Ellen's father."

His hands tap nervously on the lacquered wood, his gaze down at the paper in front of him, seeking a place to focus as he realizes the decisive finality of verb tenses. It seems that to say that he was, instead of is, her father makes him feel like he's not a father anymore. I play with the idea in my mind. Am I Tara's sister? Can I still be a sister if she isn't here? Or *was* I her sister? Did my identity as her sister end with her death too? Upon meeting someone for the first time and asking me if I have brothers or sisters, will I say I am an only child but wasn't always? In my work, I've always been amazed by the power of words—of choosing the right words, of writing and speaking with precision—and yet my thinking in this scenario feels fuzzy.

"Thank you all for coming. I know that Ellen would be honored to see so many friends and family here. Jill and I are so—"

Dennis drifts off as he glances at his wife, a weak smile on his face, acknowledging that he is equally unsure of how to proceed.

"We are so grateful for all of you. Ellen was dearly loved, and we certainly couldn't have made it through this without you."

My eyes quickly look away from him, and my back stiffens. I fear he can see me, that I will be revealed to him as a fraud. That everyone will know I shouldn't be here. I feel a trickle of sweat roll down my back. I reposition myself in my seat to appear more natural, more relaxed.

He looks out over the room, his eyes glassy and unfocused. I assume he cannot imagine that an emotional voyeur sits within it. In this room filled with photos and flowers and friends and family, bursting with the reality that his daughter is no longer alive,

Dennis can't know that I do not belong here. To him, I am just another face in the crowd, one of the multitudes of people all here because they have been touched by his daughter's life and death. I mentally prepare myself to respond if anyone asks me how I knew Ellen. I need to keep the story short and consistent. I can't overexplain. It's always a sure sign that I'm hiding something. At least, that's what I've always thought. I don't want to draw more attention by making myself seem too anonymous or too familiar.

I shift in my seat again, uncomfortable seeing the vulnerability of a father who cannot handle the loss of his daughter. I knew that I would see that here because I read all about Ellen's family. But I still came. Perhaps I wanted to see what this kind of grief looked like when someone else's father was wearing it. But it seems the same to me. Dennis reminds me of my father, powerless in the face of my sister's death, reduced to a fraction of his usual abilities and emotions. I wonder if Dennis will also leave overdue bills, miss trash pickups, and let milk sour in the fridge, all victims of my father's inability to bring order back to a life that was thrown into chaos by his child's suicide. In my father's case, and perhaps Dennis's, the death of a child is also the death of the way life used to be, the way he used to be. For it can never be the same.

Ellen's parents appear just as mine were when Tara died. Showing grief so raw, so authentic, it moves me to witness it.

I want to find Ellen's sister Julie.

She is off to the side, surrounded by a small middle school army, her expression stunned, unsure of how to act in this new reality. She seems lost and broken. She is not like me, not relieved or peaceful. Her life is now worse without her sister in it, and my cheeks start to burn with the thought I have interpreted mine to be better without Tara in it.

My life with Tara has familiarized me with the fallout of families that break down, whether by death or design. But this feels different. As I sit here, a visceral sadness brings me to tears, which did not happen at Tara's funeral. This is what I wanted, a sister who I would feel lost without. A sister whose death would leave a hole in my heart so big I would feel it would kill me too. To have had that sisterhood would have prevented all of this, all the searching. But I don't have it. I didn't have it.

I realize that part of my sadness is for what I've missed out on with Tara, both then and now.

Another speaker, Ellen's aunt, rises and tells a story about Ellen as a child. Ellen used to take in stray animals in the neighborhood, an early indicator of her gentle kindness. She was in the Girl Scouts. She volunteered at soup kitchens. Ellen was a special person.

After Ellen's aunt finishes speaking, I use the break to leave the room searching for a water fountain. I find one in the far hallway and take a long drink.

I hear a voice ask me, "How did you know Ellen?"

I turn to see a young man standing next to me, waiting to fill his cup. His eyes are wide with disbelief, his thick hair falling over his face, his breath heavy with coffee and hunger, too much cologne on the collar of his suit.

"I work for the school district." A lie I worked on in the car on the way over. I needed a reason to be here. I don't work there, had never heard of Ellen Sawyer before this week, and have no reason at all to be here. At least not one that I can share.

I ask him, "Do you go to the high school?"

He nods his head and says, "Ellen and I were in the same biology class."

I say, "It's so sad what happened to her. How is everyone doing?"

He replies, "Terrible. Especially Kevin. He was driving the car. I think he feels guilty."

After he fills his cup, he gestures to a young man on the other side of the room. I find Kevin in the crowd, identifying him by the bandage on his forehead. He looks despondent, detached from his surroundings. Friends are huddled around him, offering him comfort.

I ask the young man, "Why would he feel guilty? I read in the paper that it was the other car's fault."

He says, "It was. But Ellen didn't want to go, and Kevin convinced her to. And he is still alive, and she isn't."

I am speechless in the face of such a thought—that this young man could believe he is why someone else has died. In my rush of competing emotions, guilt hadn't yet truly entered my mind. But I could just as easily feel that way. Maybe something I did or said pushed Tara over the edge. Perhaps I didn't do or say something that could have prevented her from going to that hotel room. I brace myself on the arm of the couch, suddenly feeling emotional vertigo, a scattered orientation to my surroundings.

Ellen's story is proof that one decision can change everything. I want to know the exact moment Tara made her decision. I wonder what she was thinking.

Was it when she and Matt broke up? Was it something else?

I say goodbye to the young man and tell him that I need to leave.

I think about how Kevin, the driver of the car, feels like he had a hand in Ellen's death, even though it was the other driver's fault. My lips begin to quiver, and a pit builds in my gut. I run to the bathroom, barely making it in time to empty the contents of my stomach into the porcelain bowl, coughing and retching until I am exhausted.

The seat feels cool against my forehead as I lie on the floor of the stall. I can hear the low hum of the exhaust fan and the drip of the faucet. I am alone in this room, but not alone in my thoughts; the ghosts of Tara and Ellen and Laurie and Beth swirl around me, young women who died earlier than they should have. My purse has fallen on its side, funeral cards and obituaries spilled out onto the floor. The punched tickets I have collected on my journey to find a way to grieve for my sister. The evidence that I am trying to learn how to live with death. But cards and newspaper clippings can't get me to where I want to be. I'm embarrassed by them at this moment. It feels empty and juvenile.

Much like the driver of Ellen's car, I imagine myself as the tipping point of a final set of decisions. These decisions ultimately determined the end of someone's life. I wonder if I am complicit with Tara's death simply because I did nothing. If through avoidance and escape and deflection, I allowed Tara to wither on the vine, each time I turned away from her another emotional drought that drove her to eventually fall, rotted and cracked, to the earth, ready to decompose and generate something new.

My guilt shifts to anger as I look at myself on the bathroom floor, with the scattered papers and the bile churning in my stomach. I wipe my face with the back of my hand and think, *You did this to me, Tara*. You have turned me into this person, a pathetic imposter who needs to pretend to be sad. You have fucked me up so royally that I am pretending to be someone else again and again just to feel something.

I can't do it anymore. It is breaking me apart, and I fear I won't be able to piece myself back together.

I flush the toilet and gather my things, smooth my hair, adjust my necklace. I slip out of the bathroom and toward the back exit of the funeral home, avoiding the specter of responsibility that lingers in the space between Kevin and Ellen, between Tara and me. The sun is so bright that it hurts my eyes as I walk back to my car, but I still turn toward it.

I clutch my purse closer to me and find my hidden funeral cards and news clippings intact, even though I am not.

Chapter Twenty

TARA

MARCH

My head is foggy. I drank too much again last night. It was my typical Friday night, starting at happy hour with some work friends and moving to another bar later in the evening. Friends and strangers bought me beers and shots all night, and I didn't turn them down. I look down at my hand, still stamped from one of the bars—my Scarlet Letter.

I kept drinking because I wanted to numb myself. It has become the only way I can have a good time. It prevents me from remembering. It insulates me from my feelings. It dulls my sharp edges. And there are so many sharp edges that could shred me into pieces.

Yesterday, I was scrolling through Facebook and came across a photo. My friend Marisa was tagged in it. The picture was taken at a bar, and in it are some other friends from high school alongside Matt and Stacey. I could see that Stacey was beginning to show. I could also sense that she and Matt are now together. The pregnancy did not drive them apart. It was just me that Matt didn't want. It was never about not wanting what I wanted; he just didn't want it with me. I felt so betrayed that Marisa would be there with them. She must have heard about our breakup. She must have known what it would do to me.

When I saw that photo, it felt like the entire world was against me. That everyone had decided to move on from me as if I was never there.

I don't remember coming back home from the bar last night. It's not my home anyway. I don't have a home anymore. Matt took that away from me. But maybe he took it because I didn't deserve it. Even though I tried to keep him in my life while trying to keep it together, it was ultimately just another thing that I've screwed up, failed at, not been good enough to keep.

I roll over on my side and look around the room. My things are scattered everywhere. Shoes and papers and perfume bottles and soda cans create a chaotic counterpoint to the items neatly placed by my parents in their guest room: a vase, a clock, a photo of my grandmother. The room looks like how the inside of my head feels, like an erratic collection of objects disrupting someone else's sense of order. I never fail to make everything messy for everyone else. I've always wanted to believe that everybody else made things a mess for me. But the evidence now speaks for itself. I am failed in everything I have wanted to do, everything I wanted to be, and I don't have the energy anymore.

When I was probably about four, we went to the zoo. My parents brought me a balloon, a large cellophane lion that shone in the sun. As we walked toward the lions' den, I got distracted and let the string go, not knowing the balloon would float away. I jumped and reached for it, but it was too high. I cried as I watched it rise in the sky. I still feel like that girl every day—not knowing that my happiness could float away so easily, no matter how I try to grasp it.

I'm not even sure I know what happiness would look like

anymore. I thought for a long time that it was to find someone to love me, warts and all. I thought it was to start a family and have a lovely house. But would I be happy with all of that? I'm not sure anymore. Every day I wake up with this feeling of dread that nothing will make me happy, that the pieces will never fall into place for me. That the voice in my head that tells me I'm not good enough will be the only voice I will ever hear. That I will always be an extra in someone else's scene, or that I will be the clown called upon simply to make everyone else laugh. That I will be the poor downtrodden soul that will make everyone else feel better about their own lives.

I see myself alone years from now, still being the fun drunk at work parties flirting with married men. I see myself going to the hospital to welcome more friends' babies. I see myself getting irritated on Christmas Eve by a casual joke and starting a fight. I see myself going to the same bars and having the same conversations, with nothing ever changing.

I feel like I've been chasing that balloon ever since that day at the zoo. One day I looked around, and I was thirty-two with not much to show for it except for things: expensive jeans, nice wine glasses, and a Pottery Barn sofa, all of which were currently in storage, along with most other things I own, because I am back to living with my parents. It's not the first time, either.

I came home after one semester of college away because I couldn't handle it. I was sure I wanted to run away and be someone new, but then I came running back. I didn't have the confidence to go out on my own. It was my first time away from home. I felt awkward and out of place.

I felt like such a coward. Jennifer went away to college and then even further to grad school, and she never looked back. I never told her, but I always envied that about her—the willingness to go somewhere new, to try something different. Yet another way I can't compare to her.

The clock on the dresser says it's almost noon. I've stayed in bed too long.

I take a long drink from the faucet. Water streams over my face, and it helps revive me.

The shots of tequila were a mistake last night. I make the same mistake every time, even though I always know how it will turn out. I think it's considered the definition of insanity—doing the same thing repeatedly but hoping for a different result each time. I kneel before the toilet and begin to heave. With each convulsion, I am more disgusted with myself. I place my forehead on the seat to rest and decide that I am destined to be wretched. I will be perpetually disappointed in my life course, always resisting opportunities to transform myself. I will never get out of my own way.

Matt was the final blow, breaking me into a million pieces that I'll never be able to reassemble. I now know that life doesn't have much more in store for me. I will be doing the same thing years and years from now. Being envious of other people's lives, drinking too much, puking in my parents' guest bathroom. Meeting up with friends, convincing them I'm fine, crying into my pillow at night. Seeing my sister, starting a fight with her, storming out. In between these moments, I'll go to work where I'll exhaust myself being the picture-perfect person and model employee, then drag myself back to my parents' house to live among my clutter and do it all over again.

I feel like I'm on that ride from Disney World, sitting in a teacup spinning around and around but ultimately going nowhere. I'm belted into the ride, pretending that I'm having fun but feeling terrified. Almost every situation in my life has spiraled out of control—in a matter of minutes or a matter of years—and I have been unable to stop it. I haven't even wanted to stop it. And that has been my biggest problem. I am the emotional storm chaser, always running toward danger and potential pain. I don't know how to do it any other way.

I have tried to slow things down in my mind, to be more sensitive. I have been attempting to not fuck things up. I have been trying to live peacefully and lovingly with myself and others. I have quickly realized it's not a muscle I've flexed very often. So, I end up reverting to what is most familiar to me—getting a rise out of people. Blaming them. Mocking them. Making them hurt so they can feel how I feel. I don't want to be alone with how I feel, so I make others feel it too, so maybe they will understand. But they never do.

I rethink being a storm chaser. Perhaps I am also the storm. It scares me.

I flush the toilet.

I think I have gotten rid of all the tequila. The acid has burned my throat; my mouth tastes bitter and feels dry. I vow that I will never drink tequila again. Immediately I know that I am lying to myself.

I stand up and examine myself in the mirror. I look tired.

I've never been happy with the way I look. My teeth are too big, my nose too strong, my eyes too close together. I run my fingers across my cheek, down my cheekbones, across my chin. Sometimes I look at myself so long I don't recognize my own face. It's like I'm looking at a stranger. And I hate her.

I've become more and more distant from everything.

I feel separated from myself as if I'm observing my life from the audience. I am alienated, detached, like a puppet made to dance by its handler.

The child who never did anything right grew into a woman who never does anything right.

I want to make her go away. I start scratching my face as if I can erase it. I claw and pull at my skin. There are red streaks on my forehead, my chin. But I'm still there in the mirror.

The sister who was never wanted.

I pull my hair so hard it makes my neck tingle. My hair becomes wild, knotted, and frayed. But I'm still there.

The girlfriend who wasn't good enough.

I slap my face until my cheeks are red and swollen, but the image doesn't disappear before me.

The troublemaker daughter, the fighter, the nuisance.

I clench my fists and strike myself again. And again. But the reflection doesn't go away.

My face looks grotesque and distorted. I wipe away streaks of tears and mascara. I don't want to do this anymore.

I turn off the lights because I don't want to look at myself. I want to be anonymous and hidden. I want to disappear.

Brutalizing myself won't change anything. I have fought for so long—myself, my family, the course of my life—and nothing has changed. I still feel empty and incomplete, like a piece of art the artist abandoned for another project. A half-sculpted pile of clay that the artist could no longer envision becoming a fully formed being.

I don't want to fight anymore. I am tired of fighting every situation, fighting with my family, fighting with myself. I think about it being like someone fighting cancer. They will try everything at their disposal to fight the disease, even though it exhausts them, weakens them beyond comprehension. The chemotherapy directed at the bad cells inevitably kills many of the good ones, too. That is how I feel. And just like the person who must face the terminality of their situation, I must do the same. But while the sick are applauded for their courage in the face of the struggle they face, I've only been rejected. I know people won't understand it and how hard I've tried. I don't even think they'll see it in the same terms.

In my life, I've always walked an exhilarating line between desperation and joy, either making frantic pleading phone calls or rejecting the love that attempted to surround me. I've called

Matt's house at least twenty times a few nights after I've had too much to drink, ready to beg for him to take me back if he picked up. I've begged friends to cancel their other plans so I wouldn't be alone. But I'd also push my mother away almost every time she'd invite me to go to lunch or get manicures. I'd tell my sister I didn't need her advice when she'd try to help me out.

I've never known how to be different. No one could ever understand that.

They will not understand that I feel trapped under a glass jar, able to see outside of it but not able to be close to anything. It's what prevents me from wanting to be physically close to others, to hug them tenderly. It's because I don't feel connected to them. And I've become tired of bumping up against the walls while I see life being lived outside of the jar—people close enough to see but not to touch. And the air inside the jar is running out. It is no longer in my control. Much like for the terminally ill patient, the doctor has just entered the room in my mind and told me that no other treatments would work. That I will need to prepare for my death.

I can't continue the way I have. I don't want to continue the way I have.

I start the shower. The water is hot, and the room fills with steam. It's like I'm in a dream, blanketed in fog, lost in the dark. But I'm not scared. As the water falls over my face, it shocks my skin, and I hold my breath. It's so quiet and still. The only sound is the gentle flow of water around me, over my body, the swirling sound as it circles the drain. I am moved by the silence, the peace I feel.

There are so many things that make me feel out of control. I need to hold onto these opportunities to take control back.

I hold my breath again, longer this time. I am controlling it, determining when I will breathe again. And it's the feeling I need —peace, quiet, control.

There is a moment that comes when you can't breathe—where you stop your body from doing what it needs to do to stay alive. When it comes, you can almost imagine what it feels like to begin to die. And this time, that feeling doesn't scare me. It calms me.

I've thought about what it would take to feel better. I won't lie and say that ending my life has never crossed my mind. But it was never more than that: a fleeting thought, one pushed away by a string of good days.

Life has not delivered on its promise for me. Instead, it has controlled me, and I can't take it anymore. And I am deciding that it must end. Rather than continuing to fight the current as I am hauled downstream toward inevitable disappointment and disaster, I need to hold my breath and allow myself to be pulled under. I am tired of fighting back, of fighting in general. Every time I fight, I feel like I am both pushed up against the ropes and the one who delivers the knockout punch.

Aggressor and victim.

Winner and loser.

I turn off the water. I am calm as I think about how I can make it end. I have never felt so optimistic about a decision. It's not that I want to die; that seems too grotesque. I am simply tired of living, and I am the only one who can make it stop. I need to take the upper hand. I haven't been able to wrestle life into the order I want it. So, I am considering what control will look like for me. I arrive at the same vision every time. The only way I can control how I feel is to end it.

I think about what dying will look like, what it will feel like. I know it will be more than holding my breath in the shower. But I imagine it will be just as peaceful. Maybe it's just wishful thinking. But it's better than the alternative. How I'm living now isn't living. It's getting by.

I think about what I will miss, the holidays and birthday

parties and trips to Hawaii. I won't see my friends' children grow up. I won't see my sister ever get married. I won't get married or have kids myself. I won't grow old.

But I also won't be unhappy anymore. I won't make anyone else miserable anymore, either.

I turn the lights back on and wipe the mirror clean. I look at myself in a new light, but I don't see myself in the mirror anymore. Instead, I see someone I no longer recognize. I see the person I have become, and I don't love her. She has caused too much trouble. She has made herself unlovable by her family, Matt, and herself. I want to make her go away. I need to exorcise myself from her. I must believe that it will not only bring me peace, but also make everyone generally better off.

I can't stop thinking about it as I get dressed. The more I play with the idea in my mind, the more comforting it is.

I sit down at my desk and open my laptop. I begin to research ways to kill myself. You wouldn't believe the things you can find on the internet.

I need to remember to erase my search history when I'm done.

But then I think, *who will care what I've searched for? It doesn't matter anymore anyway.*

I learn that hanging is one of the cleanest ways to do it, and I want to limit the cleanup required after the fact. There have been enough cleanups needed in my life. I don't want my death to be any more work for anyone. I will go somewhere to do it where I'll be anonymous. I want to be alone when I do it; I want to be alone with this decision. No one would understand it, even if I tried to explain it to them.

I say the words in my head, "I will hang myself." The more I say it, the more natural it feels. But I need to do it correctly. It isn't something I can mess up.

I don't want to be awake as I slowly die. If I take pills, I might be found and rushed to the hospital to have my stomach pumped.

They might think I can be saved. But I can't. For me, being saved is not staying alive. It is the release from life and its exhausting haul from one day to the next with no end in sight to everything that infuriates me. That makes me feel small.

I need to make sure I do this right because one misstep means life on a ventilator, eating my meals through a tube in my throat. If I need to be successful at one last thing, it must be this. Because I don't want to experience going to the edge and then coming back. It's the return that terrifies me. I don't want to fail at dying. I don't want to have a chance to reconsider this decision. I don't want to live the rest of my life as the woman who tried to kill herself. I don't want people to feel uneasy around me, wondering when I'll try again. I don't want to have to live with that. So once I do it, it must be final. There is no other way.

I write down the length of rope I need. I note the bodyweight limit and proper location of the knot. I'm approaching it academically because it is a tactical solution for an existential problem. All this notetaking reminds me of Jennifer and how she approaches everything—taking notes, considering all angles, doing my homework. I wonder what Jennifer would think about all of this. I wonder if she would be shocked, sad, or relieved. I genuinely believe that my departure will cause her some distress, but I don't know which part will do it, that I will be dead, or that I will be dead because I chose to be.

But it is my choice, and that is what matters.

While I'm still feeling good in this mindset, I head to Home Depot.

My parents aren't home right now, and I am relieved not to answer any questions before I leave. I haven't sat long enough with this decision to start to lie about it. I haven't built up the lies I'll need to tell to keep everyone from sensing something is going to happen. I haven't any time to plan yet.

I arrive at Home Depot with my list. I walk around the store, walking up and down each aisle, imagining different projects I could be shopping for. They all come with other lives.

I picture myself as a young homeowner asking about the benefits of different types of tile grout. I imagine planning a huge backyard party and searching for the right décor for the patio. I think about what it would feel like if my husband had sent me to the store with a list of supplies needed for our bathroom remodel. I pretend that I'm there searching for materials for my daughter's science project. With each false errand, I feel even more empty. I feel more alone and separated from the possibility of these storylines being real for me. My chance to live any of them is in my rearview mirror.

But the fantasies also make me realize that it's easy to mask what I'm planning. I feel more confident as I walk over to the aisle with the chains and ropes. I'm not sure of the specific rope I'm looking for, so I take a few minutes to feel their textures. I resist the temptation to brush them across my neck to see what they feel like. A man in an orange apron startles me while I think about it.

He says, "Welcome to Home Depot! How can I help you?"

I quickly look down at the measurements I have scribbled on the back of a gas receipt.

I reply, "Hi there. I'm looking for rope."

He asks me, "What project are you working on?"

He is smiling too widely at me, so ready to help. If he only knew.

"I'm—um—making a rope swing for my daughter. Here's the length I need," I reply and hand him the paper. The lie comes easily.

At this moment, I can be anyone I want to be. I can be a mother wanting to surprise her daughter with a swing. I can be a woman who has her shit together and is spending a pleasant little Saturday running errands before returning to her home and the life it contains. I can be the person I thought I would be but can't.

He walks over to the rope, cuts the length for me, and ties it into a bundle.

He hands it to me and says, "Here you go. Can I get you anything else today?"

I smile at him. "No, thank you. This is everything I need."

As I walk to the register, I grab a pack of gum, some batteries, and a Diet Coke. They are simple things that remove the focus from the rope. I imagine it shining under a spotlight for other shoppers in line to see. That they know what I am going to do with it. While I know I'm just imagining it, I place the other items on the belt at the register because I feel like they make the purchase appear normal. I assume it makes me look normal to the other shoppers in line. I have felt so clearly out of place so many times, I want to blend in at this moment.

I throw the bag with the rope into my trunk. As I start the car, I pop two pieces of gum in my mouth. There are no limits for me anymore. Now that I have decided, I don't have a lot of time left and won't put any more restrictions on myself. I won't force myself to be a certain way to please others. There won't be any ramifications more significant than the ones I will deliver, so I will do whatever I want to do.

I turn the radio up as loud as it goes and blow bubbles while N'Sync blares over the sound of the engine. I speed away from Home Depot with the windows rolled down, freer than I've ever felt in my life. Because I am the one who has decided what my future will be. Even if it isn't the future I had initially dreamed of.

When the time comes, everyone will wonder why I did it. And there are no words to explain to them that being alive when you're not living is the cruelest form of existence.

Knowing that the life you want sits just past your fingertips, but you cannot grasp it is not a life.

It's waiting to die.

And I won't wait much longer.

Chapter Twenty-One

JENNIFER

JULY

Tara has been dead for almost three months.

I have been surrounded by people this whole time, but I have still been alone. I have spoken to my family, friends, strangers, and a priest and funeral director. I've asked a detective and a hotel housekeeper questions about Tara's death.

I have browsed countless Facebook pages and online guest books. I have cried next to strangers while mourning for other strangers.

Even with all of this, I have been alone. Not physically, but in my mind.

I returned from my leave of absence too early and finished up the spring semester in a haze, students asking for clarity on pages I'd marked up with scribbled and vague comments. My mind wandered off in lectures about judicial review. My impatience and distraction cut class times short. My students were the collateral damage of Tara's death. I was relieved when the summer term came up, and I didn't have classes to teach. I am not used to doing things half-assed. I am never unprepared. I never lack focus. I have simply redirected these strengths and intentions toward death.

I should text my friends back and make some plans.

But I've kept people at arm's length because I feel like if they saw the real me—the one with a drawerful of memories of dead strangers—they would leave, just like Tara did. That they would think I am a coldhearted bitch with no emotions. A type of sociopath who cries for fallen runners and stroke victims and dead grandmothers, but not her own sister. A person who needs to go to funerals of strangers to feel something. A person who stood before Tara's urn at the funeral home and breathed more freely, rather than being suffocated by tears.

I've never been out of control before. I've never shut myself off like this. I've never been this unhappy.

I wish I had a chance to talk to Tara about her decision to die. I wish I knew that she was planning to take her own life so I could have tried to stop it. I need to understand why someone would take that leap in the unknown and give up a chance at living.

I dreamed about Tara again last night. She was driving me to Laurie Phelps's funeral, the runner who collapsed on the board-walk. The brakes in the car weren't working, and we were careening through the cemetery, swerving around every turn, sloshing from side to side like overfilled drinks balanced on the edge of a server's tray. It was raining, and Tara could not turn on the windshield wipers, making it hard for us to see. I kept asking her to slow down, but she couldn't. I told her I was scared, but she didn't respond. I saw Laurie's sister Amy standing at the curb at the final turn. She was crying, wearing a New York City Marathon T-shirt. She looked at me and slowly tied a rope around her neck. I banged on the glass and screamed at her to stop. But she couldn't hear me.

I jumped out of the car door, rolling onto the wet pavement, feeling the loose gravel burn my skin. I could smell the exhaust as

236 · WE TURN TO FACE THE SUN

Tara continued to drive away, a passenger door flapping open, tires spinning fast in front of me. It was raining harder now. My mascara ran into my eyes, and my clothes were soaked. I crawled over to Amy and yelled again for her to stop. She told me that she wouldn't stop. She told me that she couldn't live without her sister.

I grabbed the rope to loosen it, but that just made it tighter, her face turning red, her eyes widening in surprise. And when she dropped to the ground, her face became Tara's. A crowd gathered around us. I became confused, not knowing who I was. I looked down, and I was wearing a racing bib over my clothes and sneakers I didn't recognize. They were all shouting at me. They were shouting that I had killed her. Tara had suddenly appeared among them and hissed into my ear that if I had loved my sister more, she wouldn't have killed herself.

I didn't open my eyes at first, afraid I would see Tara in front of me, judging me. I could feel my hair matted against my forehead and thought it was from the rain in my dream. It took me a moment to realize that it was not real and that my hair was slick with sweat and not rain. But it felt so real. I could see the pain on Amy's face. I could feel the pain in Tara's voice. I get out of bed, feeling as if I had jumped out of that car, achy and disoriented. I look out the window to see if it's raining, but it's not. It felt so real as it was happening.

In the dream, I killed Tara. But I should have protected her.

I think about a story I read in the paper a few years ago. There was an earthquake in a small town in the center of Italy. Hundreds of people died when their libraries, restaurants, apartments came crashing down on top of them. After hours of searching in the aftermath, rescuers found a young girl still alive, protected by her older sister. The older sister died clutching the young girl, protecting her. She sacrificed herself to save her sister—such an instinct to protect at such a young age. The news shook all of Italy. It shook me too.

I wonder if I would have had that same instinct; I wonder if I would have protected Tara under a pile of rubble. But then I think, *you didn't even rescue her from killing herself in a hotel room in New Jersey.*

But no one else did either.

I wonder if my parents feel the same way. I don't have the heart to ask them.

But I am trying to help them move on the best way possible.

I arrive at their house to drop off a bottle of wine I know they love. It's only available at this small liquor store near campus. Since I've been going back into my office on campus to get back into my routine, I wanted to surprise them with it.

I look at the label. It's a Chianti that they serve at my father's favorite Italian restaurant in Newark. It's where we had dinner with Tara that last time. The last time I drank this wine was when we found out that Tara was dead. Perhaps they'll see it and think of that night. Maybe they won't.

That night, months ago, I felt like everything was going to change. That everything had changed.

Tara's death altered the direction of our family's narrative, ripping a main character from the story and leaving the others to rewrite it as we went. It was a sudden red light fire drill, where each passenger had to switch to a new seat before the light turned green again. It was a band's sudden change of tempo mid-song, which left us flat-footed and disoriented.

Tara's death filled my parents' house with friends and family for three days straight in the very living room where I was standing. People cycled in and out with lasagnas and wine and fruit platters. There were hours upon hours of small talk and memories and ruminations, bookended by red wine and cigarettes, by laughs and tears. People appeared who were close but felt distant to me at that moment—neighbors, aunts and uncles, my father's bocce team—all of whom inserted themselves into our fabric of grief woven in real-time by the group, desperate to make themselves useful for every task while staying out of the way.

It seems like the most challenging time after a death is when people stop coming by. In my parents' case, it was undoubtedly true. Once the funeral was over, the house emptied, and everyone returned to their lives. My parents were left alone with their grief. Those first days of errands and plans and casserole dropoffs were distracting. But, eventually, they ended. I did what I could to fill some of that emptiness, but I have also been distracted.

But I wonder if any of those original visitors have also tried to fill the space for my parents, like Tara's friends. They were so incredibly close and present during the first few days after Tara died. I assume if they had come by to see my parents or called them, I would have heard about it.

My parents arrive home. As soon as they walk in the front door, I can't help myself. I ask them, "Have any of Tara's friends called you or come by since the funeral?"

My mother responds, "Leslie has. She's in touch about once a week."

"I don't mean Leslie. The others. Marisa, Jenna, Kate?"

She says, "No. But I'm sure they have plenty of other things to do."

I say, "That's no excuse."

My dad adds, "Jen, people don't always react like you want them to when something like this happens. You just have to accept it."

"But—"

He raises his hand to stop me and says, "Look, I don't want to do this. What's done is done."

I remember when these friends—Marisa, Jenna, Kate—came to the house during the days after Tara died.

I had never known Tara's friends very well, aside from Leslie. She has always been kind to me and strong enough to tell Tara when she was being ridiculous. I remember when Tara said my mother didn't get her anything she wanted for Christmas, and Leslie scoffed at her and told her she was a spoiled brat. Leslie had a long history with my sister. She has known our family since she was in second grade. From what I've seen, she always more assertive with Tara than her other friends had been.

But Tara's friend list was constantly changing.

These other friends, the ones I don't care for, have been on a perpetually rotating list with continual additions and subtractions based on who was currently fighting with Tara at the time. The irony is that Tara had the same level of instability with many of her friends as she did with us. These, too, were bipolar relationships that experienced the highest highs and the lowest lows. But while we saw more lows, they saw more highs. Either way, it was tumultuous. Minor missteps could ruin them forever, but they also had manic happiness that would gloss over the more challenging times, level it all out. Their friendships were intense, time-consuming, all-inclusive. Until they weren't, and then the cycle would repeat.

And then Tara died.

Those first days at my parents' house, some of these friends showed up, suddenly reappearing and acting territorial. They made themselves too close. They took advantage of my being distracted and my parents' vulnerability to gain access and claim Tara's things. They petitioned for clothes, jewelry, photo albums.

Looking back, I was too distracted at the time to realize how offensive their behavior was. I wasn't listening to the various forms of "Tara wanted me to have this" and "This will always make me think of Tara." My mind was elsewhere.

Now, I realize how manipulative their requests were. Tara's body had been cut down from the hotel room door not even forty-eight hours before. Yet, they were circling hyenas, salivating at the fresh carcass, waiting to crush her bones between their jaws.

What kinds of friends do that? It makes me look at them differently. It makes me look at Tara differently. I feel sorry for Tara and how she allowed these relationships in her life. I wonder why she didn't want more for herself. Why she didn't think she deserved better.

My curiosity takes over, and I excuse myself from the kitchen.

I walk into the guest bedroom and pull up Facebook on my phone.

I click on Tara's profile and see the messages that still appear on her timeline. Even months later, people are posting memories on her wall.

I want to see what Tara's friends have been up to, but I am not connected to any of them on Facebook. I log out, then log back in as Tara. My parents found a list of passwords in the desk drawer in the guest bedroom. Tara must have left them behind for us to access her accounts and records after she died.

Once on her profile, I scan her inbox first and don't see anything new. I realize that I never looked at any messages she might have sent before she died. I click on "Sent Messages."

I pause on the most recent message, which was time-stamped about three weeks ago. Two months after Tara died. Confused, I click on the message:

Tara Rossi to Todd Murphy: Boo

I throw my phone onto the bed and freeze. How could Tara send a message from her Facebook account? Those feelings I had the night she died, feeling like she was in the room with me, haunting me, come back so strong that I begin to shiver uncontrollably. Pacing around my parent's guest room, I am worried Tara is communicating from the dead. I am also worried that I am going insane. I am terrified, confused, hands trembling. I finish my glass of wine in one sip and feel it coat my lips. I feel how chapped and raw they are—much like how I feel inside, dried up, empty, too sensitive.

I need to know what is happening. I walk to the bed and grab my phone. I reopen the page and click on the message again, this time seeing that there is a thread attached to it:

Tara Rossi to Todd Murphy: Boo

Todd Murphy to Tara Rossi: What the fuck??!?

Tara Rossi to Todd Murphy: Hahahaha just kidding its Marisa.

Todd Murphy to Tara Rossi: That is NOT funny.

Tara Rossi to Todd Murphy: Lighten up, Todd. Tara would have thought it was hilarious you dumb ass

I can't believe what I am reading. Marisa—the worst of Tara's friends—logged into Tara's Facebook account after she died and used the account to prank someone. This online exchange makes me feel sad for Tara.

What kind of friends do that?

I click on Marisa's profile. I need to see what she's been up to. I scroll through her posts and see a photo from a few months ago. Marisa is out somewhere with Tara's ex-boyfriend Matt. He has his arm around a woman who looks like she's expecting a baby. It is clear from the photo that they are together.

That's why. That's the reason Tara and Matt broke up. My head is spinning. I think about Leslie having her baby when Tara and Matt broke up. I'm sure it made the situation so much worse for Tara. She has always been so doting with her friends' children. I wonder if she wanted to have them herself.

Whether she did or not, I still imagine that the pregnancy in the picture was devastating to Tara. She was telling people that she and Matt would get engaged soon. She always seemed so happy when she was with him.

I am so angry at Matt because he broke my sister's heart. But I am furious at Marisa. She is still hanging out with Matt and had to have known what happened between them. I can't let this happen to Tara again. I can't let her get taken advantage of.

I change the password on her account so no one could ever re-access it. I immediately text Marisa:

I saw the message you sent to Todd Murphy from Tara's account. I saw the photo of you and Matt on Facebook. How could you?

I wait for a response, but it doesn't come.

I slam my hand on the desk, vibrating the wine glass stem. I put my hands over my mouth and scream into my fists until I run out of air. My eyes are watery, and I feel like I've pulled a muscle in my chest. My fury is pulsating through my body like electrical currents seeking grounding.

Tara was my sister. No matter what happened between us while she was alive, I need to defend her now that she's dead. This doesn't feel familiar, but it feels right.

She was my sister. And I will protect her in any way I can, even if I couldn't do it when she was alive.

Chapter Twenty-Two

APRIL, THE YEAR IT HAPPENED

I am going to dinner with my parents and Jennifer tonight. It will be one of the last times I see them, but they don't know that. My parents always invite me to dinner, and I rarely accept. I have always had some reason to explain why I won't go—plans with friends, not feeling well, I don't like that restaurant. But we're running out of time, so I accepted the invitation tonight.

I need to give my family this. Maybe I need this too. So I am committed to keeping it together tonight, to not let the small things bother me. I'll smile at my dad's jokes, listen to Jennifer's stories, answer my mother's questions. I'll be the person I should have always been, but never could be because I know that I will be gone a few days from now. But tonight, we will be a family.

We are going to one of my father's favorite places in Newark, an Italian place where you can bring your own wine, and they serve veal Milanese that's the size of your head. At least that's what my dad always says. I've never been there with them, but Jennifer has.

"Tara—you ready?" my father calls into the bedroom.

"Coming," I respond.

I turn off the light and walk out to meet them. My mother smiles so widely at me like she's won a prize. And in a way, she has. I have not always been kind to them. I have often shut them out and rationed my presence like precious jewels that you take out only on special occasions. But now, I am more at ease, more willing to give them my time. I feel a new type of power now that I have made my decision. It is the power to forgive, to throw away those things that don't serve me. And making them the target of my frustrations, blaming them for my own shortcomings, doesn't serve me anymore.

We get into the car, and my parents are visibly happy, even relieved. So used to being told, "no," my "yes" has appeared to give them some optimism that things might be okay now. They are certainly not naïve; they know things can escalate quickly. But they also know their own daughter, and I assume they can tell that I am more peaceful, more content now. A pang of guilt makes my heart hurt because they don't know why. I crack open the rear window to get some air.

I have decided that I need to do what I am going to do, but I do worry about how they will react. I know that it will be devastating to them. Because they try so hard. And in my moments of greater clarity, when I'd be cleaning up the debris in the wake of whatever storm occurred between us, I would feel bad. I would see how worn down they would get with each fight and how brightened and buoyant they would become when we all got along. No matter how many times we went through this cycle, they never stopped rebounding. I never told them this because it would make me feel even worse.

They have loved me unconditionally, always let me come back

when I ran, always rebounded when I knocked them down. Over the years, I have led them on a long and winding road filled with bumps and sudden stops and roadblocks suddenly thrown across it. I have not made it easy for them, yet they still love me. That is the hardest part for me to understand, for I have been far from lovable much of the time. And there is not much time left. But they don't know that. So I shake these thoughts off before they shake me, unlevel me. I can only focus on what is in my control tonight, not in the past.

"How are Leslie and the baby doing?" my mother asks over her shoulder. "I found the cutest onesie for Kaitlyn."

"They're good. I saw them last week," I reply. I think of Leslie and Dave and wonder what Leslie will tell her daughters when they grow up and hear stories of Aunt Tara. I wonder if they will ask what happened to me and if Leslie will tell them.

I will never be a parent myself—that is not what fate had in store for me. I will never see that love looking up to me from little eyes that only see me. I will never drive a full minivan to Jersey Freeze, telling each of the kids to get their orders ready, and yes, you can get a cone or a cup, and no, you can't get both sprinkles and hot fudge. I will never have to try to understand a child like me. I will never give someone unconditional love. I have always had so many conditions.

I wonder if that is the most challenging part: loving your child even when she betrays your trust, even when she pushes you away, even when she erupts in a fury at the slightest provocation. I blush when I think about the Christmases and Thanksgivings and birthday parties where I could have chosen to see things differently, acted differently, but didn't. The Christmas when I decided that nothing my mother selected for me was right, that my preferences had changed since the day I made my list. I remember counting our presents and complaining that Jennifer's pile was larger than mine. I remember my mother crying. I think about how foolish it was and how unnecessary. I could have just said thank you and appreciated her efforts and been glad that I was fortunate enough to wake up to piles of presents carefully chosen and wrapped for me. The contents shouldn't have mattered.

And yet my parents are still here—as they've always been—seemingly ready to wipe the slate clean. Because they love me.

My father says, "Hey, Tara, maybe we can go to Jenkinson's next week. That band you like is playing there." He smiles at me in the rearview mirror.

"That would be nice," I reply and look out the window. Out of the corner of my eye, I see my mother reach for my father's hand and squeeze it. I realize I don't sound like myself. I'm being too easy, too amenable to them. So I temper it.

I say, "Actually, I'll have to look at my calendar and see if I'll be around. But I'd like to."

What I'm saying is not a lie. Except I know that I will not be around.

They will be confused when it happens. They will wonder why I did it. I wish I could explain it, but I can't. I don't remember when the thoughts started. I don't know when I began to hate myself. I can't pinpoint the moment when I focused my sights on Jennifer and my parents and the cause of everything that went wrong in my life, everything that frustrated me. Maybe I chose to take out my frustrations on them because I knew they'd never leave me. And the thought of being alone with myself is terrifying. It is why I always surround myself with friends, with strangers at the bar, with colleagues on the dance floor.

By the time I had fully dug in my heels, I believed it was too late to turn back. It was too late to rewrite the narrative I had written about us. Everyone loved Jennifer more than me, and I was unlovable. I acted unlovable, which just supported my hypothesis. And now, the life I created for myself is coming apart at the seams. The good days aren't good enough anymore. And since I've identified the problem—me—I am rethinking all the time I wasted blaming everybody else. I should have just looked at myself, tried to work on myself. Make me someone else.

I am the source of my own unhappiness, a leaky bucket that can't be filled despite fully opening the spigot above it. So, I am removing myself.

I watch exit after exit pass by on the Garden State Parkway. The joke about New Jersey and telling people where you live by the exit on the Parkway is real. I know the list by heart: Aunt Karen lives off Exit 120; my grandmother lived off Exit 148; our house is Exit 91. With each exit we pass, I know someone or some-place attached to it. It's the silent riding in the car version of "This Is Your Life." I'm glad that this ride is forcing me to think about these places and people. It's like in a movie when the end is approaching; there is a review of all the things that have happened, so the buildup to the ending is even more powerful.

My phone vibrates in my purse. It's my friend Marisa, the one who's been hanging out with Matt and Stacey behind my back. She wants to apologize and invite me to a party later. I text her back that I can't make it. It's much more PG than what I want to text, which is to fuck off and go die in a ditch. But I don't. There are so many people I have wasted time on, and Marisa is one of them. She was always attracted to fun Tara and had no interest in when I wasn't fun. She was my friend when I was arm wrestling in a bar or showing up to a party ready to dance. She had no interest in the real me, the iceberg waiting in the dark water.

I place my phone back into my purse.

I've made a mess of things. I have allowed situations in my life to control me, to destroy me. Maybe I'm an awful person who could never live a normal life, or perhaps I've just had the worst luck. I got in too deep with Matt, didn't see he was not the right one, and he ruined me. I pushed Jennifer away for years, my eager puppy of a sister who only wanted my love, and now I know that she resents me, even fears me. I've ruined friendships and relationships over the years because I felt out of control. I am now a grown woman, once again living with my parents because I have never been in control of my life.

Sitting in the back seat watching my parents, I see them differently. I witness what they are like when no one is watching. When I am not around to mess it up. They speak quickly and comfortably. They look relaxed. They are talking in the front seat about making plans to go away with their friends this summer.

My mother says, "Robert, we always go to the Outer Banks. You know there are other states to visit besides North Carolina, right?"

"But Ann, you love that little restaurant on the water. Remember?"

She laughs and says, "Yes, but I'm sure there are good restaurants in lots of other places too. Let's look at Sarasota this time. Kathy said that it's beautiful."

My father replies, "Kathy also married Joe, though, so I don't know if I trust her judgment," my father replies.

They both laugh, and my mother playfully slaps my father's shoulder.

I wish I could tell them that I wish it could have been different. That I didn't know how to make it different.

I wish I had spent more time with my parents, enjoyed their company more often, but I didn't. I wish I had the memories that Jennifer has of time spent with them, but I chose to separate from them time and again. I wish I could change course and try to do things differently.

But there's no turning back for me. I can't just walk away from it. I've planned it in practice and my mind—purchased the materials, booked the hotel room, thought about what I will write to explain everything. It's too real. I just can't unthink those thoughts. I can't go back to Home Depot and say, "You know what, I want to live now, so I don't need this rope anymore." I can't call the Ramada Inn and tell them, "Good news, I won't need a room where someone will find my body the following day." I can't say to my parents, "You'll be happy to know that tonight was supposed to be the last time I see you, but I've decided to live instead."

It seems like once suicide enters the room, it's hard to make it leave.

We pull into the restaurant parking lot, and I see that Jennifer's car is already there. Rutgers isn't too far from the restaurant. I never visited the campus, even though Jennifer occasionally asked me to. I could never understand why she kept trying to connect with me even after I would be at my worst. It always infuriated me that Jennifer took that approach because it forced me to push her away for fear that she would get too close.

Persistence has always been one of her strong suits. It just never worked with me. As I think about it now, maybe Jennifer wanted to try to save me. Perhaps she knew that I was on a path I couldn't sustain and didn't want to leave me behind. Or maybe she's just a glutton for punishment, forcing me into rejecting her so it can support her theory that I am and always have been an asshole. That's fair too. Because I was.

And looking back now, she didn't always deserve that.

I remember my cousin Marie's bridal shower about five summers ago. I had a few too many apple martinis and walked around the room in a toilet paper bridal gown, my drink sloshing around as I told jokes. I wince at the memory, seeing myself as a bride I would never be. But I didn't know that then. I believed that we would all be at my bridal shower one day, playing games and making plans. All of that doesn't seem important to me anymore.

I couldn't drive myself home, so Jennifer offered to. Maybe it was because I was loose and lighthearted that day, but I remember

Jennifer laughing with me, not at me. I remember her saying that I didn't need to worry about it; she would handle it. So, she drove me back to my place, and I blasted this song I love by N'Sync, "This I Promise You." I remember singing it at the top of my lungs and Jennifer cracking up because I couldn't hit the high notes.

We got back to my place, and Jennifer helped me out of the car. She walked me up the stairs and into bed. She even brought me a glass of water and plugged my phone in on my nightstand. I realized all of this when I woke up the next day.

I don't know why she did it. And we never talked about it again. I think I wanted to forget it because it didn't fit my narrative. I wish I would have thought about that day more, seeing Jennifer through a different light, even if for a little bit. But I didn't.

My thoughts were a little blurry that day, but I didn't hate taking that ride with my sister.

I would never admit that to her.

Jennifer is already out front when we arrive.

"Hey," she greets me, carefully.

"Oh, hey nerdy sister," I reply, trying to lighten it up between us, giving her the signal that I am not here to fight tonight. I have always defused the tension between us with sarcasm, weird offhanded jokes, light ball-busting. Jennifer and I are combustible, but I will try my best to keep it together tonight, to keep a pail of water by my side to throw on any sparks that might ignite.

She smiles at me and rolls her eyes. She says, "Let's head in. Our table is ready."

As I follow her into the restaurant, I see her shoulders tense. It's always a sign that Jennifer is worried about something. I used to joke that it was her scoliosis, but that never landed well. Jennifer always approaches me with her guard up, and that is fair. I might as well put a label on her shoulders that reads, "Waiting for my sister to fuck things up." And she's never stopped trying to calm her worry with hard work. I wish I had her approach to life, where every problem seems solvable with enough effort. To Jennifer, every mystery appears solvable with enough research.

I see a photo of the Colosseum on the wall as we head toward the back of the restaurant. I remember Jen telling a story repeatedly when she got back from Italy. She was touring the Colosseum, and the tour guide was talking about the violence that occurred there so many years ago—stories of lust and life and gruesome deaths. It had been a cloudy day, which seemed to match the somber tone of the tour. But when the sun finally peeked out from behind the clouds, the tour guide yelled to the group to turn and face it. He waved his arms frantically and encouraged them to look right at the bright beams of light. Jen told us that someone in the tour group responded that the sun was too bright and hurt his eyes. The tour guide was insistent and replied, "It might hurt your eyes, but it makes you feel alive. And it's worth it!"

I remember hearing such passion in Jen's voice as she retold the story. She asked us, "Doesn't it just make you feel so alive?"

I remember thinking, *no, it doesn't*. It was always such a foreign concept to me. The sun is the sun and nothing more.

But Jen has always wanted to find greater meaning in everything.

As we head to our table, my father greets the owner and stops to say hello to a large table of people on the other side of the room. Having grown up in Newark and worked there for years, he always runs into someone he knows. It always embarrassed me. Seeing other people give my parents so much attention and love didn't fit how I portrayed them. Tonight, I am trying to be more generous, to look at things through a new lens. My father looks so happy, so content in his surroundings, knowing what he wants from life: his family, familiar places, and friends. I have never been so self-assured and clear about what would make me happy.

I envy him.

I have historically focused on what makes me unhappy rather than pinpointing what would make me happy. That one thing has been to have a baby, to start my own family. It has been a dream I fixated on that I believed would part the clouds and allow in the sun. I stop thinking about it because I don't want to go to a painful place in my mind.

It doesn't matter now.

We are sitting at a table in the corner, under a few framed photos of the owner with his family in Naples. There are candles on the tables melted into Chianti bottles, and Louis Prima flows softly from the speakers above. I've brought a bottle of Chardonnay and fill my glass after the waitress opens it.

I open the conversation with a joke.

I say, "Here comes the bread for Jennifer—we'll need another basket for us."

Jennifer laughs. So do my parents. Joking with Jennifer is not easy, as it continually degrades into a perception of veiled criticisms that threaten her self-esteem. But I go easy on her tonight, staying light-hearted. There is no longer any need for us to fight. I am tired of fighting. She reaches for a piece of bread and hands it to me.

She says, "I think I can spare a piece."

I accept and dip it into the olive oil one last time. Moments like these give me the strongest sense of the finality of my decision. Everything is the last time: our last family dinner, my last bread and olive oil, the last time I'll order at a restaurant, the last time I'll hear Louis Prima.

But these are small things. I've also considered the more significant moments I'll miss: becoming an aunt one day, that trip to Hawaii I've always wanted to take, buying my own house. None of these things, large or small, are insignificant, and all of them give me feelings of regret that I will not have the chance to experience them, again or ever.

I'm not scared of these last times. On the contrary, I take comfort in them and realize that most people would probably not understand. I have had so many years where my happiness has had fits and starts, never genuinely taking off on any consistent basis. I have had so many rehearsals that felt out of tune and off-key. I am thinking of this as the final performance after years of practice. Measure by measure, it is my last chance to make it perfect, every final interaction polished and meticulous. I know Jennifer would appreciate my perspective if I explained it to her this way.

I need these final moments to be perfect. I am afraid that if they aren't, everyone will look back with regret rather than just sadness—or possibly relief—when they learn that I have died. It probably sounds crazy, but a part of me wants them to be sad when I die because they miss me. I don't want them to be angry at me for doing this. They were angry enough at me for what I did while alive. I don't want to go out that way.

But ultimately, their perception of my death is not something I can control.

My death is the only thing I can control.

After dinner, I say goodbye to Jennifer as if it had been a regular night. I feel a sense of relief as I see her walk away. Even though I know my next step will be a challenge for her, I imagine it will also bring her some sense of peace. I hope it does.

On the way home, I fall asleep in the back seat and dream that I am standing in front of an orchestra, baton in hand, the music swelling and receding with my every gesture. I remember thinking it was the most beautiful music I have ever heard because I was in control of it.

Chapter Twenty-Three

I turn off the bedroom light and walk into the living room. My parents are sitting on the sofa, glasses of wine in hand, watching an episode of *The Sopranos*. It's dark in the room, but the light of the television reflects on their faces, making them look supernaturally alert and focused.

It's the last time I'll see this, the last time I'll see my parents. I'm glad this is the way I'll remember them, that this is one of the memories I'll take with me. It's familiar, comforting. I regret that I couldn't feel this nostalgia until I made my decision. It was only then that I considered holding onto these small moments and considering them precious. Like our last dinner in Newark. I've felt like I'm filling up one of those View-Masters I had when I was a kid, loading snapshots of memories that I can click through in my last moments.

My parents are watching the episode where Christopher and Paulie get lost in the woods of the Pine Barrens while hunting down a target they had driven there to bury. The Pine Barrens is a massive pine forest in southern central New Jersey. As the two characters run through the woods, it's the dead of winter, and the two characters are freezing. Their bickering and frustration increase with each hour that passes.

I hear Christopher tell Paulie, "Captain or no captain, right now, we're just two assholes lost in the woods." My father laughs.

I empathize with Christopher.

I remember stories from my childhood about the Jersey Devil and the Pine Barrens—a fantastical and diabolical creature central to New Jersey folklore. As the story goes, the unwanted thirteenth child of a woman named Mother Leeds roamed the Pine Barrens, terrifying anyone it met. I can't help but think that I've always felt a parallel to my story. That I, standing before them while they watch this episode, am a mirror to that story, a sinister counterpoint to this family that would have been perfectly happy without me. Just as I would have been perfectly happy without me.

My father asks, "Hey Tara, are you going out?" He pauses the VCR.

"Yes, I'm going to meet some friends. Don't wait up. I'll probably stay at Marisa's house."

I smile at them before walking toward the front door.

My mother says, "We love you. Please be careful." She has been telling me to be careful as long as I can remember, as if she's always imagining some potential disaster that could occur. It makes me feel guilty. My mother has never stopped trying to connect with me, physically or emotionally. She has never stopped showing me love, and I have never stopped rejecting it.

I turn back to look at them before walking out the door. Maybe one day, they will understand that I have been just as sad about our lives together as they have. I have been equally unsatisfied with the ways things have gone. I can't help but feel that there is something that should be inside me but is missing. Something that was there but is no longer. I'm not quite sure what it is, but I have waited for it, repeatedly, like a child trying to find the marble under a walnut shell in an old boardwalk magic trick.

It comes down to me not having the ability to love myself. And I've identified those things that I thought would ultimately fill the void: friends, work, love, a family of my own. But they've either not materialized or just not been enough.

If I were to investigate myself and reflect, I'd probably see that I'm overly attached to a kind of grief—grief caused by my own hands. Jennifer and my parents wouldn't believe it, but I grieve for our tortured family bonds, scarred by my own hand over the years. I grieve for my inability to allow myself to be loved by someone deserving of me; not superficial admiration love or sloppy drunk love, but the love that persists in the good and bad. And sometimes, I grieve the most for the love I have never been able to show Jennifer and my parents, for the happiness I could never share with them.

My unhappiness is as much a mystery to me as I assume it is to everyone else. Maybe that's why my family kept trying. They hoped that the mysterious appearance of my unhappiness would just as quickly and mysteriously disappear. I'll never know.

I walk out and close the door behind me. I will never see my parents again. It makes me sad—for them as much as for me—but they are not enough to fix my problem. I hope they make it through.

A small flowerpot has tipped over on the front step, spilling its contents across the porch. My father is meticulous about his plants, always tending to them, pruning, watering. I stand the flowerpot upright, collecting as much soil as possible. Inevitably, some of it slips through my fingers. I brush what remains off the step and look down to my hands, which are now coated, grimy, charcoal colored. How often in our attempts to fix situations, to clean up dirty things, do we instead mess them up. We bear the evidence of our efforts in the messes they leave behind.

My family bears these marks, proof that they tried, time and again.

I can't change it now. And I am ultimately doing everyone a favor by removing myself from the equation. I can only believe that while they will be hurt and confused by it in the short run, it will also make us all better off in the long run. But it's complicated, and I know that fixing my problem will create another mess, especially for my family. So I have planned to make it as clean and painless for them as possible. My final mess won't be at my parents' house; I am going to a hotel instead. With all the pain I've caused them, I need to do it somewhere else.

I look down at the flowerpot. I think about my father and this small gesture I made for him. Of course, he'll never know about it, but it gives me some comfort that I can help him with something. That I made things right for once instead of messing them up.

I start the car and pull away from their house. As I look in the rearview mirror, I see my father looking out the window, watching me leave. I open my window and wave my hand quickly to signal that I've seen him. This will be the last visual he will have of me. His daughter, waving goodbye with little fanfare, as if we will see each other again. He will become a prisoner to my last day alive, dissecting every moment, looking for clues, replaying it in his head. He will want to see if there was a sign in my last words, gestures. If there was anything he could have done to change my trajectory. I wish I could tell him that there was not.

I arrive at the hotel about fifteen minutes later and pull into a spot on the far edge of the parking lot. I flick my cigarette out the window, watching it sail over the gleaming asphalt before it falls to the ground, sprinkling orange embers in its wake. It's my last cigarette. This I know is true. I put the car in park and turn off the ignition, leaving the keys in the cupholder.

I won't need them anymore.

My hand trembles as I grab my bag from the back seat, quickly opening it to ensure I have everything I need. Once I see that I do,

I zip the bag closed and walk toward the entrance of the hotel lobby.

I feel lightheaded. I wonder if I should have one more cigarette to calm my nerves.

I decide not to. I have decided what I am going to do, planned it, so there is no room for error. But, as calming as the thought of it is for me, I still feel anxious. I am a little bit scared. But it doesn't change my mind.

Even at 8:15 p.m., Route 70 roars with traffic behind me. Turning to take one last look, I remember how many times I traveled this highway, calling on customer after customer, peddling trays of sandwiches and mini cannolis on my sales calls. I spent so much time trading jokes and favors with colleagues, friends, and clients at the Hilton Garden Inn or the Applebee's across the street. How much of my life I lived along this throbbing section of artery running between Lakehurst and Brick Township. How unsatisfying it all was, despite the best of intentions. How different it looks to me now, background noise, a blur.

My family drives this strip of Route 70 often; I wonder if they will now take detours to avoid the view of this Ramada Inn, or if passing it will become a compulsion, a visceral need to see the scene of my crime. Either way, I know they will think of me after I'm gone. The thought comforts me that I will live on in their minds even though I can't control what they think.

But then again, I never could.

When explaining my death during those first phone calls and texts after my family learns what has happened, I imagine they will have a hard time explaining it. Because they won't be able to say the words. Because they will be ashamed, scared, and frustrated.

But they will never understand.

It is the only option, the only conclusion I'm able to come to that will quiet my anxieties and put an end to the despair that has traveled with me most of my days. I was dealt an unplayable hand that could not trump the house no matter how many cards I drew. It was not apparent to my family or most people I know, but I insist that I tried.

Unless someone has faced the emotional circumstances I have, they've likely never flexed this self-destructive muscle, never looked at the option of suicide as viable. More likely, most people have had days, months, years where things go wrong, and they believe that they cannot continue along the same track, but they summon some instinct to cope. They anesthetize, transform, reimagine. They seek options to mitigate their own suffering where and when they can because they want to survive their lives. Most people cannot understand when choices are so limited that one's relief could be so extreme, so final.

Unless a person has looked up from the damp and terrifying mineshaft of anguish that threatens to collapse around them, they cannot empathize with actively settling themselves on the floor and kicking aside a support beam to trigger the fast fall of earth onto their skin. And for that reason, most people find suicide equally terrifying and confusing because it is never one of the choices on their menu of options.

And so my decision has been made.

Most of us continually battle against the cessation of life. We strive to live longer and stave off the inevitable. We concoct stories to explain the afterlife, existential fairy tales to help us sleep at night. Yet no matter our efforts, we all die. Funny, right? Simply put, one moment we are alive, and the next, we are not. For most people, it is unknown when that moment will arrive—will it be a sudden illness, a plane crash, bad luck?

I am not most of us. I know.

I close my eyes and smell the evening air. I look up to the sky and take in the stars. Never having been a religious person, I had little frame of reference outside of a basic understanding of Heaven that I saw in books and movies. With that, I imagined myself inhabiting the air, the sky, the stars; Heaven is above, at least that's what we've been told, so the sky is where I looked. An ethereal afterlife incited by my transformation from solid to air, from living to dead. Where I will end up is unknown to me, but I have always felt it was somewhere incredibly far away but still in my sight. And the irony is, once I am there, I probably won't even know it.

I remember being at my grandmother Stella's wake. I was around seven at the time. It was my first struggle with the concept of death, seeing my grandmother in the open casket and wondering how she could be there, physically in front of me, yet no longer alive. I was fixated on her skin, waxy and shining in the soft light of the funeral home. That she was so still. I kept looking at her chest to see if it was a mistake or if she was just breathing quietly. What confusion arises from seeing a person in the same body they've always had, just without its life, its animation, the things that made them a person. Before they closed the casket, we placed photos and little packets of M&Ms alongside her, things she loved, mementos for her to travel with. I didn't understand how she would enjoy them since she wasn't alive; I know now that they were placed there to comfort us, not her. That placing senti-mentalities into the casket was a way for us to believe that there is some way she would be able to see them, wherever she was.

The idea of the afterlife is for the living alone. Any possibility of communication between the living and the dead rests solely in the minds of those who are still alive. It is something to calm us when we begin to fear death. The afterlife exists in our minds, and so we, the living — can I still call myself that when I am about to die? — can believe that it is not over when it is over. We interpret flickering lights and clutch discovered pennies and shiver at the tingling at the napes of our necks to will something into existence that is greater than us. It is our collective imagination. It is our protection from an unflinching fear. But none of us really knows.

I can't focus on the uncertainties right now; I need specifics and the stability that comes with the known to tamp down my fears of the unknown. I can't speculate on what might be; all I have left is what I have determined will be. I need to remain calm, to resist anxiety. The best way to do that is to get started with the schedule I've planned over the last month. I will take it step by step. I will follow the plan. I will do what I came here to do.

I head toward the revolving doors, pausing to let a young family exit. The youngest child smiles up at me, and I smile back. They walk away, toward their lives, and I turn toward my decision.

As I walk into the lobby, I'm greeted by the smiling face of a clean-shaven young man in a dark suit. His name tag says, "Andy."

"Good evening; how can I help you?"

"Hi, Andy, I'm checking into my room."

I hand him my license and credit card.

"Thank you. . .Tara. Looks like you're staying with us one night, correct?"

"Yes, just one night."

Just one night.

And forever.

"The breakfast buffet opens at 6 a.m.—" Andy starts.

"I won't need breakfast," I interrupt, perhaps a little too quickly. I can't think of tomorrow. For me, there is no tomorrow. It's strange to think there will be a tomorrow for Andy and the family who just left and the people eating the breakfast buffet.

"I'm sorry," I smile, then repeat more politely, "I won't need the breakfast buffet."

I take my key and head to the elevator, passing a housekeeper just starting her shift. She is young but already looks tired, as if cleaning up the remnants of so many lives lived in hotel rooms has depleted her own. She has dark hair like Jennifer and wears small gold hoops, just like my mother. I wonder if this young woman will be the one who finds me tomorrow.

I shake my head, saddened by the thought. I don't want her to find me; she looks sad enough as it is. But I don't want to imagine anyone else finding me. I don't want to imagine anything after I'm gone. Because my decision isn't about them—what's best for them, what's easiest for them. I've been trying all my life to make it okay for everyone else, even as I failed at it. But tonight, now, forever, it's about me.

I nod as we pass each other, press the elevator button, and head up to the seventh floor.

My room is comfortable, spacious enough. Not that I require much space tonight. I walk to the window. The room overlooks the rear parking lot rather than the highway, but I won't see the sun rise over it tomorrow. I won't ever see the sunrise again. I expect that is supposed to make me sad, but I have seen enough sunrises, and they never quite brought me the feeling of optimism they do others. I won't wake to the sun shining on my face, and honestly, I've never enjoyed its blinding light first thing in the morning. I prefer a darker, more somber beginning to the day, for it can only improve from there. I realize that this will be the only outside world I see again, and I am okay with that.

I am at peace with that.

I am not here to create new memories. Simply to erase the ones I have. It is the one last thing I can control. And given how wrong everything has turned out, I have never doubted it is the right thing to do.

I've had no illusions about myself—I've always known who I am and proceeded to live with that. But it wasn't enough.

I put down my bag and sit on the bed, my mind still active, alive. I can't help but think of my sister.

My plunge from the deck into the frigid waters will make room in the lifeboat for Jennifer, and even right our family's ship, re-leveling it from its perilous listing. I see now that no matter how often I wanted to connect better with them, it was impossible. My wiring planted me firmly on the other side of the glass, close enough to see them and be near to them, but never able to easily step over into their environment and make myself at home; always an observer to their existence, but able to walk away at any time, leaving them together behind the thick panes smudged with tears and prints of hands that should have been more readily embraced by mine. I don't see it as fixable.

So now I will be successful in ending my life rather than attempting to fix it. I've taken great care to get to his moment, writing and rewriting the schedule until it felt manageable. I unzip my bag and pull from it a notepad and pen, printed instructions, and a bundle of rope. I see that the Home Depot receipt has fallen to the floor. I remember the clerk who rang me up, selling me the material required to bring about my demise, yet could have no idea it was happening. Much like Andy, the desk clerk who checked me into my hotel room, or the unlucky housekeeper who will find me slumped against the back of my door in the morning. All innocents swirling within the same existential crisis, some more tangential than others, but still all unwitting players in my end game.

I lay the rope on the bed, next to the instructions. I unfold the instructions and review them one last time. I measure the rope and tie the knot as the instructions indicate, measuring and remeasuring to make sure I get it right the first time. There is no margin of error allowable, for it would be the difference between a tidy ending and a slow, painful burn to brain damage. I consider running back down to my car for that extra cigarette.

I can't mess this up. It's escalating my anxiety.

I wonder if I leave the room if I'll even return, and I don't want to give myself that option. So, I focus on the rope. I feel it again like I did at Home Depot. But this time, I place it against my neck. It feels substantial, bumpy, slightly scratchy. I tie the knot as the website instructed, tying a noose knot while sitting on the queen bed. After I'm satisfied that I have prepared the rope appropriately, it's time to ensure I have all the rest of my details in order.

It's too hot in here, but perhaps it's the adrenaline pulsing through me. I turn down the temperature in the room, and the fan turns on with a loud hum. I turn on the TV for background noise. I turn the volume down to the lowest level I can hear over the air conditioning. It doesn't matter what the show is. I just want something else happening in the room. My throat is dry, so I check the mini fridge for a soda. After grabbing a Diet Coke, I place the envelopes on the desk.

They are the notes I'm leaving behind for my parents and Jennifer.

It is not easy to write a suicide note. It is a bridge between life and death—the last act of a living, dying person—an artifact to be resurfaced and interpreted endlessly until some meaning can be extracted from it. It is a final last statement that stays while you go, one that both says too much and not enough.

My notes are short and minimally apologetic; I feel the need to say I'm sorry because I know this will create a mess. My apologies are not for what I'm about to do, but for what my decision is about to do to them. I hope that they one day see that this was the best option. The only option. My hand shook the entire time, even as I tried to steady it. I thought about their reactions as I wrote the notes. I wondered how they would be received and if they would be enough.

I'm verging on second-guessing myself, so I quickly review the notes to make sure they're legible. When I see that they are, I place them back into the envelopes and rearrange them on the desktop. My last gesture of something like love, at least love in the way that I am able to express it. My notes don't explain to them why I did it. I honestly don't feel a need to explain it because it won't make it disappear. It won't bring me back.

I wrote the notes to simply offer a final connection to my

family with words that were easier to say on paper than I was ever able to express in person.

Love is not a word I have ever used; my parents often did, and Jennifer occasionally did, but all were always unanswered by me. Jennifer would probably say that she has found it hard to love me, and I deserve that. I know I can't rewrite history. I can't change everything that has happened. But I can change the future. So while I am not sacrificing myself at the altar of sisterhood, I can't deny that my departure will relieve some of the mounting pressure between us and buff out some of the more superficial scratches in our dented exterior.

It's no one's fault. I just can't continue on the same path I've been.

No one will want to understand why I did it. No one will ever know all the details, but they will travel with me, as many of them cannot—or perhaps should not—be shared. Honestly, my last moments will prove to be as mundane as any others. I turned on the TV, adjusted the thermostat, drank a Diet Coke while slipping off my shoes. There is no need for anyone to know the intimacies of my last moments, even though I am sure someone may wonder about them, perhaps even spin out wild and tragic scenarios to explain why I did what I did. I wonder if I would react the same. I'm not sure I would, as I've always preferred to skirt emotional details.

People I love have walked away from me so many times. As Jennifer knows, I was not easy to love, and I know other people in my life have felt the same from time to time. Boyfriends and friends have turned away from me and sought love and companionship elsewhere. Jennifer has essentially started telling strangers she is an only child. I overheard her on the phone telling her friend Joanna that. It didn't bother me as much as I thought it would.

This time, I am the one walking away by my own choice and hand. I will leave behind nothing but clothes and papers, wasted opportunities and disparate recollections, my unexpressed thoughts, and my last words left in envelopes on a hotel desk. I will take some of these things with me and others I will leave behind. It is not a lot, but it is more than I could express while living.

Even though this is ultimately for the best, my parents will miss me.

But Jennifer, I'm not sure she will. And that's okay too.

While I can't control the memories Jennifer revisits or give her the tools to score them more generously. I can still hope—for her sake—that time and distance from me can soften her view. I hope that my sister can one day realize that despite all her efforts to change the course of our relationship over the years, her fate was sealed. And so was mine. Nothing she did or didn't do could have made it any different. When she reads my note, I hope she understands that and finds the peace I have found.

It's time. I feel an odd sensation of peace. Which is how I told myself I would know it was time. I raise the volume on the TV, so no one will have to hear any sounds I might make. I use the bathroom one last time, hoping that I won't release my bladder in my final moments. I place my phone in my bag so that it will be easily found. I want to make this as easy as possible for whoever finds me.

I am scared.

But I am more scared of staying alive.

I move the chair to the back of the door, and when I look up, I realize that I can see myself in the mirror over the dresser. I don't want to see myself do this. I think it will scare me even more. I go into the bathroom and grab a towel to drape over the mirror; I can't imagine watching myself do this. It's not a visual I want to take with me, wherever I'm going.

I turn off the lights and step up onto the chair.

Chapter Twenty-Four

JENNIFER

AUGUST

Tara once asked me if I would be sad if she died. And now it has been one hundred and fifty-two days since she died, and I still don't know what I feel.

I haven't gone to another funeral since Ellen's. I think I have had enough of death.

So, I am trying to refocus on life, starting with my own.

It's late summer and the fall semester begins soon. As I review the syllabus I created for my Politics of Power course that starts next week, I see Niccolò Machiavelli on the list. I take out my copy of *The Prince* and see some notes I scribbled in the margin, hasty Italian translations I pieced together in Italy. I think about the Colosseum, the sun, and the life and death thrust together on those ancient city streets.

The first time I read the book, I was mesmerized by one phrase in particular: "Men will not look at things as they really are, but as they choose them to be—and are ruined." I wonder if I have been doing that this whole time, seeing things as I choose them to be.

I used to think that Tara and I were ruined. When she died, I took on that ruin alone, breathing it in like air and seeping it back out through my pores.

I put the book down.

I had always believed that when my time eventually came, I would approach death with a ferocity unseen before, fighting for my life. For me, death is the problem and not the solution. I could never do what Tara did, bring death earlier than planned. Maybe I'm not meant to understand it. And I am learning to be okay with that.

I am the older sister of a sister who is no longer alive. I am not an only child. I can't kill Tara again by erasing her from my story. She took her own life because life wasn't enough for her. I think about what my dad told me, that we're all "doing the best we can."

I promise myself that I will do better.

I can't walk in Tara's shoes, but I can try to put myself in her mind.

I can feel for her, even if I can't understand what she felt. I need to get close to it.

I have become more aware of the things that broke my sister: the breakup with Matt, not having a home of her own, not having her own family, her perpetual dissatisfaction with herself and her life. I have seen how some of her friends behaved. I witnessed Marisa using Tara's Facebook page as a tool to scare someone, making her death a tool for a cruel joke. I now use this lens to reinterpret other ways people took advantage of my sister. They attended her house parties and trashed the place. They asked for her things right after she died as if she were nothing at all to them but the owner of 7 for All Mankind jeans.

It disgusts me.

Maybe this is a type of grief I didn't recognize because it is veiled in the need to protect someone against offenses that have already happened.

Maybe.

I think about how I fantasized, for so many years, what sisterhood should look like. Maybe I was fantasizing about grief in the same way. I envisioned it as being broken apart, irrevocably shattered into a million pieces by a loss. But perhaps grief lies in realizing that there were cracks and fissures along the foundation all along, and actual resolution is understanding that I can exist on that foundation, even if it remains imperfect. Perhaps it even makes me stronger because I have had to build the strength to keep myself upright on such a tenuous footing all along.

I am standing on the screened-in porch tonight, dripping from the humidity of a New Jersey summer. I have finally started seeing some friends again. It's a break I desperately needed, a turn toward living to compensate for my focus on dying.

I see my friends Becky and Mark out on the lawn, pointing to the moon and talking to their kids. Mark's father passed away last year. Their children are young—five and eight—and they do not yet have a full grasp of death, so they're asking for signs to help them understand. They are looking for Pop-Pop in the stars, signs of his face in the moon, memories of his life written across the night sky. It's a beautiful thought that someone we loved could be out there for us to see, a part of the beauty around us, just waiting to be appreciated.

The moment is so optimistic that I can't resist it myself, and I quietly ask Tara to send me a sign.

I feel like she owes me one. Or maybe I just want to know that she would contact me if she could. Maybe she needed the distance between us to be able to reach out to me. I dismiss my thoughts as nonsensical, pure fantasy that attributes greater power to the dead than they likely deserve.

But the thought still intrigues me.

I remember my mother looking up to the ceiling the night Tara died. I wonder if she saw something I couldn't.

Perhaps it's because the sky is so clear and sharp that I believe something like Heaven must be lying behind it, ready to relay a message. Maybe it's because I'm one bottle of Sauvignon Blanc in, with no intent on slowing down any time soon. Steely Dan is playing quietly out from the pool deck. I can't imagine a more perfect setting in which to sit quietly with my slightly slurry thoughts, once again wondering about where Tara is right now and what happened to her after she died.

I walk over to the cooler to refill my glass, turning to look toward the screen door as I hear it creak open. I turn around to see Michael, the younger child, only five years old. I smile at this innocent creature who is slightly sunburned from the day in the pool, his hair tousled, a Capri Sun ring around his mouth. He looks at me, then takes a few steps before stopping to shift his gaze to the ground. Something is lying there, and he picks it up and brings it to me. Right to me, as if it had my name on it.

He says, "Jennifer, this is for you," just as I was asking for a sign.

I look down into my hand to find a penny.

After Tara died, my Pamela saw a psychic who said that when someone we love dies, we'll find change--pennies, dimes, and nickles--everywhere. What do you know, this time, the change found me. I could easily be a skeptic, but it feels real to me, even though the sensation of watching the penny's journey into my hand felt like it came from another dimension. It feels like a gesture from Tara—she was here, and now she is not. But she can still move the penny from the floor to my hand through the intermediary of a young boy who is just following his instincts.

I clutch the penny in my hand, feeling its cool dampness turn warm from my touch. "Thank you, Michael."

He says, "You're welcome. It's your penny."

With that, he shrugs and runs into the house, after which I hear an immediate request for dessert. Such a powerful gesture squeezed between a juice box and an ice cream sandwich—the mundane and the mysterious coming together in such a beautiful way.

I wake up the following day, slightly foggy from my excess of wine, but my dream is crystal clear. Since I stopped going to funerals, my dreams have not stopped; they've just changed.

Last night, I dreamed about pennies—mountains of them. I was stacking them as tall as skyscrapers, building towers until my fingers turned green from the fetid cocktail of copper and sweat. I was trying to count them as I stacked but kept forgetting the total. With every completed tower, another pile appeared, ready for sorting, and I just couldn't keep up. I became buried under the pile of pennies, which has accumulated past the point of manageability. While I could still breathe, I had the distinct sensation that I was drowning in a cruel sea of pocket change—strangled by memories hidden in every tarnished disc.

My dreams used to be about death and dying. Now they seem to be about resolution and connection and moving on.

For someone who believes in signs, I can't help but accept this one.

I walk into the kitchen, slightly queasy from last night's wine and humidity and supernatural communication. I feel like time is moving both fast and slow for me. I feel like it could be five a.m. or afternoon right now. I sometimes feel like Tara just died, and other times like it's been years. It's all blurry in my mind.

The further I get from that day, sitting in the police station, learning about a housekeeper who discovered my sister's lifeless body in that hotel room, the more abstract it becomes in my memory. It seemed unreal when we found out at the police station. I remember thinking that I could smell my sister's perfume, that I could imagine what the rope felt like, that I could see her hanging there. But now, it's as if it happened a lifetime ago. I sometimes need a photo to remind me of every detail of my sister's face. I sometimes go days or weeks without thinking about how she died.

Everything seems a lifetime ago.

I look at the penny I must have placed on the counter when I got home last night. I take it and tape it to the refrigerator. I see a postcard taped on the freezer door. I had forgotten about it. On the front is a painting with large block colors. I know what is written on the back without looking at it. On the back is written, "Unsettle yourself toward the way you think things should be." My good friend Jeffrey sent it years ago after we met up at the Museum of Modern Art in New York City during a summer break in college. I hung it on my refrigerator the day it came in the mail. I felt like it was a mini self-help book reminding me to keep an open mind. I have always craved things that made me think.

I remember that day at MoMa well. Jeffrey and I were standing in front of a Mark Rothko painting. I was straining to understand what made these large blocks of color "art" in the same way I understood the Sistine Chapel to be art or the Monet posters I had hanging in my dorm room. I told him that I just didn't get it. Jeffrey turned to me and said, "This is art because it changes the way we think about art. It disrupts everything we thought we knew and makes us think differently about it."

His words took my breath away. I immediately felt like I understood everything and nothing at the same time.

That conversation in front of a Mark Rothko painting stuck with me for years, made me more generous to things I, at first, didn't understand. When Tara died, I became unsettled, perhaps without realizing it. But not in the way the postcard instructed. Instead of being more open-minded to unfamiliar ideas, to be better about thinking differently about things to grow as a person, I was adamant about my own perspective. Instead of growing and improving, I became unsettled by fear, regret, and death itself. I became smaller, my thoughts narrower.

I need to leave funerals behind.

I need to move on. I need to figure out what moving on means.

There is one place I can start.

In the hall closet, I had hidden a small urn of Tara's ashes and the photo of Tara and me on Easter. I take them out and place them on my bookshelf. I can't hide from them anymore. They are a part of me. As I stand there before them, I think of standing before the urn at Tara's wake. I was so angry, so resentful. I had glared at that urn in the funeral home like it could understand my rage. As if Tara were there before me and could acknowledge my feelings. It seems like years ago.

I feel so different now.

I open the drawer to my desk, and under the funeral cards and clipped obituaries is Tara's suicide note. I buried it there because I haven't been able to bring myself to read it. I have been lost in the past, unable to see a future that I can live with. Tara's death has caught me in an endless loop of old resentments, unsolved disagreements, and missed opportunities to fix things. I had cemented myself in the present with our past.

I put all the cards and obituaries in a box on my closet shelf. I don't need them anymore, but I can't get rid of them. They helped me find my sister. They helped me find myself.

I take the note and put it into my purse. I need to read it, but I don't want to do it here. I don't want to be alone with this, even if it means sitting among strangers.

I get in my car and begin to drive to Seaside Heights. It's a beautiful, sunny day. It's the kind of day where you need to shield your eyes from the sun because it's so bright, but you feel like you can bathe in its warmth. Fall is right around the corner, so each last day that feels like it could be summer is something to be embraced.

As I pass a church, I see a funeral taking place.

I don't stop. I keep driving.

I pull up to Klee's. I used to come here all the time. Once Tara and her friends were old enough to drink, they came here. Which is when I stopped coming.

Several months ago, Tara and I were here together, but not by choice. She had called me in the late evening that night, her words slurry from too many drinks, her thoughts incoherent.

She said, "Jen. Hey. What—what are you doing?"

I could hear voices in the background. The Allman Brothers were playing on a jukebox.

I asked her, "What's up? Are you okay?"

I was concerned about her because she never called me. Ever.

She said, "I drink. I had—drinks. I'm here at Klee's by myself."

She laughed at someone just out of earshot, and I heard a loud bang as she dropped her phone.

She said, "Oops! Need a ride."

I was becoming frustrated, as it was almost eleven on a weeknight. But I couldn't let her drive like that. Tara always raised such conflict in me. While I was frustrated by her taking up any of my time, I also wanted her to want to spend time with me. I wanted her to choose me.

"Be there in twenty," I responded and hung up.

When I walked in, Tara was drinking a beer that had been recently filled. She was chatting with the bartender, holding court in front of the other patrons who lingered at that hour. Tara could always make herself the center of attention like that. She had a gift for it. I wish that I had that ability. I'm no wallflower, but I've never captivated people like Tara did unless I was among my peers talking about something academic.

But Tara had always captivated everyone everywhere. I wonder if she knew that about herself. If it gave her a type of social confidence that I have always lacked.

"Hey, Tara." I said as I sat down next to her and signaled to the bartender for a drink. "Is everything okay?"

She looked at me, her eyes blurry and red. She said, "Sure, everything is great. Matt and I broke up. It's over. He's an asshole. How is your day going?"

I looked at her and could see the pain on her face despite her efforts to hide it.

I said, "I'm sorry, Tara. I didn't know that. What happened?"

"None of your fucking business," she said to me with her eyes closed, as if she couldn't even look at the reason they broke up. As if she was trying to make it disappear from her view.

I went to reach for her arm, to comfort her, but she pulled away from my touch.

"You don't have to do that," she sneered at me. "I'm sure this is what you'd expect anyway." She took another sip of her drink.

I said, "Come on, Tara. I want you to be happy."

"I'll never be happy, do you understand? Never."

She stormed out to the dance floor, grabbing the hand of a man who was sitting at the end of the bar. "Bartender, turn it up!" She pulled the man around the bar, singing at the top of her lungs, "Sweet—home—Ala*bam*a! Where the skies are so *bluuuue*—"

I didn't have the heart to pull her off the dance floor. I didn't want to embarrass her. I also wasn't sure how she would have reacted to me pulling her away. So, I let her stay. Tara stumbled over to me at the song's end and said it was time to go. I helped her out toward my car, and she fell asleep immediately in the front seat.

As I pulled up to a stoplight, I looked over at my sister. Her face was aglow in red. She looked peaceful. Moments like this made me crave my sister's love even more. Even though we had our differences, I felt terrible when something made her unhappy. I couldn't help it. I didn't want her to suffer. Except when she made me suffer.

We pulled up to my house, and I nudged her awake. She was still half-asleep. She looked at me and quietly asked, "Jennifer, would you cry if I died?"

I said, "What do you mean?"

She replied, "I mean, if I got hit by a car, would you cry? I bet you'd be happy."

I said, "Stop it, Tara."

Tears formed in my eyes, and I hit her shoulder over and over, trying to keep her awake. I had fantasized about Tara disappearing for years, but I had never come face to face with Tara talking about scenarios surrounding her death. It scared me, and I didn't know why.

She turned her head and half-smiled at me. "I'm just kidding. I need to go to bed."

We walked to my front door, and I made a mental note to talk to her about her drinking. It had gotten out of control lately. She had become sloppy and careless.

Tara fell onto the couch face first and began to snore immediately. I turned off the light and smoothed her hair. I could never touch her while she was awake; she shrunk from any display of physical affection our entire lives. I asked myself the same question she asked me. Would I be sad if she died? The answer was no, but I could never say that to her. Because it was more complicated than just "no." There was a whole calculus of suffering I used to come to that answer. I try to remember if I felt guilty about that at the time, but I don't know.

Tara was gone before I woke the following day, and we never spoke of that night again. That was two months before she died.

As I walk up to the bar, I think of that night when Tara opened up to me in the only way she could. A passing joke, her best attempt at intimacy. I take a shot of vodka to dull the pain of that memory. I now fear that she was asking me for help, but I didn't do enough. But instead of guilt and anger, I feel a growing acceptance of our circumstances. They are what they are. My sister was who she was. I can't hold on to the bad memories because that is no way to go on. The resentment I've held for so long has transformed into a real sense of loss.

We've lost so many things since she died. We've donated most of Tara's stuff from the storage space. We haven't seen many of Tara's friends. We've paid off Tara's bills and settled her accounts. We sold her car. All of it, gone.

I think about what she has left behind. An urn with my sister's ashes and the photo of us at Easter, the one I had to retrieve on the last day of her funeral. Both had been sitting in a box in my closet until I displayed them in my living room earlier today.

And her suicide note.

I reach into my purse and pull out the note. I place it on the bar in front of me. I have to finally read it. It's the last thing that connects me to my sister. It's her final communication to me. No matter what it says, I need to experience it.

I unfold the paper and begin to read. The note isn't long.

Jennifer,

This isn't anyone's fault. Life was just not enough for me. Please know that it was the only way. And I am ok with that. It gives me peace, and I hope it will provide you with the same.

I do love you – even though you're a huge nerd. Always remember what makes you happy. I couldn't do that. I hope as you travel through your life that you always turn to face the sun. I've heard that it's worth it.

Tara

I can feel Tara there with me, stronger than I ever have in my life. I run to the bathroom with it, not expecting to react the way I do. I lean against the side of the bathroom stall and hold my head in my hands, crying violent, loud sobs. My sister is dead, and I miss her. I'd rather have her back in my life and be unhappy than have her gone. I'd try harder with her this time. But I can't choose that for her; I am left to play the cards I was dealt, much as she was.

I throw two twenties on the bar and walk out into the warm salt air. I am slightly tipsy from the drinks, so I head across the street to the boardwalk to walk for a while. For the first time in a long time, I can breathe, and it's not because Tara is dead. I can breathe now even though she is dead. While I initially felt free from her, I now feel free in the memory of her. To know that she isn't in pain anymore. I didn't realize there was so much pain in her life.

This sisterhood we had wasn't what I was always wanting or expecting.

But it is what we had. I can't change it.

But I can change the way I think about it. I owe that to Tara.

I end up at the boardwalk a few towns over. I get out of my car and stand at the edge of the sand.

I look out at the ocean and remember my dream the night before I learned that Tara had died. The scene before me looks nothing like my dream.

Today the water looks peaceful. I don't envision my sister sinking below its surface. I don't see myself pushing her away anymore. I don't think about anything but that feeling of being alive. It's a feeling that I wish Tara could have had. Maybe she did, but not often enough.

I walk toward the water—I need to know what it feels like.

I take the piece of rope out of my pocket; I carry it with me everywhere. I feel its fibers again. It has become comforting to me. It's the last thing my sister felt before she died.

I walk to the water's edge.

The water is cold.

The wet sand crunches under my feet.

I am still here.

I hurl the length of rope into the water. I hope that it will help change my dreams. In my mind, I can still see Tara there, under the surface of the water, and believe the rope helps her survive.

As if I can change the past through my dreams in the future.

I know I can't change everything that happened. Throwing the rope into the water is still liberating.

I feel a warmth on my back. The sun has come out from behind a cloud. I remember the words Tara wrote to me. The last thing she said to me.

I turn to face the sun.

It burns my eyes, still wet with tears.

But it's worth it.

Afterword

My sister Melissa died by suicide on October 13, 2009. Some of the things in this book really happened and some are purely fiction.

I am not a mental health professional or an expert on suicide. This book has been my attempt to grieve. It was a project I undertook to try and connect and empathize with my sister in a way that I couldn't while she was alive. I will never know all of the things that turned my sister toward suicide, but all I can do it imagine them to help me understand her better.

If you or someone you know has a mental illness, is struggling emotionally, or has concerns about their mental health, there are ways to get help.

- American Foundation for Suicide Prevention: **https://afsp.org/**
- National Institute of Mental Health: **https://www.nimh.nih.gov/health/find-help**
- National Suicide Prevention Lifeline: 800-273-8255

Author and her sister Melissa, 1983

Author and her sister Melissa, 2003

Acknowledgments

Thank you to Andy and Tess for allowing me to sacrifice mornings, nights, and weekends with you to finish this book.

Thank you to my favorite women, my BOD, for your continued support throughout this whole process.

Thank you to Jen Braaksma, my amazing book coach for your continued support and feedback at every step along the way, and to the Author Accelerator for connecting us.

Thank you to Stephanie Spector for your incredible copy editing.

Thank you to my readers for your feedback and support as I worked through endless drafts.

And a final and very important thank you to my parents, who have remained strong despite every reason to fall apart after Melissa died. Thank you for providing me with enough love and confidence throughout my life to make me believe that I could write a book someday.